Peace & love
Rocky Barilla

# *SANCTUARY*

**BY**

**ROCKY BARILLA**



ROSQUETE PRESS

Cover and book design by Rocky Barilla © 2020

Library of Congress Control Number: 2019920393

ISBN: 978-0-9904851-6-2

# OTHER WORKS BY ROCKY BARILLA

## STARS

Award Winner of the 2020 International Latino Book Awards for Best Novel – Romance

## Esmeralda

First Place Award Winner of the 2019 International Latino Book Awards for Best Novel - Fantasy Fiction

## Harmony of Colors

Second Place Winner of the 2018 International Latino Book Awards for Best Novel - Latino-Focused Fiction

## Ay to Zi

Award Winner of the 2018 Latino Literary Now's Latino Books into Movies Awards for Romance
Second Place Winner of the 2017 International Latino Book Awards for Best Novel – Romance

## The Devil's Disciple

Award Winner of the 2018 Latino Literary Now's Latino Books into Movies Awards for Suspense/Mystery
Second Place Winner of the 2016 International Latino Book Awards for Best Novel – Mystery

## A Taste of Honey

First Place Winner of the 2015 Latino Literary Now's Latino Books into Movies Awards for Fantasy Fiction
Second Place Winner of the 2015 International Latino Book Awards for Best Novel - Fantasy Fiction

*All works are published by Rosquete Press. All works are or will be available as Kindle or CreateSpace editions on Amazon.com*

# DEDICATION

This work of fiction is based on actual historical events which occurred in 1977, 1987, and 2018 in the State of Oregon. It is dedicated to a Latino hero, Delmiro Treviño, a U.S. citizen who is the Rosa Parks of the Oregon Sanctuary Movement. Like the African-American civil rights icon who refused to sit in the back of a bus in Alabama, and overcoming all odds, Mr. Treviño fought bravely against overzealous and misguided local law enforcement officials who were engaging in ethnic profiling while acting on behalf of the federal immigration service. His powerful story inspired this book which is a fictionalized version of the events that led to the creation of Oregon's Sanctuary Law.

The actual catalytic event occurred in 1977, when three Polk County sheriff deputies and a policewoman from the city of Independence, Oregon, went into the local Hi-Ho Restaurant and harassed Treviño and his friends. The local law enforcement officer physically grabbed Treviño and asked for proof of his citizenship. Delmiro was a U.S. citizen and a long term resident of Oregon. This was racial/ethnic profiling at its worst.

Delmiro, represented by his attorney Rocky Barilla, filed a Civil Rights lawsuit in federal court against local law enforcement and the INS, and they prevailed. The Immigration Service agreed that it would no longer encourage local law enforcement officers to make arrests on federal immigration violations.

Regardless of the litigation, similar police raids still persisted in the state. In 1986, Barilla was elected to the Oregon Legislature, with the Treviño case still strong on his mind. His experience with the Treviño case, prompted the Democratic State Representative to author the Sanctuary State bill, which passed with almost unanimous bipartisan support in 1987. Everyone was in favor of local governmental controlling their own budgetary spending, and setting their own law enforcement priorities e.g., protection of persons and property.

The incident of Delmiro Treviño being racially and ethnically profiled led to Oregon becoming America's first sanctuary state.

Delmiro has courageously stated on several occasions that enough was enough, "¡No más, ya basta!"

**"The New Colossus" written on the Statue of Liberty, by Emma Lazarus, 1883:**

". . . Give me your tired, your poor,
Your huddled masses yearning to breathe free,
The wretched refuse of your teeming shore.
Send these, the homeless, tempest-tost to me,
I lift my lamp beside the golden door!"

***

**"The Sheep and the Goats" from Matthew 25:31-46:**

"When the Son of Man comes in his glory, and all the angels with him, he will sit on his glorious throne. All the nations will be gathered before him, and he will separate the people one from another as a shepherd separates the sheep from the goats. He will put the sheep on his right and the goats on his left.

"Then the King will say to those on his right, 'Come, you who are blessed by my Father; take your inheritance, the kingdom prepared for you since the creation of the world. For I was hungry and you gave me something to eat, I was thirsty and you gave me something to drink, I was a stranger and you invited me in, I needed clothes and you clothed me, I was sick and you looked after me, I was in prison and you came to visit me.'

"Then the righteous will answer him, 'Lord, when did we see you hungry and feed you, or thirsty and give you something to drink? When did we see you a stranger and invite you in, or needing clothes and clothe you? When did we see you sick or in prison and go to visit you?'

“The King will reply, ‘Truly I tell you, whatever you did for one of the least of these brothers and sisters of mine, you did for me.’

“Then he will say to those on his left, ‘Depart from me, you who are cursed, into the eternal fire prepared for the devil and his angels. For I was hungry and you gave me nothing to eat, I was thirsty and you gave me nothing to drink, I was a stranger and you did not invite me in, I needed clothes and you did not clothe me, I was sick and in prison and you did not look after me.’

“They also will answer, ‘Lord, when did we see you hungry or thirsty or a stranger or needing clothes or sick or in prison, and did not help you?’

“He will reply, ‘Truly I tell you, whatever you did not do for one of the least of these, you did not do for me.’
“Then they will go away to eternal punishment, but the righteous to eternal life.”

# Table of Contents

# The Golden Rule

**Buddhism:**
*Hurt not others with that which pains yourself.*

**Christianity:**
*Do unto others as you would have them do unto you.*

**Hinduism:**
*Treat others as you would yourself be treated.*

**Islam:**
*Do unto all men as you would wish to have done unto you.*

**Judaism:**
*What you yourself hate, do to no man.*

**Native American:**
*Live in harmony, for we are all related.*

**Sacred Earth:**
*Do as you will, as long as you harm no one.*

# ACKNOWLEDGMENTS

My wife Dolores and I have had hundreds of experiences and adventures in California and Oregon. We have met wonderful people and encountered interesting personalities. Dolores is my soulmate who supports my writing and edits my works like a surgeon. Sometimes without any anesthesia.

This book is based on a true Oregonian hero, Delmiro Treviño, who was brave enough to stand up to racist local sheriffs and repugnant immigrant officers. It is also a story based on Oregonian values and the acceptance of all persons. Thousands of people and many organizations and coalitions have kept Oregon a true sanctuary state.

The background of this story began when I moved from California to Oregon in 1975 and became one of the first Latino attorneys in the State. The total number attorneys of color in the State numbered less than twenty. I worked for a legal aid office that rendered assistance to poor people. Since I was the only ethnic minority attorney in the office, I was assigned to all the cases involving persons of color. I learned Immigration Law by assisting Micronesian students at Chemeketa College in Salem, Oregon. Then in 1976, I went to visit the legal aid office in Spokane, Washington. I met a wonderful young man, Larry Kleinman, who later moved to Oregon to help establish PCUN, the Oregon farmworkers union. We were teamed up together on many occasions, and he, along with Cipriano Ferrell and Ramon Ramirez, started the Willamette Valley Immigration Project sponsored by the ACLU and the National Lawyers' Guild.

Additionally, as a result of the petitioning of the

University of Oregon Law School by, Dana Weinstein and Peter Fels, I became a part-time faculty member at the U of O and taught Immigration Law. During my ten-year teaching tenure, I had many fabulous students, including Michael Muñiz and Congress member Suzanne Bonamici.

In 1977, Providence introduced Delmiro Treviño to me. After listening to the mistreatment of Mr. Treviño, I filed a federal lawsuit on his behalf. Marion-Polk Legal Aid Services was very supportive of my litigation efforts. My colleague Steve Goldberg was an excellent mentor throughout the process. We had a favorable settlement in the federal lawsuit against the local enforcement officers and immigration, but it seemed liked a hollow victory. The police/immigration raids continued throughout the State for many years.

Later, in 1987, I became the first Latino to be elected to the Oregon State Legislature. Because of the Treviño experience, I introduced a legislative bill that prohibited local law enforcement from enforcing federal immigration laws. The purposes of the bill were to prevent racial profiling and to allow local governments to set their own law enforcement priorities e.g., protection of persons and property. Local enforcement loved the bill. Growers loved the bill. Civil rights and people of color loved the bill. It passed almost unanimously with bipartisan support. Willamette Law School Dean Daniel Santos, Gale Castillo, Roberto Mendoza, the Hispanic Political Action Committee, the Oregon Commission on Hispanic Affairs, Al Nuñez, Luis Caraballo and Senators Jim Hill and Dick Springer were all very instrumental in its passage.

I loved the natural beauty of Oregon, its values, and its

people. But I hated the rain. So I moved back to the Bay Area. Life is good.

Thirty years later, in 2018, I started receiving phone calls from Oregon about Proposition 105 that was on the November ballot. This measure was intended to repeal the Oregon Sanctuary Law. My wife and I went to Oregon to assist La Causa Oregon, One Oregon, APANO, Oregon Voice, and Unite Oregon. We were so proud of Governor Kate Brown, the civil rights groups, the religious groups, the unions, and many other groups who fought against this racially-motivated initiative.

Then in 2020 Danny Santos and I were contacted by two of the most wonderful people. They were researching the legislative history of Oregon's Sanctuary Law. Tina Ching is the Law Reference Librarian o the University of Oregon Libraries and Shiwanni Johnson is a third-year law student at the U. of O. who produces the podcast series "Truth of the Matter Asserted" (tomapodcast.com).

What the U.S. presidential administrations have done with respect to immigrants and refugees is unconscionable, immoral, and racist. Should we be surprised since this country murdered and stole lands from the Native Americans "fair and square"? The hardships of the thousands of human beings, children, and refugees need to be told over and over again. These struggles happened two thousand years ago in Egypt. They happened under Manifest Destiny. We saw them unfold in Germany and Poland. We experienced them with Japanese-American relocation camps. Addressing these injustices has been my inspiration and my passion.

My moral compass: Love thy neighbor as thyself.

# SANCTUARY

# PART I – AN AMERICAN HERO

## Salem, Oregon - 1977

*Heroism:*

*The ultimate measure of a man is not where he stands in moments of comfort and convenience, but where he stands at times of challenge and controversy.* - Dr. Martin Luther King, Jr.

## Chapter 1 – Sheriffs in Town

***Independence, Oregon***
***Sunday, January 9, 1977***

The moonless night was camouflaged by anthracite clouds. There was a brief respite in the seasonal torrential rains. The Tick-Tock Restaurant was housed in a red-bricked building in downtown Independence, Oregon. It was a popular place with the local growers, lumberjacks, and migrant workers. Tonight was Sunday and the cozy restaurant served pot roast and mashed potatoes as its special. The American style food was good and the price was right. The City of Independence was only 13 miles from Salem, the capital of Oregon.

Justino "Tino" Hidalgo was celebrating a belated $27^{th}$ birthday with three of his buddies from the plywood factory. The restaurant was three-quarters filled with the regulars. Donna, the big-haired, bottle blonde with ruby red lipstick, brought over this group's second round of drinks. The preferred clientele was Anglo, but the Mexican customers usually consumed lots of beer, and that was good for business.

Memo Mora was bemoaning the fact that he had broken up with his girlfriend, Leti. She had wanted to get married, and he didn't.

"She's the best you ever gonna get, pendejo," said José Aguilar. "Besides she must be blind if she doesn't see how feo you are."

"Screw you!" Memo countered. "I'm not ugly. I am a

handsome dude."

The others laughed.

"I think she is smart for dumping your sorry ass," Paco Urbino piled on.

"Screw you too!"

"It's his choice, dudes," the quiet Tino said. He swished around the gravy on his plate to cover the mashed potatoes.

"You're right, Tino," nodded José. "He probably likes boys better anyway."

"Screw you, cabrón," Memo was getting irritated.

As the four Latino customers were engaged in friendly bantering, two Polk County Sheriffs' cars pulled up in front of the restaurant. Sergeant Bill Doerfler was dressed in his verdigris uniform. He got out of his vehicle and walked over to Independence Policewoman Diane Palin who was standing in front of the restaurant.

"Hey, Diane, what's going on?" Doerfler tipped his hat as he greeted her.

"Same ol', same ol'" she responded. "Just shaking the bushes. See what runs out."

Sheriffs John Trahern and Bob Campbell joined the pair.

"Ready!" Doerfler commanded, rather than asked. It was the sheriffs' weekend routine to rout apartment buildings looking for undocumented persons or arrest patrons after the closing hour near the Mexican bar for driving under the influence. The officers thought that "these hombres" should just work and be invisible the remainder of the time. Just don't even dare to look at their wives or daughters.

The four officers nodded and then they all entered the restaurant. Tonight they would begin by combing through the Tick-Tock Restaurant looking for any possible "action." At the moment, Trahern and Campbell had split up, scanning the dining room from side to side.

Trahern pointed to a table in the middle where Tino and his three companions were seated. The conversations in the restaurant started to die down as the sheriffs moved to the center of the restaurant and stood in front of Tino's table.

Tino's eyes grew big. There were four cops directly in front of him, all in uniform, all armed.

"Where you boys from?" Campbell asked in a stern voice.

"Here," Memo responded. His other three friends nodded in agreement.

"Let me see your proof of citizenship," Campbell continued gruffly. "Your passports."

"What are you talking about?" Tino responded. "We don't have passports."

"Stand up!" Trahern barked and grabbed Tino by the arm.

Tino was surprised and angry, but mostly embarrassed. He wanted to resist, but he was smart enough to know that they were cops and that they would either beat him or take him to jail or probably both.

For the next few minutes, Memo, José, and Paco were interrogated and badgered in a similar fashion.

"Why are you hassling us, man" Tino blurted out. He

couldn't handle the harassment.

"Shut your face!" Trahern shouted. "We don't want any wetbacks around here." He took his handcuffs off his belt and grabbed Tino's left wrist.

"I'm from here!" Tino said defiantly. Tino tried to pull away, but Trahern had quickly succeeded in cuffing him. Tino sighed. He knew that he couldn't resist.

Trahern took a step closer to Tino. "Okay, let's go." He started to push the young Latino toward the front door, but suddenly Officer Palin put a hand on her partner's chest. "I recognize him. He's okay. He's a local."

After the incident, Tino went home filled with mixed feelings of indignation, shame, and rage. Indignation at the unjust treatment that he and friends were subjected to and shame for not being able to stand up for himself as a man. He had been raised to always carry himself with pride for whom and what he was. Pride for his culture. Pride for his language. Pride for his family. In one instant, he had been robbed of his pride and had been publicly humiliated. Él estaba muy enojado and his wife knew how pissed off he was when he came home.

***

The Mid-Willamette Valley Legal Aid office was located on State Street, Salem's main thoroughfare, a block away from the Oregon Supreme Court building and the Capitol. The City of Salem is situated in Marion County, next to the Willamette River, and in the center of the agriculturally rich Willamette Valley. This legal aid office was staffed with seven attorneys, assisted by part-time law clerks from Willamette Law School, and six over-the-top clerical staff. The office handled civil cases for low-income clients. They did not do criminal defense.

It was mid-morning on Monday, January 10, and the grey clouds had brought in cold precipitation. Daniel Muñiz's was scheduled to do legal intake at the office. Daniel was a transplant from the Monterey Bay area. He had done his undergraduate work at the University of California Santa Cruz and was proud to wear his banana slug school mascot tee shirt. Wanting a little adventure in his life, he enrolled at Willamette Law School in Salem, Oregon in 1972. He had three major impressions. First, everything in the state was green, including Oregonians who were all uber-environmentally conscious. Second, the sky was forever gray and it rained every day. Third, everyone was white. Ninety-eight percent of the state's population was Anglo. There were less than 20 attorneys of color in the entire state!

In 1975, Daniel graduated from law school and soon thereafter, passed the Oregon state bar exam. Because he was bilingual in Spanish and English, he was hired at the local legal aid office to work with migrant farmworkers. Most of the seasonal migrant worker stream was from Texas. Daniel had to immerse himself into the Tejano language and culture. A few Latina girlfriends helped him make the transition.

Today, several potential clients walked into the crowded waiting room of the legal aid office which was furnished with beige-colored, metal folding chairs. The large-framed receptionist, Sara Reyes, instructed the client walk-ins to sign in and then quickly asked them to fill out personal information forms. Since it was legal aid, there was an upper income criterion for eligibility for services.

A young Latino couple walked in and took a seat.

"Mi amor, some of our friends say we shouldn't do this," Araceli nervously said to her husband as she squeezed his arm.

"It's not right!" Tino exploded with a fiery Tex-Mex accent.

"We shouldn't be treated like this!"

A half hour later Daniel was escorting Tino and Araceli Hidalgo into his postage stamp sized office with the César Chávez posters on the wall.

Tino looked at the attorney. Daniel had a beard and longish black hair. He looked like a hippy. *Is he a real lawyer?* Tino wondered.

Daniel asked Tino how he could assist him. Tino spent the next twenty minutes venting. His wife leaned forward. She had tears in her eyes. Daniel stared at Tino. He felt sad. Most of his clients were poor and uneducated. They had more than their share of misery. Their standard response was "*Así es la vida.*" Their "Such is Life" attitude was so fatalistic and automatic. It was ingrained in the culture. *But this guy seems different.*

"My pops fought for this country," Tino said in an angry, but soft-spoken tone. "Now we are being jacked around by the pinche cops because of our brown skin!"

***

Daniel learned that Tino's father, Luis Hidalgo, had been born in Guadalajara, Mexico in 1925. He became a mechanic and worked for Mexicana Airlines in Mexico City at the age of sixteen. When World War II started, the United States had tried to remain neutral. However, Mexico supplied Great Britain with oil during this period. Then when Germany sank two Mexican oil tankers in the Gulf of Mexico, Mexico declared war on the Axis powers. Mexico then sent its Mexican 201st Fighter Squadron, "The Katzen Aztecs," to the Philippines. The Mexican volunteer pilots, ground crew, and mechanics were trained in Texas and shipped off to Manila to assist the U.S. Air Force. They flew sorties in the Pacific and were hailed as heroes when they returned home after the war. A few stayed in Texas and made their homes there. Luis Hidalgo was one of the latter. He was twenty years old and single. He needed a job so he went to Laughlin Air Force base in Del Rio, Texas. The base captain gave him "make work" jobs and Luis was happy. Every once in a while he would have to defend himself against GI's who called him racist names and were angry about him taking a job from Americans. In the beginning, he was at the receiving end of a few attacks. But Luis had been raised in the barrios and was street wise. After a few skirmishes with him brandishing a combat knife, he was left alone.

Still Luis was not fulfilled. He was doing menial labor. A friend of his on base had a sister, Josefa Ortiz, who was from Brownsville, Texas. They started dating and the following year, 1946, they were married. They needed a place to live, but housing was hard to find. So were jobs. Most of the hires went to whites. Josefa's family had done migrant labor in Oregon, so Luis and Josefa decided to go to the Northwest. They bounced around the Mid-Willamette Valley that year, picking every type of vegetable and fruit known to humanity.

It was hard work and did not pay that well, so they went back to Texas and settled down in Weslaco, an hour away from where Josefa was from. During the next decade, the couple were blessed with four children. Justino "Tino" came first in 1950; and he was followed by José, Dolores, and Eloy. Luis had several jobs and the family lived hand-to-mouth. Josefa's parents were getting older and couldn't travel any longer to Oregon. They had a house in Woodburn, Oregon, that they owned. They offered it to Luis and Josefa who accepted the generous gift. In the early 60's Luis and his family once again moved to Oregon. He found work in a hops plant in Woodburn and made decent money. The problem was that the work was seasonal and he had very little work for part of the year.

Some of the campesinos that he worked with migrated to the sawmills. The pay was a lot higher, but more dangerous. Luis avoided the temptation to cut down trees. He had a family that needed him. The years went by and Luis and Josefa watched their children grow up.

The oldest, Tino, went to French Prairie Middle School and was its best cross country runner. He would run to and fro the three-mile distance from his home to school while his siblings took the buses. He held the school record for cross country and wanted to go to the regional finals. His family was too impoverished to get him proper running shoes. Within a week of the championship track meet, Tino stepped on some rocks on the muddy trail and tore his left Achilles' tendon. That ended his running career. His father took him to the hops plant to work on the weekends. The irony was that by the end of summer, he was able to buy a set of Adidas running shoes.

Later on, Tino had graduated from Woodburn High School with good grades. He didn't want to go to college. What for? His pops never went to college and he was doing all right. Tino was quiet, but popular, at school. He was very serious about doing the right thing and setting a good example for his younger siblings. Since he was the oldest of the Hidalgo kids, he always felt a responsibility to protect and defend them. If there was a bully that beat up on José, Tino was able to resolve the matter without violence. He talked with the kids and made them understand. He was very mature in that way. If someone was getting too friendly with Dolores, he politely asked them to back off. He never threatened, but his serious stare forced the person to back off.

Tino, himself, had a few girlfriends, but they wanted to get married and have kids. Tino wasn't ready for that. Tino wanted to save his money and buy some ol' used car. He didn't want to spend money on girls.

In the summer of 1968, Tino's best friend, Benito, moved to Independence, Oregon, to work at a plywood plant. The money was good. The work was year around. Benito invited him to join him. Tino talked it over with his dad. Luis was reluctant at first, but found out that the job was not as dangerous as lumberjacking. Besides, Tino would send money home to carry the family over during the slow times. Luis gave his blessing and Tino moved to Independence.

"Mi amor, Tino is a good son," Luis spoke to his wife who had tears in her eyes watching the departure of her eldest son. "His money will help our family. But whatever he sends us, we need to save half of it for him."

Every month Tino would come back to visit his family (and give them money). Josefa would fix his favorite meals and do his laundry. Luis had been strict, but fair, with his children. They all knew right from wrong. *Do the right thing! Show respect! Don't take crap from anyone!* These values were drilled into the minds of the Hidalgos.

Tino tried to time his visits home with the Norteño dances at the Woodburn Armory, where the locals celebrated their Mexican culture. Couples would bop up and down, circling the hall clockwise as the accordions played. It was here that Tino hooked up with Araceli Baez. She had been a grade behind him in high school. She thought he was handsome and he was mesmerized by her charms. A year later they were married at St. Luke's Catholic Church in Woodburn. As a wedding present, Luis gave Tino the money he had been saving for his son and advised him to buy a house. Because Tino had a job in Independence, the couple decided to buy a little place there. It was also cheaper.

The pair were blessed with Luisito who was born in 1971, and two years later, Iris, who was named after Araceli's recently-deceased mother. The job at the plywood plant was good and Tino received several promotions over the years. In 1977 he became an assistant floor supervisor.

***

But now, here in front of Daniel, was Tino Hidalgo, a Latino who was willing to bravely defend his rights. Tino had been outgunned by four local law enforcement officers, but he had a secret weapon: his determination to get justice. Daniel admired Tino's courage. Despite having less than two years of legal experience, he wanted to defend Tino's rights and dignity.

"Mr. Hidalgo, let me ask you some more questions," Daniel flipped over a page on his yellow legal pad. "If you don't understand the question, let me know. I will try to rephrase. Okay?"

Tino nodded his head. His wife, Araceli, stopped crying. She took a deep breath.

## Chapter 2 – Litigation

***Salem, Oregon***
***Tuesday, January 11, 1977***

Michael Cordy, the director of the legal aid office, sported a big brown handlebar moustache. He held weekly staff meetings on Tuesdays and Fridays starting as 8:30. The attorneys who had done legal intake discussed cases that had not been immediately resolved. Did the case have legal merit? Did the office have enough resources to handle the case properly? If there was consensus among the attorneys, then they would take the case. That could mean anything from sending a letter to full blown litigation.

This morning when Daniel Muñiz reported on three of his intakes from the previous day, he brought up the Hidalgo matter. Normally, the reporting out of cases involved landlord tenant disputes, marital dissolutions, or breach of contract issues. The Hidalgo situation was different. It was a civil rights case.

Daniel narrated the facts of the case. "Mr. Tino Hidalgo is a United States citizen. He was born in Weslaco, Texas. . ." Afterwards, Daniel was barraged with questions.

"What are the legal issues?" Michael began the questions.

"I'm thinking unlawful arrest and civil rights violations. Discrimination," Daniel responded. "Probably not kidnapping. Some kind of harassment?"

"What does this guy want?" Ken asked. "Money?"

The attorneys around the room knew that most clients would

say “A million dollars!”, just because. Then they were told that damages had to be proven. The clients would still persist in asking for a million dollars. In the rare instances when a case was settled out of court, it was usually for less than $5000.

“No,” Daniel answered. “Just justice.”

There was a groan from one attorney. “Let’s spend hundreds of hours to get an ambiguous apology with no acknowledgment of culpability,” Josh threw out cynically.

“What would be the cause of action, Daniel?” asked Charlie, their director of litigation, who was only one year older than Daniel.

“For sure, violation of the federal Civil Rights Act,” Daniel had already done some preliminary research. “And, we don’t know yet if the police were following standard operating procedures.”

“So you’re saying that we would take this to federal court,” Charlie further inquired.

Daniel nodded in the affirmative. The others were stone faced. The moment of truth was upon them. If they all agreed that they should move forward, one of them would be in charge of the case. This Hidalgo complaint would take hundreds of hours. Nobody wanted to sacrifice a lifetime for this type of case. It was not sexy enough. It didn’t even rise up to the level of a police brutality case.

“I suppose you want to be lead on this case, Daniel?” Charlie really wasn’t asking. Although Daniel had been in the office for less than two years, he already had two federal courts under his belt. On the positive side, he had the most federal court experience of any of his colleagues.

Daniel's legal training consisted of the centuries old practice of trial by fire. He remembered that in his first month at legal aid, a gigantic Micronesian client had come into his office. His student visa was being revoked because he had dropped out of school. Daniel knew nada about Immigration Law. After cramming during a weekend and making a few calls to the local Chemeketa Community College, Daniel was able to get the student reinstated, and a letter was sent to the Immigration and Naturalization Service that rectified the situation. Thereafter, every immigration case went to Daniel, including one involving a South African.

As to his federal court experience, his first case involved a little old African-American lady, Beryl Jones, who wanted to buy a house in the most rural, redneck city in the county. The realtor said that he didn't sell to Blacks. The case was filed in federal court. The good news had been that the realtor recanted and was more than willing to sell the woman a house. The bad news was that Beryl passed away before that could happen.

Daniel's other federal case involved Chemawa Indian School that was run by the Bureau of Indian Affairs. It was more of an "off the res" young adult center. The school administrators, although they were Native Americans, did not appear to care about providing a meaningful education to the students. Basket weaving was the number one activity. At that time, "Apple" was a derogatory label for a Native American who was red on the outside, but white on the inside. The Chemawa "Apple" administrators maintained a draconian discipline system. The students were older adolescents, so sex and alcohol were always issues. School enrollment in September started at about 125 students; but by the following June it was less than 50. Students were expelled and sent back home (as far east as North Dakota) for trivial infractions. It was here that Daniel met Neil Katz, the U.S. Attorney. Katz was a political appointee and was tasked with putting out fires. The Chemawa case was eventually settled with several students reinstated if they chose to come back to the school after being sent home to Montana or North Dakota.

"Okay," Charlie made some notations on this legal pad. "I'll need a legal memorandum on this case in a week. Causes of action. Legal issues. Precedents. Defenses."

"Anybody want to assist Daniel?" Charlie looked around the table. "Chance to get your feet wet in federal court."

Peter Raksin raised his hand weakly. "I worked on a police misconduct case back in Boston when I was a law student." Peter was very self-effacing. He had finished in the top 1% of his class at Harvard Law School. He had turned down some very lucrative job offers in Manhattan to work at this legal aid office.

"Great, Peter," Charlie smiled. He loved his staff. They were always willing to help one another. "And don't forget to include research on governmental immunity and the Tenth Amendment."

***

For the next six weeks, the legal aid staff attorneys, Daniel and Peter, drafted federal court pleadings. They would be suing the Polk County Sheriffs and the Independence Police Department. Juventino "Tino" Hidalgo would be the lead plaintiff in the class action. His three companions from the Tick Tock Restaurant were being pressured from work and the church not to make waves with local law enforcement. They refused to participate in the lawsuit. They all had to live and work in Independence. And besides, *asi es la vida.* But Tino was all in. He was determined not to be a second class citizen, just because he was Brown and Latino. In the meantime, the two staff attorneys also plotted out their legal Discovery strategy. They would submit Interrogatories to each of the defendants to get written responses from each of them.

The City of Independence is located in Polk County. Peter had dug through the county archives and found out that the four-thousand-person city was founded by pioneers from Independence, Missouri. Moreover, the neighboring town of Dallas had been a recruiting site for the Ku Klux Klan during the early 1900's. Some of this county's residents were still wedded to the philosophy of white supremacy.

Sheriffs Doerfler, Campbell, and Trahern were served the legal papers along with policewoman Palin. The Polk County Counsel didn't want to handle the case. He persuaded the county commissioners to hire a private law firm that specialized in federal litigation. The sheriffs were represented by Reed, McClain, and Paulus. They were good and they were expensive. The City Attorney for Independence was retained on a limited contract basis. She recommended that the city retain the same legal counsel as Polk County since the facts were the same for all.

For the next month there were a lot of legal machinations. The defendants filed general denials to the federal complaint. Daniel and Peter immediately sent Samuel Reed, the lead attorney for the defense, some Interrogatories, Request for Admissions, and other related information. This was part of their legal strategy to discover the facts and background of the defendants' actions. The defendants were dragging their feet in answering. At $300 per hour the county and city were cash cows for the law firm. Or to be more accurate, the local taxpayers were on the hook for the legal fees.

On April 1, Sheriff Bill Doerfler was sitting for a deposition in a small room in the Polk County Courthouse in Dallas, Oregon. Attorneys for both sides were present along with a court reporter. Doerfler was dressed in full uniform, including his patrolman's hat, and carried his service revolver. He also was wearing his dark green Ray Ban sunglasses. Mr. Hidalgo was not present.

Daniel and Peter looked at each other and rolled their eyes. *Oh, really?! A Strother Martin, Cool Hand Luke look alike?!*

Doerfler was sworn in by the court reporter. Peter took the lead on the interrogation of Sheriff Doerfler. Peter was super bright and could cite any law at any time, but the night before he hardly slept. He was nervous. He didn't want to blow it. The Hidalgo family was already being hassled by their neighbors for being troublemakers. The local sheriffs were driving by their house on a daily basis. Peter was under pressure. He wanted to protect the Hidalgos.

"Please state your name and occupation for the record," Peter took a deep breath and calmly began the deposition questioning. He was going to help get justice for the Hidalgos.

"William Doerfler, Polk County Sheriff."

"How long have you been employed by Polk County?"

For the next five minutes Peter asked a lot of background questions. Doerfler had a smirk on his face when he answered.

"And what are your duties as a sheriff" Peter continued.

"To enforce the law," Doerfler said with a wry grin. He had been well coached. "We protect people and arrest the bad guys." Doerfler was getting a little cocky and started to ad lib.

"On January 9 of this year, you entered the Tick Tock Restaurant in Independence, is that correct?"

"Yes."

"You were with Sheriffs Trahern and Campbell and Policewoman Palin, is that correct?"

"Yes."

Samuel Reed, the legal counsel for the defendants, thought that plaintiff's attorney Peter Raskin was doing an okay job, but wasn't finding out much. *Why is this youngster asking closed-ended questions?* he thought.

"Why?" Raskin struck.

"Why what?" Doerfler was thrown off balance.

"Why were you there?"

"To enforce the law," Doerfler gave the default answer.

"What laws?"

"We thought there might be illegal aliens there."

"Is that a crime?"

"Sure it is."

"Did you read Mr. Hidalgo his Miranda rights?"

"What for? We thought he might be here illegally."

"So you believe that if he is here illegally, you don't have to read him his Miranda rights, is that correct?"

Doerfler did not respond.

"Did you arrest him?"

"No," Doerfler was looking nervous. He glanced at his attorney, Samuel Reed. No help there.

"Did you grab him?"

"I don't recall."

"Did you question him?"

"I don't recall."

"Did you ask Mr. Hidalgo to show you his passport or proof of citizenship?"

"I don't recall."

"Sheriff, do you carry a passport?"

Reed jumped in. "Irrelevant! Don't answer!" Doerfler's head was moving from one attorney to the other.

"Have you arrested other individuals for being illegal aliens in the past?"

"Objection! Relevance!" Reed was now awake.

"Please answer the question. This is a follow up to his previous answer."

Reed thought a moment and nodded for Doerfler to respond.

"Sure, that's part of our job."

"Is this written down somewhere in a standard operating procedures manual?"

"I don't know. It's what we do. We've always done it."

"Counsel, please furnish me a copy of this policy," Peter

stared squarely at his opposing counsel and kept starting until Reed nodded in the affirmative.

"Officer Doerfler, how do you know what people are illegal?"

"Because most of the Mexicans around here are."

"Do you ever interrogate or question Canadians?"

"Don't have to," Doerfler was trying to act tough. "They speak good English."

Raksin leaned over to Daniel and they whispered for a moment.

"Mr. Reed, what do you say to a ten-minute break?"

Everybody assented. Peter was on a roll and really didn't want Reed to coach Doerfler anymore. On the other hand, he wanted to consult with Daniel to make sure that he was getting everything they needed.

During the break, Daniel complimented his partner and handed him a legal pad sheet with a few more questions.

After fifteen minutes, the deposition resumed.

"Just a few more questions, sheriff," Peter said. He could see beads of sweat on Doerfler's forehead. "After you arrest people for being illegal aliens, what do you do?"

"I don't understand," Doerfler was now fidgeting in his chair.

"After the arrest, what is the follow up procedure?"

"We call up INS and let them know."

"What does the INS do?"

"Well, usually within a week or so, they drive down from Portland and haul them off in a van."

"Where do the illegal aliens stay until the INS arrives?"

"In our jails."

"Who pays for this?"

"I don't know."

"Has the INS ever told you to stop arresting alleged illegal aliens?"

"Heck, no. They love it when we find them some wets," Doerfler was getting excited. "They encourage us to round them up. They haven't got the manpower."

"So you are doing the INS's work for them?"

"Sure, why not," Doerfler was talking freely. "Just enforcing the law."

***

After the first deposition, Daniel and Peter debriefed as they drove back to Salem. They had a quick lunch at a local Mexican restaurant and then met with Charlie, the director of litigation, in the afternoon. By the end of the week, the Hidalgo complaint was amended to add Edward Miller, Director of the Portland Office of the Immigration and Naturalization Service, as an additional defendant. Miller was served papers on Friday.

A few days later, a young woman with short, brown hair showed up at Marion-Polk Legal Aid and asked to speak with Daniel. The receptionist buzzed Daniel and gave him the message that a Greta Nelson wanted to speak with him. Daniel asked Sarah to send her to his office.

Greta entered the tiny office, glancing sideways at the César Chávez posters mounted on the wall. "Hi, I'm Greta Nelson with the Capitol-Journal. "Do you mind if I ask you a few questions?"

Daniel looked at the blue-eyed Salem newspaper reporter who gave him a big crooked smile. *What was this all about?*

"I want to ask you about the Hidalgo lawsuit," she jumped right in. She turned on a portable recorder. "You don't mind if I record this?"

Daniel nodded no. *Was he allowed to talk to the press about pending litigation? Maybe I should check with someone?! I think I'm okay as long as I just keep to the facts. Can't violate attorney-client privilege or work product.*

For the next fifteen minutes, Daniel recited a sterilized version of the Hidalgo case. Greta kept nodding her head. He kept talking. She seemed to be on Tino's side.

"Just a few more questions," the reporter smiled again. "How would you characterized Mr. Hidalgo?"

Daniel blew out a breath. "Tino's brave. He is still putting up with the constant harassment by the local sheriffs. He's like Rosa Parks. He's courageous. He is not a quitter."

They were almost finished and then Greta asked, "Is there anything else that you want to say?"

"Well, how did you find out about this lawsuit?" Daniel was curious.

"I cover all local government," she responded in a peppy

manner. “I heard about it at the Polk County Commissioners’ meeting. One of the commissioners was angry because of the high attorney fees. He had campaigned on a balanced budget platform and now expenditures were running out of control.”

“Another thing,” Daniel sensed an opening. “What do you know about the harassment of Mexicans in the area by the local sheriffs. Do you have any information about this?”

Greta started to say no, but finally said, “Let me see what I can dig up.”

***

As expected, a few weeks later the feds also filed a general denial. Daniel kept Tino abreast of the legal machinations. Tino was not backing down. The court set a preliminary trial date and ordered all the parties to meet for a pre-trial conference. The meeting was conducted by a federal magistrate who had three main functions: first, to expedite the pretrial discovery process and resolve legal motions; second, to “coax” the parties into settling; and third, to ensure that a trial was a last resort. All the parties were represented by counsel. The plaintiff’s attorneys, Daniel Muñiz and Peter Raksin wore their bargain basement sport coats. For the defense, Samuel Reed wore a charcoal gray three-piece Brook Brothers suit, and the U.S. attorney, Neil Katz, wore a navy Italian double-breasted suit with Bruno Magli loafers. The prior Monday, the attorneys for the sheriffs had tried to file a motion to dismiss, but the judge said that he wanted all the parties to meet before any trial to try to work things out. The defense attorneys argued against this, but the judge was firm in his decision.

Today all the parties were before the magistrate for a pre-trial conference. Henry Stern, short, chubby, and bald started to ask questions of the parties. He began with the plaintiffs.

"Mr. Muñiz, what does the plaintiff want out of this case?" Stern asked, getting straight to the quick.

"Your Honor, we are seeking an injunction against the sheriffs, the police, and the INS, and a declaratory judgment," Daniel asserted.

"I understand that, Mr. Muñiz, I have read the pleadings," Stern adjusted his wire-rimmed bifocals. "But what does he really want?"

"He wants the sheriffs to quit harassing Latinos and he wants an apology from the sheriffs."

Samuel Reed didn't want to spend all morning playing paddy cake. He wanted to force the issue, "Your honor, our officers were just doing their job."

"But they have no authority to enforce federal immigration law," Daniel jumped in. "This was racial harassment."

"Your honor, I object," Reed had baited Daniel and the young attorney had bitten.

"Mr. Muñiz, Mr. Reed is correct. You did not allege racial discrimination," the magistrate said.

Daniel knew that he was getting too emotional, but remembered what his boss, Charlie, had advised him, "Sometimes cases do not prevail on legal merits. They win on public perception or the threat of bad publicity. Politicians don't like to be embarrassed. They could lose an election."

"Your Honor, I think the enforcement of immigration laws by the sheriffs was racist. At trial we will present such evidence," the legal aid attorney said with self-assurance.

The defense attorneys were dumbfounded. *This was not good for them.*

"Your honor, our sheriffs and police were only enforcing the law," Reed retorted. "Nothing racist about that."

"Well, firstly, they have no legal authority to enforce federal immigration law," Daniel asserted. "And secondly, they only harassed brown-skinned Mexicans." Daniel knew he was pushing it, but what the heck.

"They have the authority to enforce these laws. The INS has said so. They work in cooperation with the INS on these raids," Reed was playing his fed card.

"We have not authorized any sheriffs to do these things," U.S. Attorney Katz jumped in. He needed to cover the federal agency. "We haven't deputized any of them."

"Well, our sheriffs have been taking orders from someone at the INS," Reed proclaimed. He wasn't going to let the feds dodge their role in these incidents.

"I think the sheriffs may have assumed things that are not true," Katz tried to counter diplomatically.

"Your honor, we are planning to depose INS Director Edward Miller as soon as possible," Daniel added. "That should help us resolve the discrepancy between both defendants' positions."

***

Magistrate Stern was very astute. He made the parties work through the lunch period without food. At about 1:30 they reached a settlement. The federal government would not encourage local law enforcement agencies to unilaterally enforce immigration laws. Local law enforcement could provide secondary assistance in any INS situation, like traffic control, but could not be involved in initial contacts.

As they exited the building, Katz pulled Daniel and Peter aside so they couldn't be overheard. "You gentlemen did a fine job. I think the settlement is fair." He reached out to shake their hands.

As he walked away, Katz thought, *these two young attorneys made law enforcement look like the keystone cops.*

## Chapter 3 – The New Guy

***Salem, Oregon***
***1986***

Nine years had elapsed since the Hidalgo case and Daniel Muñiz was no longer an attorney with the legal aid office. On this particular day, he was busy reorganizing files for the Telecommunications Committee Chair, State Representative Jeff Pennington, after a legislative meeting on telephone surcharges at the Oregon Capitol. The six other legislators had left the room with their respective staff.

"I think the telephone companies are jacking up the rates on poor people in order to give big corporations price breaks," Pennington said in his baritone voice, shaking his head. "Daniel, do me a favor and check out the political contributions from the phone companies to all the other members of the committee. I know that Bush gets a ton from the them. And so does the Republican Caucus."

"Will do, Representative," Daniel replied.

***

On 1980, after working with Mid-Willamette Valley Legal Aid for five years, Daniel Muñiz had moved to a staff attorney position with the Oregon Legislature. He was seen as politically non-partisan, and that was an advantage for working with some of the legislative committees. Most of the legislators were not lawyers, even though they were making the laws. They needed to rely on staff for objective analyses, not political propaganda. Daniel made friends with all the legislators, Democrats and

Republicans. He worked for the Senate Labor and Education Committees, and was Legal Counsel for the Assembly Judiciary Committee.

Life was simple. In 1982 Daniel had gotten married to a Latina bilingual education teacher, María Adan, who worked for Salem Public schools. She had two children from a previous marriage. They had a little white wooden-framed house a few blocks away from Bush Park. Most of the time Daniel would walk to the Capitol where he worked. It was less than a mile.

***

"Have you heard the rumors, Daniel?" State Representative Jeff Pennington was giving him a strange smile.

"No," Daniel furrowed his eyebrows. *Is everything okay?* he wondered. Pennington was a 6'2'' handsome African-American who represented South Salem in the Oregon Legislature. His trademark was his sincerity and folksy manner. When he spoke, people listened.

"Let me say this," Pennington said like he was practicing a speech. "I'm running for the South Salem Senate seat."

"When?" Daniel knew that state senate terms were for four years. The incumbent, Lionel Weeks, was a very popular Republican. *Surely, Pennington was not going to run again Weeks this year. Most likely, in four.* The legislative district was super Republican, but somehow Pennington had been elected as a Democrat twice. Most of the constituents cared about integrity and moderate political views, rather than partisanship.

"Right now," Pennington said manner-of-factly.

*Is he crazy?* Daniel thought. Lionel Weeks runs this city. Being the state senator in Salem, the capital city where most of the lobbyists reside, made him a formidable incumbent.

Pennington gave Daniel an abbreviated stump speech. It was like he was practicing on Daniel. Daniel nodded.

"And I have a favor to ask of you," Pennington continued. Daniel knew that this was "la mordita." Politics ran on money. Office holders and candidates always had their hands out. And once a person contributed, he or she was expected to give again. Daniel would feign poverty and probably write him a $25 check.

"Okay," Daniel said meekly.

"I want you to run for my Assembly seat," Pennington looked Daniel squarely in the eyes.

***

The November general election came. Against the staggering odds against him, Daniel Muñiz became the first Latinx elected to the Oregon Legislature. He had not been politically connected. He did not have deep pocket backers. He was a relatively a new comer to the district, but Muñiz had canvassed tens of thousands of houses, one by one. He had forced himself to ask his family and friends for money. That was really hard for him. Coming from an impoverished background, he knew that they didn't have much to give. Daniel went to local civic events, coffees, and debates. He had been fortunate enough to be endorsed by the local newspaper. His Republican opponent was unpopular in the district. A significant number of Republicans supported the Muñiz candidacy. People of color, women, gays, environmentalists, unions, and civil rights groups also backed the young attorney.

As for Pennington who was fighting an uphill battle against Weeks, a deus ex machina event occurred one month before the general election. State Senator Weeks died of a heart attack. Pennington breezed into victory.

The Republican Assembly Minority Leader was irate that Muñiz had stolen a Republican seat. The Republican seat that would have made him Speaker. On the other hand, State Representative Mayra Koffman was elated that she would remain as the Assembly Speaker in a landslide 31-29 Democratic Party victory for the State Assembly. Daniel Muñiz had worked for her and she liked him. She appointed him to several choice legislative committees.

The legislative session was scheduled to begin in January of 1987. Muñiz had barely two months to get his Capitol office organized. He hired several staff persons. Shawn Kille was his chief of staff and an IT genius, and Sharon DeShane became his executive secretary. They had staff meetings once a week. The first order of business was to draft legislation. Muñiz met with the American Cancer Society and promised to help make tobacco products inaccessible to minors. He also collaborated with State Senator Elizabeth Tong who asked him to be a joint author on a resolution to build the Chinese Gates in Portland to commemorate what was once the second largest Chinatown in the U.S. While Shawn was busy having Legislative Counsel draft their legislative bills, Muñiz went about the business of finding co-authors for his legislation. He asked both Democrats and Republicans. He knew many legislators because he had worked at the Capitol for the last five years. He was friends with several of them, including their staffs.

It was just before Christmas and the spirit was joyful. Everybody was ready for a break before the legislative session commenced the second week in January. Muñiz was walking downstairs toward the lobby. He liked using the stairs because it was a modest form of exercise. Besides, he wouldn't be waylaid by lobbyists. But on this day, he ran into Milt Cromwell, the Assembly Minority Leader, who looked like Glen Campbell.

"Merry Christmas, Milt," Muñiz greeted him as he continued down the stairs.

"Merry Christmas, Daniel. Congratulations on your win," his archenemy said, stopping for a second. That forced Daniel to stop.

"Thank you."

"You know I have seen the good work that you have done in the building for the last few years," Cromwell smiled.

Daniel gave a reciprocal grin. During the campaign, Cromwell's political minions had come after him like a group of vigilantes. *He's playing nice today. Must be the Christmas spirit,* Daniel thought.

"You know, many of our Republican Assemblymen colleagues like you. And respect you," Cromwell was singing sweet praises. "You represent one of the most Republican districts in the State. Any time you want to switch parties and have an easy re-election you just let me know."

Muñiz knew that Cromwell was blowing smoke up his rear end. First, Daniel didn't trust the guy. Second, if he did switch, the position of Assembly Speaker would be up for grabs. He was loyal to Speaker Koffman. He would not betray her.

"Just tell me what committee you would like to chair," said Cromwell with an unctuous smile as he started back up the stairs.

# Chapter 4 – Pedro's

***Salem, Oregon***
***January 19, 1987***

The first of the year arrived and Daniel Muñiz was officially sworn into the Oregon Legislature, representing South Salem. He was on the Housing, Environment and Energy, and Education Committees. The first week was usually hectic for freshmen legislators who had to become acquainted with the floor plan of the Capitol and locate the eating places and restrooms. As for Daniel, he was right at home because he had worked in the building for the last five years.

His major challenge was juggling the endless appointments with lobbyists. Everyone wanted a piece of him. People who had tried to assassinate him a few months prior, now wanted to be his best friend. "Hey, do you want to go a Trailblazers game?" "How about we take you out for a steak dinner next week?" "Hey, it wasn't anything personal, just business."

Then came the nightly political fundraisers and parties. Daniel's mentor, Senator Pennington, advised him to make token appearances at as many as possible. Daniel promised his wife María that he would try to be home no later than eight o'clock every night. Nine o'clock at the latest. He wanted to see his kids, Mario and Selena, before they went to bed, and spend quality time with María. After the first week, the entire family was exhausted. They knew that it would only get worse.

It was the third Monday in January. The Martin Luther King Day ceremony at the Capitol was very nice, with Governor Norman Brown giving the keynote speech. Daniel was in attendance and bumped into his close friend from law school, Johnny Cruz. Cruz worked with the Oregon Rural Legal Assistance program and was also president of the Latino Advocates, a group that promoted Hispanic issues in the state.

"How are you, Daniel?" Johnny shook Daniel's hand. "I should be calling you Assemblyman Muñiz."

"Hey, man, just Daniel," Muñiz was still not comfortable with his new position and title, and the corresponding social implications. "Otherwise, I'm thinking you want something."

Johnny paused for a second and smiled. "I do want something. Do you have time for lunch?"

Daniel really wanted to go back to his office. The legislative bills had started to trickle in and he had to read them. He also needed to talk to his staff. But Johnny was a friend and a "carnal."

"Okay. On one condition," Daniel turned to walk side by side with his colleague. "I buy."

"Dude, are you kidding? I know how much you make," Johnny pulled his head back. "Or don't make." Since the Oregon legislative session was part-time, the monthly pay was roughly $900. Daniel didn't get any housing or travel reimbursement because he lived in Salem.

"Okay, we'll go Dutch," Daniel smiled. "Besides I can't afford your beer tab anyway."

***

Pedro's Mexican Restaurant was within walking distance of the Capitol. The place was crowded, with Norteño music playing softly in the background. The smell of carnitas from the kitchen was overwhelming.

A young waitress with black coiled braids, dressed in a white Mexican blouse with red and green ribbons and a colorful skirt, took their drink orders. Daniel and Johnny both ordered iced tea. They dug into the chips and salsa. It could have been a meal in itself. Carlita came back and took their meal order. Johnny wanted a wet chile verde burrito. Daniel was tempted, but he knew that he was getting very little exercise and did not want to gain weight. The joke around the Legislature was that everyone gained ten pounds during the first month of the session. Daniel ordered the chicken taco salad. His wife would have been proud.

Johnny stopped inhaling the chips and said to Daniel, “I need a favor.”

They were close friends. The request could be a $100 loan or helping someone with a legal problem.

“The local sheriffs are putting up roadblocks on Highway 99E,” Johnny began to explain. “They’re stopping Latinos. If they don’t have papers, they call INS.”

“How far does 99E go?” Daniel was having an unsettling feeling in his stomach and it wasn’t the salsa.

“From down south in Eugene/Junction City, up north to Canby.”

“How many incidents are we talking about, Johnny?”

“Several dozens. The different county sheriffs have rolling roadblocks. A new place every few days. But the common denominator is the INS.”

“But how do you know all this?” the state representative pressed his friend. As an attorney, he knew there was usually a big difference between what people said and what people could prove.

"Pepe has been tracking the immigration holds where local police incarcerate people in local jails at the request of the INS (Immigration & Naturalization Service)." Pepe Saenz was the Director of the Oregon Migrant Workers Union. The program had several field offices throughout the State of Oregon. When Daniel was working for legal aid in Salem, he was co-counsel with Pepe on cases involving the poor working conditions of dairy workers. The defendants were the organic milk producers. Pepe was also very active working with Johnny at the Latino Advocates program. Daniel trusted Pepe implicitly.

"What do you need?" Daniel offered.

"Remember that old lawsuit that you filed ten years ago?"

"The Hidalgo case?"

Johnny nodded affirmatively. "In spite of the lawsuit, not much has changed. Frontier justice prevails."

Carlita, the waitress, came back to the table and asked if the two wanted dessert. They both declined. She refilled their iced teas.

"What exactly do you want, Johnny?"

"I think we need legislation to prevent the police from circumventing the Hidalgo case."

"What do you mean?" there was quizzical look on the state representative's face.

"The police are stopping Latinos and other people based on skin color. If they don't have proof of citizenship, they are sent to a city or county jail. They stay there until the INS picks them up. It can take a few days or a few weeks, until the INS comes for them."

"Well, who is paying for their detention?"

"You and me, for sure, brother," Johnny gave a cynical smile, "and local government."

"You mean we're subsidizing the feds?"

"Yup!"

Representative Muñiz thought back ten years. The Hidalgo case was still heavy on his mind and burning in his gut. He felt something between being sad and being angry. An hour later, State Representative Daniel Muñiz called Shawn, his chief of staff, into his office. "We have a new bill we need to introduce. It's at the request of the Latino Advocates."

"No problem."

***

A week later at their staff meeting, Shawn Kille and Muñiz discussed positions on bills already in the legislative pipeline. They both read all the bills. If it was anti-labor, Muñiz would oppose it. If was pro-environment, he would support it. Because Muñiz was an attorney, he often spotted weak spots in good legislative proposals. In these cases, he would have Shawn talk to Legislative Counsel to draft potential amendments to the defective bills.

Today, they also went over six legislative bills introduced by Muñiz.

"Representative, here is HB 2314," Kille made his next

presentation. "It would codify existing law prohibiting local law enforcement agencies from enforcing federal immigration laws."

An Act, HB 2314, Relating to law enforcement.

**Be It Enacted by the People of the State of Oregon:**

**SECTION 1. (1) No law enforcement agency of the State of Oregon or of any political subdivision of the state shall use agency moneys, equipment or personnel for the purpose of detecting or apprehending persons whose only violation of law is that they are persons of foreign citizenship residing in the United States in violation of federal immigration laws.**

**(2) Notwithstanding subsection (1) of this section, a law enforcement agency may exchange information with the United States Immigration and Naturalization Service in order to:**

**(a) Verify the immigration status of a person if the person is arrested for any criminal offense; or**

**(b) Request criminal investigation information with reference to persons named in service records.**

**(c) For purposes of subsection (1) of this section, the Bureau of Labor and Industries is not a law enforcement agency.**

"Looks good to me," Daniel read it. He was pleased. He would have to call Johnny. Now it was time to work this bill.

Daniel and Johnny divided up the lobbying efforts for HB 2314. For the most part, Johnny would concentrate on moderate and liberal Democratic legislators. Daniel would have to handle the rest. They split the task of talking with special interest groups. Again, Daniel would take on the more conservative or difficult ones.

A few days later, State Representative Muñiz was getting ready for his House Education Committee hearing when Shawn handed him a dozen bill folders. Daniel gave him a tired thanks. *This legislative business is like running a daily marathon if you do it right.*

They started walking together to the hearing room three floors down.

"Representative, two quick things," Shawn was a master of stealing minutes and seconds from Muñiz. "Joel from Senator Dinkle's office asked if you wanted to be a co-sponsor on his Rogue River dredging bill."

"What's the bill say?"

"It would basically create an aquatic park and tourist spot in Grants Pass."

Normally, Muñiz would be amenable to working with any legislator, Democrat or Republican, but he had to be vigilant about political traps. The well-publicized Republican agenda for the session was to cut off Workers' Compensation benefits.

"See what the Sierra Club thinks about it," Daniel was being political. Shawn nodded his head. "And the second thing"

"Our law enforcement bill HB 2314 is scheduled for a hearing in Judiciary on February 4."

*My God! That was fast! No sleep this week!*

# Chapter 5 – AB 2314

## *January 26, 1987*

Daniel and Shawn had been getting their witnesses lined up for the hearing. Daniel had met with the Chief of Police of Salem, Michael Louys, at the Civic Center coffee shop. There was mutual respect between the two. Daniel had several relatives in law enforcement.

"I like the bill, Representative," the Chief said. "The INS leaves these guys in jail and we have to pick up the tab. I'm using a lot of my funds and staff for the feds. We already have to deal with inmates released from OSP (Oregon State Prison) and patients from the State Hospital. Not to mention their families. It's a mess."

"Would you be willing to testify in support of the bill next week, Chief?" Representative Muñiz looked him straight in the eye.

"I'll have to run it by the City Attorney," Louys said. "But I don't see any problem."

They shook hands and went their respective ways.

Concurrently, Pepe Saenz, the Director of the Oregon Migrant Workers Union, had talked to Bob Sawyer, lobbyist for the Oregon Agricultural Bureau.

"We need a stable labor force, Pepe," Bob spoke in a slow manner. "Can't afford crops to go unpicked. A couple of years ago the INS raided my plum orchards. I almost went bankrupt."

“Can we count on your support of HB 2314?”

“I can do one better, Pepe,” Bob gave him a Jimmy Stewart impression. “I can put in a word to the Rural Caucus (the Republican legislators who had a lot of agriculture in their districts) to support it.”

“Gracias, amigo,” Pepe shook his hand.

“De nada.”

The next day Johnny Cruz of the Oregon Legal Assistance program met with Andrea Meissner, State Director for the League of Cities and Counties. She was a natural ally. The feds used local funds to finance their operations, never paid their bills, and tried to micromanage everything.

“I’ll be at the hearing,” she said.

***

On Wednesday, February 4th, Representative Muñiz was given a “legislator courtesy” by the committee chair and was allowed to present his bill HB 2314 first on the House Judiciary agenda.

“Mr. Chairman,” he sat at a table in front of the committee. He was wearing his best suit (he only owned three). It was a navy wool pinstripe. A solid red tie completed the attire. “and members of the Committee . . .

“House Bill 2314 is a bill that allows local law enforcement agencies to set their own priorities, and to concentrate on the enforcement of laws that protect our communities from crimes against persons and property . . .”

After Representative Muñiz introduced the bill, there were

three other witnesses who gave brief statements and two more with "me too" comments. Josh Starr from the ACLU testified about the continuous discrimination against Oregonians who were perceived to be non-white. Sheila Sanders from the County Counsel Association talked about the unnecessary exposure to civil liability that the INS was dumping on local governments. "We're worried about being sued if someone gets hurt while we're trying to assist the INS. The feds will deny responsibility and leave us hanging."

The one opposition witness, Cheryl Dearborn, was from a rump group of the state sheriffs' association. Her complaint that alien criminals were invading Oregon.

The Committee Chair thanked everyone and banged his gavel. "Next bill!"

After the session, Daniel, Johnny, and Shawn met back at the state representative's office to debrief.

"Great job, Daniel! El primer paso," Johnny was jubilant.

"It went as well as could be expected," Shawn noted. He was always objective and honest in his analyses and opinions. Daniel liked him because Shawn was not a sycophant.

"What about lobbyist Dearborn?" Muñiz wanted to know who the opposition was and why they were objecting.

"She is just making a show to justify her lobbying fee," Shawn said. "She's not a player."

***

Twelve days later, the House Judiciary Committee scheduled HB 2314 for a legislative work session. There was another hearing and the bill was voted out of committee unanimously with a 7-0 vote. Now the real work began. Daniel's executive secretary, Sharon, and Shawn started whipping votes for the floor vote. The Assembly Democrats were supportive. The Republicans were either supportive or non-committal. While Republican Minority Leader Cromwell may not have had a personal opinion, he was against it because he didn't want State Representative Muñiz to get any credit. Maybe Cromwell could paint Muñiz as being anti-law enforcement in the next election.

On February 20, HB 2314 was presented on the House floor. A vote was taken and the bill was passed 54-3. The three nay votes coming from Republicans in rural counties. The bill was then sent to the Senate side where it was put on the back burner by the Senate President, Paul Kingsley. There was always a little gamesmanship played between the House and Senate sides of the Legislature. Freshman legislators would simply have to wait their turn.

On March 19, in the midst of the usual legislative commotion, State Representative Daniel Muñiz presided over the House as Speaker Pro Temp for the day. His wife, María, had baked his favorite raisin walnut oatmeal cookies to celebrate this auspicious occasion. Their children, Mario and Selena, were allowed to stay up an extra hour. They were proud of their father. "Maybe this is a sign of things to come," María smiled.

There were more hearings and more testimony on HB 2314. More law enforcement agencies were climbing on board, along with civil rights and religious groups and unions. The bill was amended and finally found its way to the Senate floor where it passed 29-1. One Republican senator, who was a friend of Muñiz, voted "no."

The bill was then sent back to the House which passed HB 2314, 58-1, concurring with the one minor Senate amendment.

Two days before the Fourth of July, HB 2314 was signed into law by Governor Norman Brown.

# PART II – TWIN OAKS

## Twin Oaks, Oregon

## 31 Years Later – 2018

*"The more things change, the more they remain the same."* - Jean-Baptiste Alphonse Karr

## Chapter 6 – Knock! Knock!

***Twin Oaks, Oregon***
***March 16, 2018***

Twin Oaks, Oregon, is one of those small rural settlements that gives the impression that time has stopped. The thirty thousand or so inhabitants are a microcosm of Oregon rural traditions with their farming and mining industries. Although its residents are mostly of White heritage, there is a sizable Latino population. The nearby Klamath Native-American reservation also has a strong influence on the town's culture and activities.

Twin Oaks is never mentioned in any Oregon tourism pamphlet. It is deemed unremarkable. No special buildings or churches. Nobody famous has ever hailed from this town. But it does have its great outdoors, where there are the mountains that shelter its inhabitants, lakes and rivers that nourish their souls, and trees that give clean air. This is a Garden of Eden for Nature's children.

For the last several decades, Twin Oaks has been a place of safe haven for its peoples, but now a dark blustery wind seemed to be blowing in, threatening this sanctuary.

***

It was the end of the week, but the sun had not yet set in the sylvan town of Twin Oaks.

The tall standing lamp gave Lorenzo enough light to examine the test papers strewn between his lap and the lumpy brown corduroy couch. *Jan made such a silly mistake!* He was grading the exams of his high school sophomore algebra class.

There was talk from the school board about dropping math as a graduation requirement. The argument was that everyone had computers and cell phones. Who needed to study math, when the answers popped up magically at one's fingertips? Besides, it was very difficult to recruit math and science teachers in this rural area that bordered Oregon and California.

The wood burning stove gave off a smoky evergreen smell. Some Sergio Mendes music played in the background. Suddenly, there was a loud pounding on his front door. It was late. Lorenzo frowned. Chispa barked and drew himself closer to Lorenzo. Lorenzo knew that his wife Corkie was upstairs reading Denise Chavez' "Loving Pedro Infante," in preparation for her monthly book club gathering. He had better get the door. *Crap! I hope it's not those Jehovah's Witnesses again. We're Catholic and not about to change.* Methodically, Lorenzo put down the unscored exams on the wooden coffee table.

"Just a minute!" he yelled out as he arose from the couch. Lorenzo slipped into his comfy moccasin slippers and started to make his way to the door, with Chispa on his right.

In this mile-high settlement of rural Twin Oaks, Oregon, it was an oddity to receive visitors in the evening. Magazine salespeople, delivery persons, and election year canvassers all came during the day.

There was a louder, more insistent knock. "Señor Becerra!" a female voice cried out. "Are you home?"

*Of course, I'm home. My house lights are on!* He hurried. "Coming!" *¡Cómo friega!*

The five-foot, eleven-inch-tall math teacher unlocked his front door and opened it. In front of him stood a short, auburn-haired Latina, with a multicolored striped shawl wrapped around her shoulders. Lorenzo did not recognize the woman.

"Señor Becerra, Yesenia didn't come home from school today," the brown-skinned woman blurted, totally out of breath. "And they took Gloria away."

*What's going on?*

"I'm sorry," Lorenzo was trying to be polite. "But who are you?"

"I'm Cristina. Cristina Navarro," the Latina blurted out. "I went to your wife's immigrant rights class."

"Okay." Lorenzo was perplexed about why this woman was on his porch at this late hour.

"Gloria is my neighbor. We live in Loma Linda. The police came and got her today." Loma Linda was the poor part of town that was situated in California proper, but administratively run by the town of Twin Oaks.

Lorenzo's eyes blinked. His mind was confused. He didn't know what was going on.

"Come in," Lorenzo needed a moment to collect his thoughts. "Please sit over here." He escorted Cristina to a floral upholstered chair in the living room. He turned on another lamp.

"I don't know what to do," the young woman lamented as tears rolled down her cheeks. She didn't take off her jacket. "My friend, she talked about you."

"Who is your neighbor again?"

"Gloria Ocaso," the woman replied anxiously. "And her daughter Yessie."

"What happened?"

"I come home from work around noon time. I work at the hospital," Cristina began. "Gloria is my neighbor. She lives across the court from me. I take care of Yessie when she comes home from school until her mom gets off work."

Lorenzo and his wife, Corkie, were involved with the local Latino Learning Center. They did a lot of community action work. Although Hispanics made up only nine percent of the population, it seemed that fifty percent of all local issues involved Latinos. The matters ranged from a need for bilingual education, to the issuance of drivers' licenses, or for being pulled over by law enforcement for "driving while brown." Corkie was an informal immigrant rights resource, even though she was not an attorney. Lorenzo taught Civics, as well as Math, at the local high school.

"Yessie didn't come home from school today. I called her mom," Cristina continued. "Gloria was at the middle school. She came right home."

"Mi amor, who are you talking to?" shouted a female voice from upstairs.

"A neighbor!" yelled Lorenzo back up to his wife.

"We walked back to the school, but can't find Yessie," Cristina sighed again. "We even asked at the school. But nobody had seen her. We went back home."

"Hi, I'm Corkie," Lorenzo's wife suddenly popped into the living room. She extended her hand to the young woman. "Haven't I seen you in one of my classes?"

"Yes. Mucho gusto," replied Cristina. "The police were at our place when we got back. We told them that we were looking for Yessie. But they didn't care."

"What do you mean?" interjected Corkie, as she imposed herself into the conversation.

"They arrested Gloria and took her away."

# Chapter 7 – Desperation

## *Sunday, March 4, 2018 – Two Weeks Earlier*

Almost two weeks earlier, Corkie had gotten up from the moss green armchair that was smothered with velvety grey cushions and a Pendleton blanket in their cozy living room. She and their black and tan German Shepherd "Chispa" had been enjoying the fire as the March rains pattered outside. She picked up the near empty coffee cup from the table with her left hand.

"Mi amor, do you want more coffee?" Corkie asked her 43-year-old husband Lorenzo as he systematically went through a stack of math papers that he had to grade. It seemed that he spent half of his life marking papers and scoring tests. Their Sunday morning routine was to sleep in and enjoy their half-caf, soy lattes.

***

Lorenzo was born in Mount Angel, Oregon in 1975 to Raúl and Mercedes Becerra. He was the third of four children. His father, Raúl, was a year-round employee at Wilkes Co-op, an enterprise that dealt with grass seed. The mother, Mercedes, was a part-time caretaker at the local Benedictine Center.

When Lorenzo turned five, the family moved to nearby Woodburn, Oregon, where his parents bought a powder blue, vinyl-sided house. Woodburn was a trilingual, tricultural enclave of Mexicanos, Anglos, and Old Believer Russians. All four Becerra children attended the local public schools. Their parents did not smoke or drink and didn't haven't any racial biases. They had already seen too much prejudice and discrimination in their lifetime. In high school, Lorenzo earned his money by playing in a Chicano rock group. Their music wasn't that good, but the band got free eats at the parties and met a lot of girls.

***

The 41 year-old Corkie, on the other hand, née Corcoran Hansen, was born in Salem, Oregon. Her Latina mother had been born in Mexico City and worked for the State of Oregon Employment Division in the Unemployment Hearings Division, while Corkie was growing up. Her father was a newspaper editor for the Salem Capitol Journal. Corkie was the youngest of three sisters. She graduated number one in her class at South Salem High School, in addition to being a varsity track star three years in a row. By the time Corkie enrolled at Willamette University, her sisters were married and lived out of state.

Lorenzo had met Corkie at the Ashland Shakespearean Festival when they both attended a performance of "Romeo and Juliet." He was caught off guard when he saw this 5'5" blue-eyed young woman with long brown braids leaving the theater. He approached her and asked if he had a class with him (knowing this was a lie). She went over the list of her classes knowing he was giving her a line. But they did discover that they were both attending grad school at SOSU (Southern Oregon State University). Lorenzo was pursuing his teaching credential and she was earning her Master's degree in Spanish.

That evening found them having coffee and chocolate croissants at the Mixed Sweets Café. He found out that she could speak better Spanish than he. She had spent the last four summers at a language school in Cuernavaca, Mexico.

"It's very cool to finally meet a Latina that I can really talk to," he teased.

"Your mom doesn't count?" she quipped. They both laughed.

They started dating. Once or twice a week they would jog together around the Ashland hills. Lorenzo also found out that Corkie was a gym rat and an excellent soccer player. They would argue about sports for hours. But in the end, Corkie fell in love with this guy with Latin lover looks and black curly hair parted on the side.

They were married in Ashland as soon as Corkie graduated with her Master's degree in 2001. Lorenzo had gotten a job teaching high school math, but she had no job. They decided to put off having children. A few years later, Lorenzo was offered a nice teaching position in Math and Civics, with a little coaching stipend on the side, at the high school in Twin Oaks. They moved, and Corkie got a job working for the city's community outreach center because of her bilingual skills.

Fifteen years slipped by and somehow the children never materialized. Now Lorenzo spent his Saturdays coaching either the Twin Oaks High School Cougars baseball games in the morning or the track meets in the afternoon. It was a nightmare when one of the competitions was an away from home affair. It was a nuclear bomb when both athletic events were out of town since Lorenzo couldn't be in two places at one time. *It won't matter anyhow,* Lorenzo thought, *most of these kids won't be playing any sports once they get to college, even if they go to college.*

***

Corkie picked up the twelve-page community newspaper that had more advertisements than real news. She wondered why they bothered with the local rag. Both Lorenzo and she read the New York Times, Huffington Post, and Washington Post online anyway. *Must be the comics and the sports.*

Answering her offer of another cup of coffee, Lorenzo shook his head no. He was in a comfort zone. He was drained from the prior day's baseball game in which his team lost 7-6. *Need to practice the fundamentals.*

"I'm starting breakfast in a few minutes," Corkie sat back down and resumed reading the paper. Without looking at him, she casually said, "You're getting oatmeal . . . with raisins."

Lorenzo nodded his head and gave her a silent "whatever" look.

A minute later, Corkie stood up abruptly and yelled out, "This sucks!"

"What happened?" Lorenzo was startled at this wife's sudden outburst.

Corkie began to read him an article:

**DESPERATION**

***"They scaled the terraced hillside in a single line, their machetes tapping the rocky grounds.***

***Pablo Guzman and his two brothers walked up to the door of his 16-year-old ex-girlfriend's shack. With the butt of the machete he pounded on the door. No answer. Pablo then started chopping into the thin wooden door, easily splintering it into pieces.***

***His ex-girlfriend, Jazmina Rojas, had left him two weeks earlier, escaping to her parents' home in southwest Guatemala. She was six months pregnant. Her mother stepped in front of the daughter and asked him to leave. Pablo swung his machete and instantaneously killed the mother. The father cried out***

***and was taken outside byPablo's two brothers. Jazmina could hear him begging for his life until there was no longer a sound. Jazmina was left unharmed.***

***At the end of the ensuing trial, Pablo was sentenced to four years in prison. Upon his release he would have visitation rights to see his son.***

***While Pablo was in prison, Jazmina sold the house and paid to be smuggled to Los Angeles. She applied for asylum, but was denied due to draconian policies made by U.S. Attorney General Sessions. She still lives in Los Angeles waiting for the appeal of her case. She is deathly afraid that Pablo will come to Los Angeles to find her once he is released from prison."***

"The only people more frigged than the corrupt Guatemalan government is the frigging U.S. President and his immoral A.G.," Corkie was infuriated by the article.

Lorenzo tried to calm her down, "They know the risks of trying to come here."

"But it's not fair," Corkie was one step away from deflecting her anger toward Lorenzo. "She should not be the victim there or here. She's still a child, for Christ's sake!'

"Well, what can be done about it?" Lorenzo tried to mollify his wife.

"I don't know yet," Corkie blurted out. "I'm too pissed to see straight."

## Chapter 8 – The Exodus

***1998***
***San Salvador, El Salvador***

Gloria Ocaso had been born on the hilly slope of a little pueblo outside of San Salvador, El Salvador on April 5, 1998 to Ysaac and Albina Ocaso. Her older brother was named Felipe and her younger brother was Fernando. Throughout the years, Señor Ocaso worked at a coffee plantation harvesting the beans. On Sundays, the entire family would walk two miles or so to the little adobe church for services.

When Felipe turned ten in 2005, he went to work with his father. The younger siblings went to a little rural school with other neighborhood children. Although the mother, Albina, had not had much schooling, she tried to read to her younger children every day. Life was tough, but the Ocaso family persevered.

Then in 2012, Gloria turned fourteen and she was getting ready to receive the sacrament of Confirmation with the other boys and girls. Her mother had made her a white dress. Her various madrinas had supplied her with a white veil, shoes, and white stockings. She looked angelic.

Relatives and friends of the Ocasos attended the Pentecost Sunday mass and watched Gloria receive her Confirmation. As the family was leaving the church, a weathered older man in a wrinkled dark brown suit and straw hat, blocked Ysaac's path. Elias Díaz was Ysaac's boss from the coffee plantation.

"Congratulations, Ysaac," Elias said, putting his right hand on Ysaac's shoulder. "Your daughter looks very pretty."

Ysaac nodded. He didn't know where this was going, but something felt wrong.

"I hear that your son, Felipe, is doing a good job at the plantation," Elias looked at him with his lazy eye and continued. "I think you have another son. I don't remember his name." He paused and rubbed his chin for a moment. "But one of these days he's going to be working with us too. ¿Es verdad?"

"Well, I think so," Ysaac replied weakly. The rest of his family had walked ahead of him.

"Your daughter is blossoming beautifully," Elias gave an unctuous smile. Ysaac had never thought of it, but Gloria was a fully mature 14-year-old girl with a well-defined bosom. But Ysaac didn't like where this tête-à- tête was going.

"My son, Rodrigo, needs a girlfriend," his boss gave Ysaac a slimy smile.

"But she is so young, jefe!" Ysaac blurted out.

"She looks ripe to me," Elias said in a firm tone.

"Oye, compadre," another grey-haired man with a big sombrero called over. "Are you ready? I'm starving!"

Seconds later, Elias was being led away by his close companion. Ysaac was in shock. *What am I going to do? He could get me fired! And Felipe too! Should I tell Albina? No, I'm the man of the house. I need to take care of this.*

All week Ysaac and Felipe left for work at 3 a.m. The father avoided contact with his boss. He didn't say a word to his wife. The next Sunday the Ocasos went to mass as usual. Elias was at church with his family, but made no effort to contact Ysaac. *¡Gracias a Dios!* Ysaac murmured to himself. However, on Tuesday he was confronted by Elias after his shift.

"Have you given any thought to what we talked about, amigo" Elias asked with a tightly lipped smile.

Ysaac was caught off guard. He tried to collect his thoughts. "My wife thinks she is too young."

"Too young?!" snickered the boss. "She is like a summer flower, ready to be plucked."

"But she is so innocent! She's only 14!" Ysaac protested.

"She has to learn someday. Now's the time," Elias leaned in. "There are 12 and 13 year-old putas in the City. Maybe even younger."

Ysaac was stunned. "Please don't ask this of us!"

“I’m doing you a favor,” Elias said in a firm tone. “I’m sending Rodrigo over to your casa next Saturday. Make sure it happens.”

Tears of sadness and despair were pouring down Ysaac’s face when he arrived home.

“What’s wrong, mi amor?” Albina asked with her shoulders scrounged up.

Ysaac told her the whole story. They both prayed extra hard that night.

Saturday came around, and Ysaac and his oldest son Felipe were working at the coffee plantation. Meanwhile, a greasy-haired youth stopped his motorcycle in front of the Ocaso casa. He was wearing a short-sleeved plaid shirt over his jeans. He banged on the ancient wooden door that was falling off its hinges. Señora Ocaso was surprised to see the young man, but knew it was Rodrigo, Elias’s son. He was polite, but had a strange air about him. Albina offered him coffee, but he declined. He sat down on a wooden chair. Twelve-year old Fernando sat close by. Gloria entered the room. She was wearing a modest white blouse with a coffee bean rosary around her neck. The rosary had been a Confirmation gift from her parents. Albina offered Rodrigo some cookies, which he took.

Rodrigo was trying to make small talk with Gloria, but was very nervous trying to do so in front of two other persons.

“Hey, do want to ride on my motorcycle?” he said jubilantly.

"No," Gloria said, popping his balloon.

More chitchat. "Hey, do want to take a walk?" Rodrigo tried again.

Gloria looked at her mom who said, "Fernando has to go with you."

A few minutes later the threesome walked down the dusty, dirt road.

"Gloria, hold on a minute!" Rodrigo grabbed Fernando's shoulder and pushed him over to the side of the road. "I need to talk to your brother," he excitedly said to her.

Gloria saw Rodrigo trying to give Fernando something. Fernando was adamant and said no. Rodrigo was agitated.

"Let's go back!" the youth shouted.

As they returned to the casita, Rodrigo went straight to his motorcycle without saying goodbye to anyone.

On Sunday there were no problems at the church. Ysaac and Albina thought that the storm had passed.

Two days later, however, Gloria was walking to the grocery store at the edge of the pueblo. She heard the loud sound of a motorcycle pull up beside her.

"Hey, Gloria, want a ride?" Rodrigo said.

She nodded her head no.

“Wait a second!” he stopped and pulled his motorcycle off to the side of the road. “I’ll walk with you.”

Gloria didn’t know what to say. She knew her mother always wanted her to be chaperoned.

“I think you are cute. You could be my woman.”

Her brown eyes became dilated. She was afraid, but did not want to show it.

“Hey, wait a second. Let me see that!”

Gloria was confused. *What was he talking about?* She stopped and faced him. His hand went up to the coffee bean rosary. He started to play with the beads. Then he grabbed her and pulled her toward him, his hand dropping down to stroke her breast. He tried to kiss her, but she turned her head. Gloria wanted to scream, but couldn’t. He pressed harder and harder against her. With the speed of lightning she freed her arm and scratched his face.

“You friggin’ puta!” He was holding his bleeding cheek. “You’re going to pay for this. Your father will be out of job.” Rodrigo ran back to his motorcycle and jetted away.

Ten minutes later Gloria arrived home sobbing. That night, Ysaac was livid when he heard what had happened. Gloria and her mother were babbling messes. Fernando was sent to the small room in the back of the casita where all three children slept. He could hear everything.

"I'm going to kill that little puto," raged the older brother, Felipe. "He's a cabron. He hangs out with some asshole punks. They go whoring in San Salvador on the weekends."

"Mijo, you can't do anything foolish," Ysaac was trying to sort out everything in his head that was pounding. "We could lose our jobs! We could get hurt! We could even disappear!"

Ysaac and Albina knew that they could not go to the police. The local policias were controlled by the gangs and cartels. Violence against women and femicides were part of the domestic culture. Men, especially powerful men, could literally get away with torture and murder.

***

Saturday came. It was payday for the coffee plantation workers. Ysaac was in line to collect his and Felipe's money.

Elias rushed up to him and got in his face. "Where is your son?" he demanded.

"I don't know. He came to work this morning," Ysaac stammered. *What was going on?* he was nervous.

"Someone is going to pay for messing with my son!" Elias was slobbering as he shouted. "It's because of your puta daughter!"

***

That night Ysaac, Albina, and Fernando said goodbye to Felipe and Gloria as the two youngsters boarded a municipal bus. Ysaac had given his eldest son all of the family money that was the equivalent of $100. The two siblings each carried an old flour bag filled with some clothes and a little food.

The following Sunday, parishioners asked the Ocasos where their two older children were, since they had not been seen at mass. Ysaac said that they were visiting a sick aunt in San Miguel and that maybe Felipe would look for work there.

A week later Felipe and Gloria had crossed into Mexico. They later found a coyote who made space for them in a container truck crowded tightly with men, women, and children. The truck was destined for the U.S. border. The sun was hot and the metal box baked the inhabitants. There was no water and no bathrooms. The container reeked of sweat and urine. Every other day they were transferred to a different container truck. Sometimes they got fruit to eat or maybe a tortilla with rice and beans; other days they got nothing. Everybody was dehydrated.

They finally arrived in Reynosa, a Mexican border town. They spent the next two nights in a safe house. The smugglers wanted $500 each to cross the river into Texas. Gloria and Fernando told the smugglers that they only had $100. The smugglers then grabbed Fernando and took him away from the house. They took Gloria across the river after raping her for three straight nights. She was picked up by Border Patrol near McAllen, Texas. Some Project

Corazon volunteers interviewed her while she was in detention and filed a petition for asylum on her behalf. Gloria spent a week in a facility with no windows or air conditioning. She saw dozens of other adults and minors squished together in crowded cells that resembled cages. There was no privacy.

Gloria was put on a bus with other unaccompanied minors and driven to San Francisco. Once there, she was housed in a detention center for young girls. Gloria started to get sick in the morning, and after complaining for several days was sent to a local public hospital. Her body seemed to be changing. She was getting bigger and bigger. The gynecologist confirmed that Gloria was pregnant and ordered the immigration service to give her private quarters back at the detention center. Gloria made friends with the other pregnant Latinas.

One day, she showed signs of vaginal bleeding and was rushed to the hospital Emergency Room. Gloria stayed in the hospital for three days, missing her asylum application hearing. The patient next to her was also Latina and was being released the next day. Gloria noticed that there was no security watching her. She asked the Latina if she could catch a ride with her.

"Why, sure, chica," the young Latina said. "But we're going home to Oregon." Her new found friend took pity on Gloria and gave her a place to stay while she waited for her pregnancy to come to full term.

During these following months Gloria spent her days either crying or being catatonic. On February 14, 2013, Gloria gave birth to Yesenia Ocaso in Twin Oaks, Oregon.

## Chapter 9 – Over The Hill

***Klamath Volcanic Legacy Highway***
***Wednesday, March 7, 2018***

Holly drowsily pushed off the warm quilted yellow with tiny white polka dots comforter from her bed, slid her feet into the fuzzy brownish plush slippers, and slowly made her way to the bathroom. The floor was cold, even though there was a small throw rug. She threw a little water on her face. Brr! It was freezing! She was 5’6” with black hair, cut in a pageboy that accentuated her half Latinx, half Yaqui ethnicity.

Thirty or so minutes later she clomped down the creaky stairs wearing an olive green pullover sweater over her jeans and sheepskin boots. Holly Acevedo lived with two roommates in Jacksonville, Oregon. The twenty-nine-year old had been born in Merenci, Arizona, received her bachelor’s in Political Science from the University of Arizona, and attended Willamette Law School in Salem. After graduating and successfully passing the Oregon Bar, she went to work as a staff attorney for the Oregon Legal Project (OLP) out of the Medford office. She was partnered with Manny Raven at OLP.

“The cafecito is ready!” yelled out Carlos as he pushed more kindling into the wood stove that heated the house, especially on those nippy March mornings. Carlos Nieto was the youngster of the trio of roommates, being only 22 years old. He worked at the Red Sage Winery that was less than five miles away. He was the supervisor of the syrah, merlot, and cabernet sauvignon vineyards. He usually left the old house between six and seven a.m. every morning.

"Oye, Carlitos," Holly said as she sank into a high-backed chair, resting her steaming mug on the red and white checkerboard table cloth. "Do you want some toast? I have some loganberry preserves."

"Sure, why not?" he responded, although he had just finished his breakfast. *Young men always have an appetite,* she thought.

"Did Joel come home last night?" she asked about their other roommate.

"Yeah, he came in late. He and Tyler partied hard after the performance," Carlos added. "They're both upstairs sleeping."

"Won't see them til noon," Holly gave a little grin. The third roommate, Joel Small, was a costume designer for the Oregon Shakespearean Festival. He was fifty, had a long pony tail and thick beard, and wore hoop earrings. His blonde partner was quite a bit younger and was a thespian with the Shakespearean company.

"I put two bottles of the syrah by your backpack," Carlos said "You'll be back tomorrow night?"

"I hope," Holly mumbled, as she devoured her last piece of toast and went upstairs to use the bathroom.

Today she had to drive over the Cascade Mountains to the Twin Oaks Community Center where she would conduct legal intake for the financially-disadvantaged residents in the area. Weather permitting, she made the trek every other Wednesday. The Community Center would do the initial screening to check for legal services eligibility, get a brief description of the problem, and if necessary, set up an appointment. It seemed that the more inclement the weather, the more appointments there were. Holly and Manny made it a policy not to give legal advice over the phone or by email or text. That meant that both were doing circuit duty a few days a week.

Holly grabbed her backpack that contained her laptop, three yellow legal pads, dozens of files and forms, and now two bottles of wine. “Thanks, Carlos!” she yelled as she went out the front door. It was raining, as she ran to her muddied white Prius AWD. It was so cold she could see her foggy breath.

Twenty minutes later she was approaching White City, after having passed Medford and the Rogue River. The morning commute was in full swing as her windshield wipers slashed through the sheets of water. Her car heater was going full blast. Today, Holly was listening to “The Red Sparrow” audiobook. At other times she would listen to soft jazz music or NPR (National Public Radio). The highway was flat here and the traffic traveled at maximum speed. She was now on Highway 140.

She made one pit stop before reaching the Highway 97 interchange. The trees were beginning to show off their spring colors. Holly’s butt was feeling numb from all the sitting during the drive. Her cell phone had rung twice during the journey, but she knew the reception was really bad. She would have to return the calls later. She decided to make a strategic stop to gas up. Her motto was “be prepared.” Holly purchased a large coffee that tasted like battery acid.

The scenery was beautiful as she started the climb the Cascades. There was snow in the mountains, and the Upper Klamath Lake was majestic. Holly was delayed about 25 minutes due to road repairs. It was almost noon when she reached Lakeview and turned south on Highway 395 toward Twin Oaks.

Holly punched #7 on her hands-free speed dial.

“Twin Oaks Community Center,” an elderly woman’s voice

answered at the other end.

"Hi, this is Holly Acevedo," she enunciated as she drove toward her destination. "May I please speak to Corkie Becerra?"

A half-hour later, Holly was dipping corn bread into her chili at Las Tres Comadres Restaurant. Corkie was briefing her on the three intake cases for the afternoon. Holly handed her a bottle of the Red Sage syrah. This was her biweekly tribute to the folks on the other side of the mountains.

The previous Monday, Corkie had called Holly to ask her about the recent ICE (Immigration and Customs Enforcement) raids in southern Oregon. The Oregon Legal Project had been concerned about the illegal ICE practices and the unlawful cooperation of local law enforcement agencies. They discussed what could be done at the community level. Holly had volunteered to give a workshop on "immigrant rights" at the local community center. Corkie had been working on publicizing it and managing the logistics. Holly had given dozens of these types of workshops and even had a PowerPoint presentation on the subject.

Sometimes, if Holly had a light intake afternoon, she would try to drive back home to Jacksonville that same evening. However, most of the time she crashed at the Becerra's place since they had an extra guest room. Corkie liked the Red Sage Syrah; so life was good.

"Do you need anything else for tonight?" Corkie asked.

Holly nodded. "How many people are we expecting for the workshop?"

"I think about a dozen or so."

# Chapter 10 – The Workshop

## *Thursday, March 8, 2018*

Lorenzo carefully handed off a steaming hot mug of citrus chamomile tea to his wife. Corkie was sitting on the lumpy brown corduroy sofa in front of the fireplace with a multicolored crotcheted quilt over her lap. She had just gotten home from work. She wrapped both of her hands around the cup. She loved the sweet, soothing scent. "Thanks, mi amor."

"Din will be ready in about fifteen or twenty minutes." Lorenzo was a master chef with a rice cooker. Since he had come home from school first, he was making a southwestern veggie and tofu dish over brown rice and quinoa.

Corkie nodded. Chispa was near her feet. The German Shepherd never knew when he might get a gratuitous scratching under the neck or maybe even a morsel of food. Who could resist those sad brown eyes?

Corkie was tempted to pull out some of her notes from work, but this was a quality moment with her husband. By the time she and Holly had come home the prior night, Lorenzo was fast asleep. And this morning he had left the house before she had woken up.

"How was the workshop last night?" he asked.

"Actually, it was pretty good," Corkie beamed. "Holly is really good. Confident. Knowledgeable. She can relate to the audience. And she does her presentation bilingually! Whew!"

"How many people showed up?"

“Almost thirty!” Corkie’s eyes rolled upwards, trying to visualize the crowded meeting room from the night before. “There were a couple of teachers and a nurse. And even a couple of Anglo cowboy types.”

The kitchen timer went off. Outside it was getting dark and gloomy, and the winds brought more rain that pounded on their roof.

“That Holly is very sharp,” Corkie commented as she plopped a piece of tofu in her mouth with chopsticks. “She’s really a hard worker.”

“Sorry, I missed her this time,” Lorenzo said as he was inhaling the black beans and corn kernels. “Did she bring any wine?”

Corkie pretended that she didn’t hear him. “How was your day?”

“Same old pedo,” he took in a deep breath. “You know Luke, the other PE teacher? The guy I coach with?” The 33-year-old, tree stump Luke Esquivel was a religious fundamentalist. He sported a black lock moustache and goatee, disguising his weak chin. He had earned his teaching credential in 2008 from George Fox University, a Christian college in Newberg, Oregon.

“He’s kind of short and wide?” she answered.

Lorenzo nodded. “He heard about the workshop last night. He went on and on, in an anti-immigrant rage,” Lorenzo paused with disgust. “‘The law is the law,’” he said. “What a pendejo! I hate Latinos who drink the president’s racist Kool-Aid.”

“You can’t educate these right wing types,” Corkie started getting incensed. “They’re racist, ignorant, or both.”

"Luke's pastor, Paul McConnell, is a fundamentalist preacher and really anti-immigrant. He believes that God wanted this president elected," Lorenzo added. "I think there are some city council members and cops who are members of that congregation. So much for the Christian 'love thy neighbor' philosophy."

"You're kidding!" Corkie's mouth was slightly open in the state of shock. "He can't be that screwed up?!"

Lorenzo rolled his eyes and nodded.

***

The next week or so was fairly quiet. Corkie was trying to set up another immigration law presentation at the local Catholic Church. But old Father Beto Murphy didn't want to rock the boat by involving the church. Although most of the parishioners were poor Latinx, the agricultural growers and city business interests made significant monetary contributions to the Church. The priest did not want to bite the hand that fed him.

This was one of the reasons that Lorenzo and Corkie did not attend mass, except for maybe Christmas and Easter. They also didn't like the Church's positions on women's rights and gay rights. And since Lorenzo was a History scholar, he couldn't condone the colonization, slavery, and genocide by European countries of indigenous people all of the world, the complicity of the pope with Nazi Germany, and the Inquisition.

After Father Beto refused to host the immigration law presentation, Corkie had to keep looking. Finally, it was Preacher Wendell "Dell" Starmont who came to Corkie's rescue. Preacher Dell, as he liked to be called, was in charge of the Armadale United Methodist Church. He was 32-years-old with black wavy hair and blue eyes. He was from Texas, with his bachelor's degree from the University of Texas at Austin and his master's from Southern Methodist University in Dallas. His wife Sandra had a perpetual smile that was like the first flower of spring. They had two sons, Matthew and Mark. The entire family spoke Spanish. Preacher Dell invited Corky to have Holly make a presentation at his church any time that was convenient.

At school, Lorenzo had been hearing rumblings about ICE threatening to come onto the school grounds to round up children who were suspected of being in the country without papers. One day after school, Principal Erin Kokoro, popped his head into Lorenzo's office. This was a highly unusual event.

"Lorenzo, how are you doing?" the principal was very polite and seemed to have bowed. He was wearing thick black glasses, a yellow bowtie, and displayed freckled liver spots on his face and arms.

"Fine," Lorenzo was in shock. *What did he want? What did I screw up?*

"I understand that Mrs. Becerra helped organize a presentation with Ms. Holly on immigration last week."

Lorenzo nodded.

"I was wondering if we could get Ms. Holly to come to the school to do an after-class in-service workshop on how to deal with ICE on campus. Could you please ask Mrs. Becerra if this is possible?"

"No worries," Lorenzo was relieved. "I'll talk to her tonight."

"Thank you," the principal smiled, gave a slight bow, and left.

Lorenzo liked the old man who had to be in his seventies. He had heard rumors that Principal Kokoro's family had been interned in a detention camp in Tule Lake, California, during WWII. They had lost their 88-acre family farm in Central California. After the war, Kokoro had pursued his academics at Oregon State University in Corvallis.

Later that evening Lorenzo shared Principal Kokoro's request with his wife. Corkie was overjoyed and immediately called Holly.

"And tell Holly to please bring extra wine," Lorenzo smiled. "Red!"

## Chapter 11 – Chiloquin

### *Friday, March 16, 2018*

The atmosphere in the Becerra living room was very tense with Cristina's surprise visit. Lorenzo and Corkie looked at each other as Cristina told them that the local police had arrested Gloria. *This didn't sound right,* they thought.

"We should call the police," Lorenzo blurted out in an excited voice. "They should tell us what is happening."

Lorenzo called the police station and talked to the officer on the night shift. He told Lorenzo that no one had called in an arrest of a Gloria Ocaso. He also suggested that Lorenzo should call Police Chief Chiloquin the next day.

The next few hours were hectic. Corkie called Holly Acevedo over in Jacksonville. Holly was at the Caldera Pub having a few. Corkie explained what had happened. Holly had to keep hanging up so she could contact some of her immigration sources to find out what had happened to Gloria and Yessie. On Corkie's end, the land line and cell phones were also in constant motion with texts and voice messages. Corkie had over 40 emails on her laptop. She tried to contact her friend at the county Department of Human Services, but the office was closed for the weekend. She left a voice message.

Rather than wait until the next day, Lorenzo decided to contact Police Chief Marty Chiloquin that night. The chief replied that he had no knowledge of any ICE activities, but he expressed concern. They made arrangements for Lorenzo to bring Cristina Navarro to the police station on Saturday morning.

Chiloquin would personally be meeting with them.

Lorenzo also called around to his teacher colleagues. One of them, who taught at an elementary school, told him that the ICE police had tried to force themselves onto campus earlier that day. Lorenzo called Principal Kokoro at the high school, who was very gracious despite being called at ten o'clock at night. Normally, the principal was Zen passive when there was conflict, but in this case, Lorenzo could tell that the principal was enfadado. They talked about the upcoming immigrant rights presentation that was planned with Holly Acevedo. Kokoro was going to contact other K-12 administrators within the school district to expand the presentation. Kokoro was making this a mandatory meeting for his teachers and staff.

Cristina finally went home. Lorenzo said he would drive over and pick her up the following morning to take her to the police station. The clock struck two when the Becerras finally went to bed. The next morning arrived early, with neither of the two getting much sleep. With a coffee mug in his hand, Lorenzo grabbed his grey parka as he started out the door. There was a gentle, but persistent rain. Pitter-patter. Pitter-patter. Lorenzo gave Corkie a peck on the cheek as he was leaving. She was on the phone.

"Sorry, Trish, can't meet you today," Corkie was leaving a voice message on her friend's phone. "Something has come up." She turned and waved goodbye as her husband left.

Their marriage was a team effort based on deep love and a loyal friendship. Corkie had wanted a puppy many years earlier and there had been intense negotiations between the couple. In the end Corkie was in charge of dog poop cleanup and Lorenzo had to vacuum the house at least once a week to clean up the dog hair. They promised each other that they both would be responsible for exercising Chispa. Most of the time, though, Lorenzo took the German Shepherd out for early morning or evening walks. When possible, Corkie would join the two. On the weekends, Corkie took Chispa to meet with some lady friends and go to the city dog park. She had fun socializing after her stressful week at the community center. Homemade pastries from her friends also helped.

Lorenzo swung by Cristina's place and picked her up. "Señor Becerra, it was all my fault!" Cristina wailed throughout the drive.

"It's nobody's fault," Lorenzo tried to reassure her.

At just past nine they arrived at the police station. It was a one story brick building, nothing fancy and always understaffed. Currently, there were only twelve police officers, one community outreach person, and several support staff, including an intake person.

Cristina was nervous. Her eyes were bloodshot. Police tech Rita Pearson escorted Cristina into a little conference room to get the facts of the missing mother and daughter. The 5'2" huskily-built Rita was fluent in Klamath-Modoc, Spanish, and English. Lorenzo gave Cristina a calming pat on the shoulder, mouthing to her that everything would be all right. Then he headed toward the police chief's office.

Marty Chiloquin's office had a miniature U.S. flag flanked by the Klamath tribal banner and the Oregon State flag. The fifty-one-year old police chief was full-blooded Klamath. His jet black hair was pulled back into a ponytail tied a thin leather strap. He had dark brown weathered skin that covered a muscular body. Smiling was not part of his vocabulary.

"What's this about, Lorenzo?" the police chief asked

solemnly, sipping his cold coffee from a tin cup.

"We think that ICE has been conducting some covert raids in town," Lorenzo leaned forward in the uncomfortable wooden chair. In front of him, the chief sat behind his desk that had stacks of papers piled on it.

"Wouldn't surprise me," Chiloquin said in a slow, drawn out tone, scratching his beardless face. "Heard one of the guys say something about it."

"What pisses me off, chief," Lorenzo started to get animated, "is that these ICE guys announce themselves as 'police.' They're not police. They just try to get people to open up their doors."

Chiloquin nodded that he understood. He had a poker face.

"How can people trust the police, if ICE is going to lie?" Lorenzo was almost out of his chair. "They're targeting schools and hospitals. And even courts! That's not right, Chief!"

Chiloquin didn't say anything. His Klamath-Modoc tribe had been sent to a reservation in 1864 by the U.S. government. In spite of their isolation, the Klamaths became prosperous. So much so that the U.S. government terminated its tribal sovereignty in 1954. It wasn't until 1986 that tribal recognition was reestablished. Chiloquin's father was still on the Tribal Council in Klamath Falls. Although Chiloquin had served in the Air Force, he had no love or trust of the federal government.

"I think what you say is true, Lorenzo," remarked the police chief. "They are supposed to notify us of any activity in the area. But they don't."

Lorenzo went on to talk about the case of Gloria and Yesenia.

“I can’t promise much, mi amigo,” the chief swallowed the last of his coffee. “Let me ask around.”

“Thanks, Chief.”

They shook hands and Lorenzo left the office.

Lorenzo sat in the waiting room for another ten minutes before Cristina emerged from the intake room. She looked tired, but relieved. Rita, the police tech, came over to Lorenzo.

“Mr. Becerra,” Rita said confidently. “We are going to look into this. We should have a better idea on Monday when the government offices are open.”

“Thank you,” Lorenzo said, as he held Cristina’s arm while leaving the building.

“Gracias,” Cristina looked over her right shoulder.

The weather was misting as the two walked over to the local café that was always crowded on the weekends. They both ordered coffee and breakfast.

“Are you all right, Cristina?” Lorenzo wanted to make sure everything was okay.

Cristina repeated what she had said to Rita. They would just have to wait and see. Rita advised Cristina to go to Gloria’s apartment and remove those things that were of value and to store them someplace safe. Also, Lorenzo suggested to her to go through Gloria’s mail and pull out anything that looked like a bill. The good news was that Gloria was too poor to own a computer and that made things simpler.

The fried eggs with chorizo and corn tortillas came. Cristina ate them with gusto. She hadn’t eaten anything in the last twenty-four hours. As for Lorenzo, he ordered the "two by two by two," since Corkie wasn't around to nag him. Two eggs over medium, two chicken-apple sausages, and two buckwheat pancakes. *Love that maple syrup!*

After dropping Cristina back at her home, Lorenzo dialed Corkie on his car's hands free phone.

After the third ring, Corkie picked. "Are you on your way home?"

"Finally," Lorenzo. "I need a nap. Do you want to join me?"

"Sounds tempting," Corkie's tone was relaxed. "Made some calls. The friggin' ICE rounded up at least twelve folks. Mostly elderly or little kids."

"I can't believe it," Lorenzo shook his head as he concentrated on the wet highway in front of him.

"And there are rumors that the local police were involved."

## Chapter 12 – B.B. Barnes

### *Monday, March 19, 2018*

Lorenzo's hair was unkempt as he began his Monday morning math class. He and Corkie had had a hectic weekend with the Gloria and Yesenia Ocaso affair. Lorenzo staggered into the teachers' lounge. Some nice soul had baked some cardamom cookies. He snagged three to dunk into the battery acid coffee.

Luke plopped down beside him also with a handful of cookies.

"Good job with the meet," Lorenzo said. He had asked Luke to cover the out-of-town track competition because he was busy trying to find out answers for Cristina. Lorenzo had managed to find time to coach the Saturday baseball game which they lost 4-3.

"No problem," Luke chomped on a cookie. "That Louie Lopez is really fast. He won two firsts."

"I tried to recruit him as a shortstop," Lorenzo said. "He was a good hitter, but not so good on defense."

A short brunette, sans cookies, came over and sat next to the two jocks.

"Any of your students missing?" Hazel Arden, the Language Arts teacher, inquired.

"None of mine," Lorenzo answered.

Luke, rubbing his fingers on his black lock moustache and goatee, added. ""Well, I heard that the police and ICE picked up some kids last Friday. I don't think any were from this high school."

Lorenzo's ears perked up. "You heard this from whom?"

"I was at Pastor's McConnell's congregation yesterday. He was telling us about the sinners that are invading our country," Luke was reciting the talking points of the fundamentalist preacher. "And B.B. told me that he was working with ICE to apprehend these immigrant criminals."

"B.B. who?"

"You know, my buddy from the Oregon National Guard." Luke tried to describe his friend. "Has a reddish brown crew cut. The police officer."

"He's a cop?!" Lorenzo was shocked.

"Yeah," Luke nodded. "He likes things neat and tight. No foreigners, you know. No gangsters from Central America. The law is the law."

During the lunch break, Lorenzo texted Corkie and told her about the ICE police raids. On her end, Corkie texted back that Holly had found out that ICE had been picked up Gloria. What she didn't know was if Gloria was at the county jail under an ICE detention retainer or if she had been transported to the Portland immigration office. No one seemed to know what happened to her daughter, Yesenia. Holly was still working on it.

***

Four hours later, officer Branson "B.B." Barnes walked into the police station ready to leave work.

"Chief, wants to see you," Rita told him.

B.B. rolled his eyes. He wanted to go home. Actually, he would stop by the bar and have one, or two brews, with the local boys. He knocked on Chief Chiloquin's door and walked in to the small office. The chief waved him in to sit down.

"How are you doing, B.B.?"

"Okay, chief."

"I heard that ICE did some raids here in town last week," Chiloquin asked seemingly innocuously. "What do you know about it?"

Barnes knew that Chiloquin knew everything. He couldn't lie or plead ignorance. He decided to double down. "Well, ICE is doing some strategic targeting raids. They requested our assistance."

"Who asked you specifically?"

"ICE agent Stoker," Barnes responded. "He's from the Portland office."

The name rang a bell for Chiloquin, but he couldn't place the face.

"He contacted you directly?"

Barnes nodded his head as he squirmed in the chair.

"By phone?"

Another nod.

"Any email, text, or paper follow up?"

"No, chief."

"Since I wasn't contacted by ICE, I am assuming that this

was a rogue operation. I will contact the Portland Immigration office. They did not follow official protocol. This seems like an end run."

"I don't see what the problem is, chief. The law is the law. These people are breaking the law," Barnes wanted to have the matter dismissed. *What is the friggin' problem?*

"Well, Barnes, do remember when you took some of those law classes in order to become a police officer?"

Barnes' head was swaying. He was bored. "Sure."

"Do you remember that in 1987, the Oregon State Legislature in a bipartisan vote enacted the Sanctuary Law?" Chiloquin looked as his officer straight in the eye.

Barnes shrugged. "I guess so."

"This Oregon Sanctuary Law says that local police shall not assist in the enforcement of federal immigration laws. Do you remember that? That is our practice here in Twin Oaks!"

"Well, I was just trying to help," Barnes argued weakly.

"Here's the deal. You will go to your office and reread this law. You will refrain from working with ICE in the future without my specific authorization. You work for the town, not for the feds, do you understand?"

Barnes nodded.

"I can't hear you."

"Yes, sir."

"I will not discipline you. I am assuming that it was an honest mistake," Chiloquin knew that Barnes was concerned about his job. “Just make sure that it doesn’t happen again.”

“Yes, chief.”

“One more thing,” Chiloquin said slowly. “You will need to help find the location of those people who were apprehended by ICE last week. I’ll need daily updates.”

## Chapter 13 – Community Outreach

### *Wednesday, March 21, 2018*

“How was the drive?” Corkie asked Holly as the latter removed her bright red ski cap and crimson scarf.

“Fine,” Holly exhaled as she dumped her briefcase and some files onto the café table.

A roundish waitress came over and asked if they wanted coffee.

“Decaf, please” said Corkie.

“Just water, please.”

“Lorenzo insists that you stay with us until Sunday.” Corkie had been busy scheduling all the immigration rights presentations for the rest of the week. Tonight’s talk was again at the community center. Additionally, Kokoro, the high school principal, had asked for a Friday afternoon teacher and staff in-service, and Preacher Dell Starmont wanted a presentation at his Armadale United Methodist Church.

“I really need to get back,” Holly hedged. “This ICE raid has set me back a week. Poor Manny has to cover the entire office.”

“Well, Lorenzo wants to chill with you and drink a little wine.”

“Hmm. I guess that would be a good plan.” Holly looked at the half case of wine she had brought with her.

The waitress came back and the two ordered. Holly had a

Southwest egg scramble and Corkie had steel-cut oats with fresh strawberries.

"What did you find out about Gloria and Yesenia?" Corkie was anxious.

"The first thing is that about six to eight people were apprehended by ICE last Friday. Gloria was one of them," Holly began.

"How?"

"Gloria is a cafeteria worker at the local middle school. ICE stopped several of the school employees as they left work.

"Where is she now?"

"She is in custody at an ICE facility near Portland."

"What's going to happen to her?"

"One of our attorneys with the Oregon Legal Project is in the process of filing a notice of appearance for Gloria. There will probably be some type of hearing. In Portland, of course." Corkie knew that this meant that an attorney was now representing Gloria Ocaso. That was good news.

"And the girl?" Corkie continued.

A basket of whole wheat toast, preserves, and butter was placed between the two. They both grabbed a slice.

"That's the bad news," Holly said, talking with food in her mouth. "Nobody knows where Yesenia is."

"That's impossible!"

"Not with the president's 'let's beat up on little old ladies and little kids' policy'."

"What can we do?"

"A friend of mine at Family Services is trying to look into it," Holly continued. "The problem is that there are hundreds of private immigration detention centers from here to the Mexican border. Nobody knows anything. And what is worse, they don't care. It's all about the money."

It was late that Wednesday night when Corkie brought Holly over to their house. The wind had picked up and it was stormy. The ladies hadn't eaten since breakfast and Lorenzo had fixed some bruschetta accompanied by broccoli cheese soup. They opened a bottle of wine and sat in the comfy, cozy living room.

"Well, how did it go?" Lorenzo asked.

"Fine."

"We had about twenty-five people," Corkie chimed in.

Holly was tired. She was scheduled to do her regular legal intake the next day. She hit the sack by ten.

As Lorenzo brushed his teeth, he told his wife that he really enjoyed the wine that Holly had brought. "Any news on Gloria and Yesenia?"

"Naw! Frigging feds!"

They got into bed.

"Are you going to read, sweetie?" Lorenzo asked.

"Naw! Too stressed."

"Kokoro is pretty cool about Holly giving a presentation to

the teachers and staff at the high school on Friday," Lorenzo added.

"That's very progressive of him."

"Well, some of the teachers are very conservative."

"Don't tell me they voted for the bozo president?"

"Okay, I won't," Lorenzo grinned. "Teachers are a microcosm of the entire voting population. No smarter. No dumber."

"But they teach our kids. They should be tolerant and progressive."

"The reality is that a few of them are to the right of the NRA (National Rifle Association). Their motto is: if it moves, shoot it. Just don't ask questions."

"Sweetie, something is bothering me. There was something strange happening outside the community center today," Corkie was hesitant to share this with Lorenzo. "There were some redneck types hanging around outside the building. Somebody thought they were taking down car license plate numbers."

"You're kidding?! That's crazy."

"One of them was your teacher friend Luke."

## Chapter 14 – Desiree

### *Thursday, March 22, 2018*

Holly had just finished the second of her three scheduled legal appointments at the community center in Twin Oaks. There was no such thing as a simple question or problem. Her first case had been an elderly Latino gentleman who had been hit by an oncoming car while he was driving on the highway. Mr. Limón did not have car insurance. No one was injured, but there was major damage to both vehicles. Limón was not cited by the police and wanted the whole thing to go away. He went down to the insurance company of the other party and signed some papers. Unfortunately, he was not very proficient in English and did not know what he was signing. Now, his paycheck was being garnished at $300 a pop. He couldn't afford to pay his rent.

Limón did not remember the name of the insurance company nor did he have a copy of the signed document. After forty-five minutes of phone calls by a community center staff person and Holly to the bank and to the insurance company, a copy of a new agreement between Mr. Limón and the other party's insurer was procured. It was in English. Holly had to translate the document to Mr. Limón. Although she was proficient in Spanish, translating legal documents was very difficult. Eventually, the elderly man signed the document and a PDF copy was sent to the insurer. Holly would follow up with a hard copy.

*Well, that was exhausting! I need a double espresso!*

Her next case was simpler. It was a marriage dissolution. Oregon Legal Project didn't usually handle domestic relations cases. She referred the case to one of the attorneys on her local county bar referral list.

She now had a half hour before her third and last appointment for the day. She was looking forward to a libation that night.

Holly was just about to contact her partner Manny in Medford, when there was a knock on the door. The door swung open. It was Corkie and a young woman.

"Hey, Holly, I know you're busy," Corkie gently pushed the youngster inside the interview room. "This is Desiree Patten."

Holly stood up and shook Desiree's hand. Corkie motioned her to sit back down.

"She stopped by and has a quick legal question," Corkie advocated. "I figured that you might know the answer off hand."

Desiree was 5'5" with blonde hair and blue eyes. She had high cheek bones speckled with freckles. She began relating her narrative to Holly. There was a serious frown on Holly's face as she listened. Desiree was nineteen years old and had been working as a store clerk since graduating from high school.

She had met a young man, Ysidro Trujillo from Mexico, and they had started dating. She was now three months pregnant with his child. He wanted to marry her. Her mother said no. He was not a U.S. citizen and the mother was concerned about Desiree not getting health services if they got married. Desiree and Ysidro wanted to keep the child. The local Catholic priest would not marry them. Currently, Ysidro was working at a commercial laundry facility, working six days a week. Desiree wanted to leave her mom's house and find an apartment with Ysidro.

Desiree didn't know her legal rights or the rights of Ysidro. *Could he get a visa? If so, how? Could they get married legally?*

*Could he be deported while he applied for legal status?* Desiree's mother was less than helpful.

"Do you love him?" Holly asked.

Desiree nodded yes. Holly thought about how many young girls had been seduced by forbidden fruit. The Latinos were good at paying attention to naïve girls and making them feel special. After that, it was like picking ripe fruit.

"Does he love you?"

Again, Desiree nodded affirmatively. *What else could the young woman say?* Holly thought. The majority of the time it would work out. The man would be honorable and do the right thing. But sometimes stuff happened and it landed in Holly's lap to fix.

"Give me your address," Holly requested. "I will send you some forms to fill out to try to legitimize Ysidro's status if you get married."

Desiree wrote down an address and handed it to Holly.

Five minutes later they all said goodbye. Desiree thanked Holly profusely. Corkie said that she would see Holly later on that evening.

Holly's third appointment was a no-show.

*Finally, I can catch up on my rest. But maybe after a glass of wine or two.*

She decided to leave the center early and started to trudge across the civic center parking lot. It was twilight and the parking lot lights were not yet on. As Holly approached her car, four burly male figures moved in to cut her off. She stopped. She did not recognize any of them.

“Hey, missy,” the 5’10” skinhead spoke to Holly. “We don’t like outsiders around here.”

Holly did not respond. She knew that there were no other people around. She attempted to walk through the guys.

“If you keep this up, you might get hurt,” the 45-year-old redneck subtly threatened.

Holly stopped again. She was only ten feet from the gang of four. “Wait a second!” She pulled out her cell phone at lightning speed. “Just a second! Tell me your names and repeat what you said to me.” The flash of the cell phone flared on the rednecks.

The four guys looked at each other in bewilderment. One started to bolt. The others immediately followed.

Later that night, Holly, Corkie, and Lorenzo sat in the living room, imbibing in another bottle of wine.

“How was your day, Holly?” Lorenzo asked.

“Typical,” she answered.

# Chapter 15 – Holly Goes to School

## *Friday, March 23, 2018*

Lorenzo had driven off to school early that Friday morning. Corkie lingered at the house longer than usual, drinking coffee and doing lady talk with Holly. The sun was breaking through the clouds and the two women decided it was time to go to work. Corkie threw her green raincoat in the back of her metallic green 2014 Toyota Corolla sedan. Holly followed her into town in her own car.

"Morning, Manny," Holly called her office in Medford. "How's it going? Do you miss me yet?"

"Fine," Manny bantered back. "You owe me."

"Any time you want to trade, just let me know."

"No. We're good." Manny said. His travel from the Medford office was minimal.

They talked about ongoing cases and a few new ones. "That guy is a slumlord and should be put out of business," Holly reacted.

"The lady with the broken collar bone came in again. She wants to get back with her husband." Manny remembered that six weeks prior, the woman was calling the police on her hubby and wanted a quickie divorce. *Now she wants to reconcile. Within six weeks, she'll be back here with a broken arm,* he thought.

"What's happening with the Gloria Ocaso case?" Holly

asked.

"Our Portland office is drafting a complaint for federal court in Portland," Manny reported. "Should have the initial complaint by Tuesday."

Holly had been barraged with phone calls from Gloria and Christina asking for the status of Yesenia's case. Holly shared some of what she knew. However, Holly did not let on that the immigration detention centers that were filthy and lacked basic services. What made it worse was that they were private, for-profit concerns sanctioned by the federal government. Her blood boiled with anger and frustration.

"What is our legal strategy?"

"We're going with asylum," Manny said. "We want an expedited federal court hearing. Not an administrative one." Holly knew that a hearing with a federal judge would be fairer than a political kangaroo Immigration court.

"Can we do that?"

"I don't know, but the normal asylum approach is DOA with this president," Manny continued. "Our Portland office wants to push the envelope."

"Okay," Holly was thinking.

"They also want to add a federal habeas corpus petition because they think that Gloria is being charged for a criminal violation of the immigration laws." Holly knew that most of Immigration Law was civil in nature. When the Republicans tried to criminalize certain actions for political reasons, it opened up a can of worms. People accused of crimes have certain rights, like the reading of Miranda right when they are in custody. Detainees can't be hidden away in a holding cell forever without a hearing.

"Whoa! That sounds interesting," this was way beyond Holly's pay grade. She had only done a handful of federal cases. And nothing as complex as was being proposed.

"And what about the child?"

"Still haven't found her. That's one reason they wanted the writ of habeas corpus as the second cause of action. This could keep Gloria in the country until someone finds her daughter."

Holly grabbed a quick Subway sandwich in town, near a little 5&10 department store. The sun was actually out. Lorenzo had offered to take her to lunch, but she declined.

Around 2 p.m. Holly drove to Twin Oaks High School. Principal Kokoro came out to the waiting room and greeted her. Whatever she needed, he would arrange for her to have. He escorted Holly part way to the school auditorium and left her in the very capable hands of his secretary, Chai Mazzoni. The computer projector seemed to be working properly as did the microphone.

Classes ended at 3 p.m. The teachers and support staff were not exactly happy to have a mandatory in-service on a Friday afternoon.

Lorenzo was the first to arrive and offered to assist Holly. The school provided oatmeal cookies and Hawaiian punch. The additional benefit of a sugar rush high helped assuage the grumbling staff. By 3:30 the auditorium was almost full. Principal Kokoro introduced Holly. Everybody acted respectfully.

"We are blessed to have the responsibility to educate our youth. They are our future. They will be running our country one of these days," Kokoro was known for his somber attitude. "They couldn't do any worse than what is happening now." There was a little laughter. "Attacking our children at schools, hospitals, churches, and courts. This is not right. This is not the American way. Ms. Holly Acevedo has been gracious enough to share her insights with us. We need to have a united response to these draconian actions. Ms. Acevedo, please join me," The principal extended his right hand and Holly approached the dais.

"Thank you, Principal Kokoro," Holly shuffled some papers on the podium and began with the first slide of her presentation.

"What is the law?" she began. There was a silence. "Don't be shy. Today you're all lawyers." A few smiles appeared in the audience. Very few hands went up.

"A set of rules set up by a community," a short, round Latina cafeteria worker volunteered.

"Good!" said Holly as she wrote the response on newsprint. "Well, who makes laws?" Holly continued.

More hands went up.

"Congress."

"The Legislature."

"The mayor."

"The judges." The crowd was getting a little more animated.

"Why do we have laws?"

"To make us behave."

"To punish criminals."

"To make us pay taxes." More laughter and head shakes in the audience.

"To promote racism," the sole African-American teacher, Mariah Cooper, stated. A pall was cast over the attendees. A few teachers gave Mariah dirty looks.

"Unfortunately, she is right," Holly interjected. "The United States was founded on preferential treatment for English Protestant male land owners." The teachers and staff nervously looked at one another.

"Let's have a little history lesson. Is that all right with you?" Holly asked. There were several nods in the audience. So she proceeded.

"A couple of centuries ago, slaves were counted as three-fifths of a human being. Women were considered chattel or personal property, as were slaves. George Washington even gave back the colonists' slaves to the British whom he had just defeated. The thirteen colonies increased their land by purchase, genocide, and war. But the 'sins of the past' seemed to evolve with time. Now we have 'sins of the present.' There are no longer anti-Irish laws. There are no longer anti-Italian laws. There are no longer anti-Asian laws. On the other hand, some things that are now 'illegal,' were not always so. There is no inherent 'illegality' where immigrants are concerned. Immigration laws are more of a political expediency than something set in stone.

"The United States waged war on Mexico and stole the Southwest when Mexico refused to sell Texas. That might have been karma because Mexico had taken over the same lands from the Spaniards who had stolen them from the indigenous peoples." People were squirming in their chairs.

Holly went on and on. The mouths of the participants were left hanging.

"All of this leads us to today. Only the U.S. Congress can regulate federal immigration laws. States and cities have no legal authority to do so."

"And in our wonderful State of Oregon, we have the Sanctuary Law that was enacted in 1987 with bipartisan support. Our local law enforcement agencies can determine their own priorities and not be minions for the feds. Our local police can't enforce immigration laws or assist in their enforcement. Neither can teachers or school staff."

Five minutes later Holly ended her presentation and opened it up for questions.

"The law is the law! Why can't we help ICE?" Luke asked. Lorenzo rolled his eyes. His friend was a loser.

"As you said, the law is the law. Oregon has a sanctuary law which says you can't do it."

"But what if we do it anyway?" Luke persisted.

"You can open yourself and your governmental agency to legal liability. You don't want to get sued. I'm sure you don't want your house taken away or your wages garnished."

# Chapter 16 – Easter

## *Easter Sunday, April 1, 2018*

The sun was out and the air was crisp. The white dogwood trees were in full bloom all around town. The fragrance of roses permeated the air. Everybody was driving to and from churches celebrating Easter. Little girls had on white gloves. Boys wore little bowties. Strawberry booths and tamale stands were lined all along the highways.

Some families threw blankets on the grass in the parks, getting ready for their pascal feasts. Fathers were throwing balls to their children while mothers prepared the meals. Life was good in Twin Oaks.

In the early afternoon, the police station received a call from an angry Pastor Paul McConnell from the Christian Apostolic Congregation. He was a fundamentalist preacher originally from Tennessee who led a large assembly about three miles northwest of town. There had been several hundred members of his flock in attendance at his Easter services. He was yelling about the fact that at least a dozen of his parishioners' cars had been burglarized in the church parking lot. His people were angry. They were afraid of a crime spree coming to their neighborhoods. Some parishioners thought they saw "brown" kids in the vicinity.

Police Chief Chiloquin was on duty because it was a holiday. He always worked holidays because that was when strange and bad things seem to happen. He knew it was worse at the hospital emergency rooms. *Well, today is also April Fool's Day. Going to be a busy day.*

There were at least three other phone calls reporting the burglaries at the Christian Apostolic Congregation. Chiloquin hopped into his police AWD cruiser with his policewoman assistant Rita Pearson. Within fifteen minutes they pulled into the large dirt parking lot next to the giant church. There were groups of people milling around. He immediately spotted Pastor McConnell wearing a frock type garment. Next to him were several middle-aged gentlemen.

*Oh, crap!* Chiloquin's head jerked. He's talking to the mayor. Mayor Mitch Keough was a political animal who could smell dead meat a mile away. He was the ultimate opportunist, always blaming others for problems, but taking credit for anything good.

"Rita, please go and take statements from each of the victims," the chief said to his assistant. "Make sure you do them independently. We don't need any cross contamination of witnesses."

"Yes, chief," Rita grabbed her clipboard and a stack of report forms.

"And don't forget to take photos," the chief added. "We don't want these people repainting their entire cars at someone else's expense."

"Howdy, pastor. Howdy, mayor," Chiloquin shook hands with both men. "How can we help out today?"

Pastor McConnell jumped in immediately in an agitated tone. "Those damn immigrants broke into our cars. They are terrifying our congregation. We need to make our community safe again, chief!"

"We'll do our best to see that the culprits are apprehended.

Right now we will investigate and gather the facts."

"We know it's those illegal alien kids." The preacher was vehemently opposed to all immigration from Mexico and Central America.

"I have a call into Congressman Joshua," huffed Mayor Keough, who was big and tall with carrot-colored sideburns and a bald top. Keough had been raised in conservative Marshalltown, Iowa, and was also anti-immigrant.

"Tomorrow I'm calling the governor's office and requesting assistance from the Oregon national guard."

"Mayor, I think that is a bit premature," Chiloquin said firmly. "We don't even know all the facts yet."

"But the president says we are being invading by those MS-13 gangs from Central America!"

"You know, today is April Fool's Day," Chiloquin said in a soft voice. "Kids are doing crazy things all over the place. We want to spare any embarrassment to the town and both of you, if this was just a prank."

The mayor wanted to say something, but held his tongue. He understood what Chiloquin was implying.

"Maybe the police chief is right, Mitch," Pastor McConnell was starting to calm down. The mayor would make sure things got done. "But we still have issues with these illegal aliens and all the problems they are causing."

In the meantime, Rita had started interviewing the victims. She gave them all forms to fill out. Fortunately, she had enough pens for everyone. When a person was done, she interviewed them inside the AWD police vehicle for privacy.

She verified contact information, property damage, and property loss. She then took photos of their driver's license and proof of insurance. One or two of the victims took the forms and left saying they had to get home and would turn the forms in later. Rita knew that they were probably scammers who just wanted to make a few bucks.

It took her over an hour to question everyone and take photos of the cars. In total, there were eight cars involved. Four had been parked unlocked; the other four had broken driver's side windows. Chiloquin helped Rita finish up the last few interviews.

The mayor had left and the pastor thanked Chiloquin and Rita. The two police officers left.

"April Fool's!" Chiloquin shouted to Rita as they left the premises.

Rita grinned. She was exhausted from doing all the paperwork.

"You hungry?" the chief asked.

Rita nodded yes.

"Las Tres Comadres okay?"

Again she nodded yes.

"So what did you learn?" Chiloquin's style was to mentor his staff, not to lecture them.

"Most of these people seem to have legitimate claims," her dark brown eyes looked up, trying to recall all the salient facts. "Some claimed they lost money. Hard to believe since they were supposed to be giving money to the church today. Why would they keep money in their cars? Especially, unlocked."

Chiloquin smiled. "Go on."

"At least five tablets and two game boys are missing. A couple pair of sunglasses. A raincoat. Bottles of water."

"Good job, Rita!" as a rule, Chiloquin believed in giving positive reinforcement.

"One more thing," Rita said excitedly. "Did you know that someone in Twin Oaks owns a Rolex watch?"

They both laughed.

## Chapter 17 – Federal Court

***Medford***
***Monday April 23, 2018***

Holly parked her white Prius about two blocks from the James A. Redden U.S. District Court Building in Medford. She was walking with intense concentration. Her colleague and co-counsel, Manny Raven, was equally pensive. Although she had practiced law less than four years, she was lead on this case. *Why me? Manny has over twice as much experience! And he is a Harvard Law grad!* She felt a knot in her stomach.

Inside the renovated post office, now a federal court house, the two lawyers passed through the metal detector. It was just past eight a.m. and the Motions docket did not begin until nine. They were scheduled to meet with their client, Gloria Ocaso at 8:30. She was still in federal custody.

Manny decided that he should use the Men's restroom. The hearing room hallway was almost empty. A tall man with a salt and pepper Afro suddenly approached Holly. He was carrying a notepad and a black North Face logoed shoulder bag.

"Hey, I'm Abe Zucker with Associated Press. I've been trying to follow the Ocaso case," he had a nice smile. "May I ask you a few questions?"

Holly was not accustomed to talking with the media. *Just be calm. Pretend I own the place. Crap! I gotta go pee!* "Sure. I am Holly Acevedo with the Oregon Legal Project."

"Shall we sit over here on the bench?" he suggested, not really asking. "Do you mind if I record this?" He pointed to a tiny handheld recorder.

She sat down without answering.

"Can you give me the background on the case?"

Holly explained that the arrest of Gloria Ocaso and abduction of her daughter Yesenia on March 16 by local law enforcement happened without a warrant or probable cause. She tried to sound lawyerish. Holly asserted that this woman and her daughter were filing an asylum claim and should be afforded the opportunity to make such a claim.

Abe interrupted her every once in a while to ask a clarifying question.

"But where is the daughter, Yesenia?" he pursued his interview.

"We still don't know," Holly began showing her frustration. "And the feds don't know. We hope we can find out today. We are all worried about her."

Holly was saved by the bell. Manny had come back and she introduced him to the AP reporter. Holly excused herself and hurried to the Women's restroom. She was getting pumped up. *I'm going to nail those SOBs.*

Abe continued the interview with Manny and asked him, "Why are you in court today?"

People started to congregate in front of the courtroom. The noise level was high, and everybody was either talking loudly into their cellphones or texting.

Manny had to raise his voice to be heard when he responded to Abe. "Three weeks ago the Oregon Legal Project filed a lawsuit against ICE and Homeland Security in federal court in Portland. The Department of Justice has refused to answer the complaint and instead filed a Motion to Dismiss. At the motions hearing, the Oregon Legal Project moved to hold the Motion to Dismiss hearing in Medford. To our surprise, the U.S. Attorney General agreed. Both parties agreed that Gloria Ocaso would be transferred to the Medford federal lockup where she could be interviewed by the Oregon Legal Project."

"That seems highly unusual," Abe said. "Politics? Public perception? Why do you think that the U.S. Attorney General allowed the transfer?"

Manny gave a little laugh. "Maybe because the A.G. knew that this could be another P.R. nightmare for the presidential administration. Medford would make it low profile."

Holly was back and reminded Manny that they had to go see Gloria.

"Thank you for your time and the information," Abe shook both their hands. "Here's my card if you think of anything else."

Fifteen minutes later a U.S. Marshal let Holly and Manny into the private prisoner interview room.

"Abe was pretty cool," Holly said as they waited for their client to appear.

"Yeah, he knows some of my friends up in Portland."

The door suddenly swung open and the female marshal led the petite, skinny Gloria Ocaso to a metal table, to be seated across from Holly and Manny. The dark face of the twenty-year-old looked like it had been drowned by years of tears. Her hair was disheveled and her clothes smelled ripe.

"Where's mija?" Gloria cried out in Spanish, her skinny arms lashing out. Luckily, both Holly and Manny spoke the language.

"We don't know yet," Holly tried to calm her down by putting her hands over Gloria's. "But we are trying to find out." Gloria looked like she had been living in a concentration camp.

Manny asked permission of the female marshal standing outside the door to get Gloria something to eat and drink. The guard gave an affirmative nod. In the meantime, Holly wanted to go over the facts of the incident with Gloria. She would be arguing them in court in an hour.

"They going to hurt me!" Gloria screamed, pounding the table. "I never see my mija again! Oh, God, help me!"

Holly leaned in and started rubbing Gloria's back. "We're going to protect you. Who is trying to hurt you?"

"The migra!"

"How do you know this?" Holly asked.

Then a torrent of sobs came. Between crying and yelling, Gloria shared that when she was arrested in Twin Oaks back in March, the ICE had sent her to Portland to be detained. She was with other young woman and a few older women. On the way up, they were handcuffed and seated in a prisoner transport van. They were not allowed to talk. They were not provided any water or food. One older lady told one of the two guards watching over them that she had to go to the bathroom. The tall, muscular ICE agent told her to shut up and hold it. Finally, after almost three hours of driving, the van pulled over at a rest stop. There were no other cars. The prisoners were let out, one at a time. One guard stayed on the van with the remaining prisoners while the other escorted one prisoner at a time. They were told that they had to take care of their personal business as quickly as possible.

When Gloria's turn came, the guard grabbed her.

"I need you to show a little appreciation," he said in Spanish with a Tejano accent.

She tried to pull away, but he pulled her closer. He tried to grab her between her legs.

"¡A la chingada!" he yelled.

"He mad at me. I had made pee pee in my pants."

"What happened after that?"

"He let me go. Told me to hurry. Told me that he would hurt me if I told."

"Did he leave you alone after that?"

"Yes, but I think he did bad things to other girl. She crying when she go back to van."

Manny knocked on the door and came right in. He laid an egg and ham-filled English muffin in front of Gloria.

Holly motioned Gloria with her eyes. "Eat up. We'll talk after you eat. Remember, everything you tell us is confidential. We're here to help you. Do you understand?"

Gloria stopped crying and nodded. She wiped her eyes, and started wolfing down the food like she hadn't eaten for days.

Knowing that time was growing short, Holly tried to start the information gathering. But before she could begin, Gloria interrupted.

"Where's mija?" Gloria kept repeating with her face contorted with a sorrowful grimace.

Holly tried to establish some control and after a minute Gloria calmed down. Holly then asked, "Please tell us what happened to you on Friday, March 16."

Gloria said, "Like I tell police, I take bus from middle school where I work. It drop me off at Stateline Street. I see a white car follow me. I cross railroad tracks. I going to my apartment, another block away. The white car was police car. It turned on its loud sirens. I was scared! Really scared! Then lights go flashing. A policeman make me put up my hands. He ask me a lot of questions. I tell him I go home to my daughter. He not let me go. He said I had to wait. My mija is very worried if I get home late."

"Was this a police officer or an ICE agent?" Holly was confused.

"I see him around town a few times. Big gringo with red brown hair. Short hair. Blue eyes. Not very nice. Talk loud voice. Yell at me."

*Was she saying that the arresting officer was a local police officer?* She would have to talk to Corkie. She would check with the local police chief. *What was his name? Chilaquiles? Chiloquin?*

"Then what happened?"

"After long time, green van come," Gloria said. "The ICE men arrest me. Put me in jail. Don't let me see my daughter."

The interview continued for another twenty minutes.

Afterwards, the female marshal took Gloria away.

At 9:50 Holly and Manny were in the courtroom waiting for their case to be called. Corkie and Cristina had driven over early that morning and were seated in the back. They were bleary-eyed.

The first two cases called went very smoothly.

"Case 20190302732A, Gloria and Yesenia Ocaso versus U.S. Immigration and Customs Enforcement (ICE)," the bailiff called out. The sitting judge was the Honorable Magnus Wingaard who had been appointed by President George W. Bush. Gloria Ocaso was led out of a side door by a female marshal to sit next to Holly and Manny.

"Dennis Milbanks for the U.S. Attorney General, representing ICE, your honor."

"Holly Acevedo and Emmanuel Raven representing the respondents, your honor."

"Okay, Mr. Milbanks, why should we dismiss this case?"

"Your honor, this court has no jurisdiction over this case," stated the 42 year-old balding Milbanks, in a pinstriped suit that complimented his French cuffs and gold cufflinks. He handed some documents to the bailiff and to the opposing legal counsel. "As you can see, by the affidavits of the Twin Oaks County city clerk and the county property tax assessor, the alleged incident took place in California, not Oregon."

"I object, your honor!" Holly jumped up from her chair. "We haven't seen these affidavits before. This is an unfair surprise!"

"Your honor, the respondents' complaint sets out the address," Milbanks smirked. "They were aware or should have been aware that the incident occurred in California."

The gavel came down hard. "Both sides, in my chamber! Now!"

## Chapter 18 – Be Prepared

*Medford*
*Monday, April 23*

Lorenzo checked his cell phone just after his first period class. There were text messages from Corkie. The first one at 8:03 a.m. read:

> "Oye, mi amor, Christina and I arrived safety. Nice drive. Not much traffic, except logging trucks. See you tonight. Might stop at Costco for a supply run. Want anything? Love, C."

Lorenzo texted back "chewing gum." The second text from Corkie at 10:39 said:

> "Something strange just happened. All the attorneys had to go meet in the judge's chambers. He looked pissed. Pobrecita Gloria."

***

Meanwhile, there was quite a commotion in Judge Wingaard's office. "Ms. Acevedo, surely you knew that the arrest took place in California," Wingaard's blue eyes steeled right through her.

*What a f**king disaster!* Holly was unhinged. *How in the hell did she blow it?* A court's legal jurisdiction over a legal action usually took place where the events occurred. A New

York court could not usually adjudicate matters in the State of Florida. Here it looked like the detention took place in California. She could argue that Gloria Ocaso was a resident of Oregon or the police were from Oregon, but she knew her chances to prevail were between slim and none. She had been played beautifully. It was her fault.

"Unfortunately, your honor, I did not know that Twin Oaks is a bifurcated city. I take full responsibility. I am very sorry," Holly groveled, feeling that she should almost kneel in front of him and kiss his ring.

"You know, Ms. Acevedo, I know that you are young, but we have three very strict rules around here," Wingaard said sternly. "Be prepared. Be on time. And be fully prepared."

"Yes, your honor," there was a lump in her throat.

"Does that mean that you are going to grant our Motion to Dismiss?" Milbanks was trying to hide his smile and wanted to strike while the iron was hot.

"That was a brilliant legal maneuver on your part, Mr. Milbanks," the judge turned his attended to the Assistant U.S. Attorney. "But a better approach for good collegial lawyering would have been to inform the other side of the jurisdictional defect. Instead you have unnecessarily wasted this court's time."

"Yes, your honor."

"I'm granting petitioner's motion to dismiss on the asylum issue. Ms. Acevedo, I'm dismissing the case without prejudice. You may refile your claims in the proper jurisdiction."

The attorneys bowed slightly and politely thanked the judge.

"We would like to continue with Ms. Ocaso's deportation,"

Milbanks requested. "She signed the voluntary departure papers."

"Was she given her Miranda rights?" asked the judge.

"The file says yes. There is an indication of an oral waiver."

"Was her legal counsel present when she signed?"

"I don't know," Milbanks was fudging.

"Ms. Acevedo, were you or any member of your organization present when she allegedly waived her constitutional rights?"

"No, your honor," she was glad for the reprieve.

"Where is the daughter, Yesenia Ocaso, now?" the judge's eyes narrowed as he tried to penetrate Milbanks' soul.

"I don't know, your honor." Beads of sweat appeared on the government attorney's forehead. He knew what was coming.

"Were the mother and daughter charged with civilly and criminally violating federal immigration laws?"

"Yes, your honor," Milbanks tried to regain his composure.

"The daughter's supposedly at some juvenile detention center, your honor," Holly interrupted. "But we don't know where."

"Which one, Mr. Milbanks?" the judge's eyes were raised.

"I don't know," Milbanks responded.

"Please find out the details immediately and report the information to me and Ms. Acevedo."

"Were the petitioners, Gloria and Yesenia Ocaso, in the custody of ICE from the Oregon office?"

"Yes, your honor, Gloria Ocaso, for sure," Milbanks was ad-libbing. "Not sure about the child."

"Are you saying counselor, that you don't know which ICE agents apprehended the child?"

"Well, I don't know for sure. I would assume it was the Oregon ICE agents."

"In that case I am granting the relief for the federal habeas corpus for the Ocaso mother and child." Holly knew that the judge was basically saying that Gloria's detention was unlawful and that she was hopefully going to be released.

"But your honor," Milbanks tried to argue. "We may never find the child. And Gloria is under an order of deportation."

"You understand that the Ocasos are entitled to Due Process, correct?" the judge never took his eyes off Milbanks. "How are they supposed to present an asylum case, if one of the parties may be locked up in a privately-run zoo with cages?! They fled from El Salvador, for God's sake. This situation is totally disgusting! Ms. Ocaso is free to go, subject to a possible reinstatement of the deportation order at a later date." The judge slammed the gavel.

Milbanks was silent. Holly and Manny were shocked.

An hour later Holly and Manny were treating Gloria, Cristina, and Corkie to breakfast at a local diner a few blocks away from the federal courthouse.

"I can't believe we won!" Corkie said as she ate her blueberry buckwheat pancakes.

"Well, technically we lost the battle, but won the first war," Manny tried to show off his legal acumen.

"I couldn't believe the judge helped us," Holly said.

"Well, even judges are human sometimes," Corkie smiled.

Gloria couldn't stop crying. Corkie made a few stops to buy Gloria a few pants, tops, and running shoes. Cristina also bought her a blouse. They were on the road back to Twin Oaks by three.

Manny and Holly debriefed on their drive back. Holly told him about the attempted sexual harassment of Gloria by the ICE agent on her transfer to Portland. *That mother frigger!* They wanted to file a formal complaint against ICE, but the administrative process would take forever and never be adjudicated.

The two attorneys were the first customers at the Happy Hour at the Caldera Brewery in Ashland in the late afternoon.

"Congratulations! We did it!" Manny clinked Holly's mug.

"Now, we have to refile," Holly's mind had been racing all day. "The real sh*t is going to hit the fan."

# Chapter 19 – Oregon National Guard

## *Wednesday, April 25, 2018*

The Rotary Club had just finished its monthly meeting in the banquet room of the Red Lion Café. Mayor Keough decided to stay behind and hold court in the venue and get serious about his re-election bid coming up in November. He had no Republican challenger, but he never took anything for granted. There had been hints that Gerry Hill was thinking about running. However, the latter withdrew after Keough appointed him to the City Planning Commission (a plum political appointment). There was, however, an organic produce grower by the name of Chris Ramsey who was the Democratic Party candidate. *I don't need to worry about this socialist piss ant,* Keough thought.

Around his table were Randy Miller (a skinhead), Andy Jackson (head of the Utah American Freedom militia), Pastor Paul McConnell (fundamentalist preacher), and B.B. Barnes (Twin Oaks City police officer). They were all on their third cup of coffee.

"What's new, men?" Keough gave his good ole boy smile.

"They let that 'wet' we caught last mouth back out on the street," B.B. contributed.

"How in the hell did that happen?"

"Some attorneys from Medford and those Commie activists Lorenzo and Corkie Becerra were behind it," the police officer said.

"You need to keep an eye on them," Keough commanded.

“They’ve been giving ICE a hard time,”

“How so?”

“The schools won’t allow ICE on their campuses without warrants.”

“That’s bull shit,” Keough yelled out with a country accent. “Those wets are breaking the law. I’ve called the governor’s office, but he blew me off. I also called Congressman Smith’s office. He wanted to lean on the governor just to mess with her, but he said he would contact the President’s office instead. He knew that they would be supportive.”

“I want you and all your people to attend the City Council meeting tonight,” Keough ordered. “We have an important issue to consider. It may be the centerpiece of my re-election campaign.”

***

The Twin Oaks City Council was called to order at 6:30. The agenda and the prior meeting’s minutes were approved unanimously. Old Business flew by in less than five minutes.

When New Business came up, there was only one item. Keough moved a formal request on behalf of the City that the Oregon National Guard be called in to round up aliens. He spoke vociferously on the drain of public funds and the burglaries at churches.

The city council was stacked 3-2 in favor of Republicans. The real estate agent and insurance company employee were solid Keough supporters. However, Nelson Kirby, the third Republican, was really more of a Libertarian than anything else. He hated government.

"Mr. Chairman, does our City Attorney have an opinion on the legality of this motion?" Kirby asked.

The contracted city attorney, Donald Berger, was put on the spot. He hated to be put in the middle of politics. His solo practice only survived with city and county contracts.

"Members of the council, nothing prevents you from passing such a resolution," he tried to avoid the real question. However, the council saw right through him.

"But is it legal? Is it binding on anybody?" one of the Democratic council members followed up.

"In my opinion, no," Kirby stated. "This city council has no authority or jurisdiction over the Oregon National Guard. It would be up to the governor."

There was discussion and arguments for the next ten minutes. Keough's motion failed by a 3-3 vote.

***

"How was your day?" Lorenzo grabbed his wife's hand as they sank onto the sofa.

"Busy, busy, busy," Corkie took a sip of her red wine.

Lorenzo had prepared some cheese, salami, and pesto bruschetta for their light dinner. There was also a side of broccoli. Chispa placed himself at their feet. He still needed a walk, and was waiting patiently.

"This is really good," Corkie gave a look at her wine glass.

"It's one of the Willamette Valley Vineyard pinots we bought last year when we went to that awesome Salem winery."

"Well, let me tell you about my day," Corkie began. "Gloria spent the night with Cristina. They needed to reconnect. Cristina felt terrible about Yesenia being swept away. Gloria's rent is due on the first. But she doesn't have any money since she hasn't worked. Cristina offered to let Gloria live with her. She can sleep on the couch until they find Yesenia. Poor Gloria is suffering. I was tempted to offer our place, but knew you would have a conniption about another body in our house. But I feel so bad."

"Good call, mi amor," Lorenzo nodded. "Have to draw the line somewhere."

If Corkie had her way, every stray person or animal would have a place in their home. But she was a realist, and her marriage came first.

"We went over to the Catholic Church and talked to Father Murphy. You know, the old guy from Boston with the heavy accent. We wanted to know if he could offer sanctuary or some kind of housing, but he wasn't any help. He doesn't want to rock the boat. His big donors in the parish are the growers and the conservatives. He did, however, give us the name of the local Catholic Charities. We're going to check them out tomorrow."

"What about Gloria's job?" Lorenzo questioned.

"For the short term, no problem. She starts back in the morning," Corkie leaned forward and poured herself more wine, forcing Chispa to move. "The bad news is that once the middle school shuts down for the summer, she has no job. That's my next biggie."

"Sounds like you're doing the Lord's work."

A half hour later Corkie was cleaning the kitchen and Chispa was leading Lorenzo down the unpaved road. *Am I being too selfish by not offering more help to Gloria?* he wondered.

## Chapter 20 – Bart Stoker

***Thursday, April 26, 2018***

There was a fine spring time mist falling. Officer B.B. Barnes was sitting in his patrol car on the main highway hidden by a giant billboard that advertised the local steakhouse. He had written three traffic citations that morning. He observed the cars coming from both directions. If he knew the vehicle and it was local, he left it alone. But if was from out-of-state, especially from California, it was full lights and sirens. *They can afford the fines. They are so rich and famous,* he thought.

Today was his traffic duty day. He had to average at least one ticket an hour. That was how the city of Twin Oaks made money. That was how he got paid.

His personal cell startled him as it went off. It was a rare occurrence when he received a call on this phone.

The screen I.D. said, "B. Stoker." Bart Stoker was his ICE friend that he had assisted a couple of weeks earlier.

"Catching you at a bad time?" Stoker said at his end.

"Naw! Just some traffic garbage. Been slow in the office," B.B. reported. "It was my turn in the crapper."

"Did you hear that they let that woman go that we caught a few weeks ago," Stoker said. "We do all the heavy lifting, and the next thing you know they are roaming the streets again. How are we supposed to do our jobs?!"

"Yeah, I know. The mayor can't get any local support."

B.B. Barnes had formerly been a Clackamas County Sheriff (25 miles south of Portland) for a while until he was asked to leave for bending the rules too many times. The last incident was the use of excessive force on an African-American man who used profanity. B.B.'s personal life was no better than his professional one. He had poor luck with women and was divorced. These failings gave him a sour outlook on life and added to the chip he carried on his shoulder.

"Hey, bud, we're planning to do a few raids around some schools on Friday. Want to have some fun?" Stoker asked. "We can have a good time. Maybe even arrest that Ocaso woman for jaywalking."

They both laughed.

"I think we have some kind of strategic planning meeting on Friday," Barnes lied. He did not want to let on that Chiloquin didn't want his police force cooperating with ICE.

"Hey, we're getting some new Kevlar vests in. Maybe one could come your way."

Barnes thought that working for ICE might be a kick. Probably more money. They could be law-biding vigilantes without all the crazy constitutional protections. See someone that looked suspicious (or was a person of color), arrest them, and send them to some Third World country. *We need to make America great again.*

"Maybe next time," Barnes said quietly.

"Heads up. Some of my buddies are coming up from Utah this weekend," Stoker shared. "I think you've met them before. You know Andy Jackson, that ex-Marine. He's bringing up half a dozen guys to see the sights of Twin Oaks, if you know what I mean."

Barnes knew who these guys were. They were part of a renegade splinter group of the Utah state militia, known as the American Freedom group. They were a private, right-wing, paramilitary organization that were anti-government. This "citizen army" traveled to Oregon, Idaho, and California to "safeguard" American values. That usually meant harassing local citizenry and Latinos in particular.

***

The following Sunday morning, Barnes was passing a tray of food to an incarcerated individual who had a military haircut and snake tattoos inked on his arms. This middle-aged member of the American Freedom group had been arrested for beating up a Mexican at a local bar.

"Name's Jim. Jim Collins," the prisoner squinted.

Barnes said nothing. The jailhouse policy was not to talk to the prisoners and B.B. thought it was good advice.

"Hear you're friends with Bart Stoker," Collins gave a suspicious grin. "Hear you're one of us.

"I just do my job," Barnes had bit.

"I hear that you do more than that," Collins was a slick salesperson. "Hear you're a real believer."

***

Chiloquin knew that there would be trouble when Jackson's group of redneck, paramilitary types arrived into town in a black Humvee. The phones had been ringing at the police station all weekend. People (those with brown skin) had been accosted by these Utah thugs and asked to produce citizenship papers. Latino workers were pushed and shoved and chided for stealing American jobs. The Utah guys even made a couple of drive-bys at the local hospital. The locals were scared.

The police chief had his entire force report for duty. He found out that the Utah group was staying at a campground about five miles out of town. Chiloquin did not want to drive out there. Too many unknowns. There were also other innocent campers in the vicinity.

Chiloquin couldn't risk a direct confrontation with the group. His police force was understaffed and underequipped. He figured that Jackson's group probably had automatic weapons in the Humvee. The risk of a blood bath was too great. He decided to have one of his men follow the Humvee wherever it went. He wouldn't stop the Humvee unless he had sufficient cause. Hopefully, the Utah guys would get tired of the tail and leave town.

The arrest of Jim Collins went without incident. Jackson's crew had split up and had dropped two of the guys off in front of a local Mexican bar. Collins attacked one patron and was beating on him, until the bartender pulled out a shotgun. A police car came. Collins was arrested and taken to jail. The police let the other guy go.

***

Barnes retrieved the food tray from the prisoner.

"Hey, B.B., we have expertise in explosives."

## Chapter 21 – Assault and Battery

### *Monday, April 30, 2018*

The bailiff in the Twin Oaks circuit court called the next case on the Monday morning Criminal docket. "State of Oregon vs. Jim Collins, case number A-23930945, aggravated assault and battery . . ."

Collins was wearing an orange jumpsuit and shackled with his hands in front of him. He was escorted over to the defendant's table and was seated next to a short, round, ruddy-faced man dressed in a wrinkled grey suit.

"Alvin Beckham, for the defense, you honor. Waive reading. My client pleads not guilty. Requests to be released on his own recognizance." Beckham had practiced locally for over twenty-five years. He was part of the good ol' boy system in town. He knew that Judge Lyndon Cummings liked expedited proceedings. He put his hand on his client's shoulder and gave him an ear-to-ear smile.

A woman with short dark brown hair and bangs wearing a navy business suit and a faux pearl necklace pushed her chair back at the prosecutor's table. "Marsha Squires, for the People, your honor. The defendant has a criminal record and is a high flight risk."

"Objection, your honor. Mr. Collins has never been arrested in the State of Oregon," popped up Beckham.

"Your honor, the defendant is an out-of-towner," Squires asserted.

"Out-of-towner!" Cummings voice was raised. He hated riff raff from other places. "Where do you live, Mr. Collins?"

"He lives in the State of Utah. He is up here visiting with some friends. He needs to get back to work," Beckham asserted.

"Your honor, the defendant is part of a vigilante gang from Utah who came here to harass our local people," Squires blasted.

"I object, your honor," Beckham responded.

"How much bond are your requesting, counselor?" the judge asked the city prosecutor.

"$100,000. The defendant has a criminal record and no incentive to show up back here for a court date."

"What? Your honor, that's outrageous!" Beckham's face was apoplectic.

"Mr. Beckham, I think that you are in a weak bargaining position," the judge was not going to be okee-doked by the defense. "I'm going to give you a fifteen-minute recess to confer with Ms. Squires. Bailiff, call the next case." The judge banged the gavel.

Beckham and Squires met in a small conference room on the opposite side of the hallway. Collins was escorted back into the custody holding cell.

"Come on, Marsha, be reasonable," Beckham groveled. "This is a simple case."

"First, Alvin, this is more than a simple case. Your boy and his friends came to town to harass Mexicans. We don't tolerate Minutemen and vigilantes coming here."

"But they're all willing to leave and not coming back. No

harm, no foul," Beckham tried another tact.

"Second, the fact that someone hired you to defend Collins tells me something. I don't see these rednecks being able to afford you," The prosecutor burned her eyes into her opponent. "That tells me that there are people here who called them in. And I don't like that."

"No one else is involved," Beckham squirmed.

"Well, then, who is paying your legal fees?"

"I can' tell you. That's privileged!"

"Fine. Then the number is still $100,000. We both know that the defendant is never going to show and the co-signer will have to eat it. Collins is tough. He can hold up in jail until the trial begins. He did plead non-guilty, correct?"

Twenty minutes later Squires and Beckham were in Judge Cummings' chambers.

"What did you two work out?"

Squires laid out that bail would be set at $50,000 and that William Masters would be the cosigner. Masters was the owner of the Cook Brothers Gold Mine. He had a reputation for being an outspoken anti-Hispanic critic. He called everyone Mexican, even if they came from Central America or simply had brown skin.

"Do you both agree to this?" the judge asked.

The opposing attorneys nodded in agreement.

"No, this is not going to work," the judge was shaking his head incredulously. "We all know that this guy is never going to show, we'll only get a little money out of the forfeited bail, and our office will be deluged in months of paperwork."

"But your honor, that's the way the system works," Beckham felt more confident now dealing with the judge.

"Alvin, this is what you are going to agree to do on behalf of your client," the judge started writing on a yellow legal pad. He didn't need any stinkin' computer. "First, the defendant is going to plead guilty to aggravated assault. The sentence will be six months in county jail."

Both attorneys looked shocked.

"Second, the sentence will be suspended on the following conditions: defendant pay a cash fine of five thousand dollars before the close of business today. No checks. Next, a civil compromise of $25,000 be paid to the victim before the close of business today. Lastly, the defendant leaves town and stays away from here forever."

"Your honor, my client can't raise thirty grand by five o'clock today," Beckham pleaded.

"I'm sure that your co-signer could probably find fifty thousand, if he had to. This is non-negotiable, counselor."

"Fine, your honor," Beckham surrendered.

Squires also assented.

The judge left his chambers while the two attorneys made the arrangements and drew up the necessary papers.

"This is bull shit!" Beckham complained to Squires. "My guy is innocent until proven guilty."

Squires ignored the whining. "Oh, Alvin, a piece of friendly advice. Make sure that your boys leave town. I heard a rumor that the FBI is coming here to investigate a federal case of conspiracy to cross state lines in order to commit hate crimes."

# Chapter 22 – Pastor McConnell

***Tuesday, May 1, 2018***

The mayor was livid. He needed to put a spark into his re-election campaign. He had received an irate phone call from Masters at 6 a.m. that morning.

"I'm out almost $50,000 for the jackasses you called in from Utah," the gold mine owner had ranted. "Somebody needs to reimburse me, Mitch. And sooner rather than later!"

Mayor Keough was now scrambling to come up with a strategy to motivate his voting base i.e., Republicans, fundamentalists, conservatives, uneducated, rednecks. He pulled out his personal cell phone and dialed. The person at the other end answered immediately.

"Hello, mayor," Pastor McConnell greeted him. "What can I do for you today?"

A half hour later Mayor Keough and Andy Jackson were meeting in the office of the fundamentalist preacher. Pastor Paul McConnell was the spiritual leader of the Christian Apostolic Congregation, one of the biggest, if not the biggest church in the area. He was originally from Tennessee and his parents were cotton growers. He hated Yankees, and all that they stood for.

"We've had a minor setback, gentlemen," the mayor was beginning his ploy. "The judge ordered Andy's men back to Utah. Getting our message across will be getting a little harder now."

"Collin's a good man," Andy Jackson was trying to defend

his Utah American Freedom militia member. "Sometimes he gets a little over enthusiastic."

"There are some real trouble makers in town. Like the Becerras," Pastor McConnell added with his Southern drawl. "Esquivel told me that Lorenzo has been having school meetings and his wife Corkie helped that 'wet' get out of jail. We can't allow that to continue. We need to maintain control."

"And that outsider, Holly What's Her Face, keeps causing legal problems. Is she Jewish or just a Communist?" the mayor asked.

The trio kept complaining about this and that.

"And pastor, when do you want me to speak to your congregation? I'm available any time for your flock," the mayor made his pitch.

McConnell had worked with Keough a long time and knew how the mayor imposed himself into every major gathering in the city. *What the heck?!* Grimaced the pastor. *At least he's not trying to shake down my congregation like he does the downtown businesses. I have my own house to support.*

"Let me check with my assistant, mayor. I'll get back to you."

The three chatted some more about nothing, and Keough and Jackson soon walked out of the parsonage. The two men stopped in the middle of the parking lot to say their good byes.

"It was good seeing you, mayor," Jackson started to shake the mayor's hand.

"When you leaving?"

"Probably within the hour. The men should be all packed up by now," Andy said in a subdued tone. "We'll try to be home by midnight."

"Be safe, Andy," the mayor patted Jackson on the back.

"Too bad all of us gotta go because one guy was too gung-ho," Jackson walked toward the Humvee. He was at the driver's door when the mayor called him back.

"What did you just say?" the mayor said in an excited voice.

"We'll be home by midnight."

"No! You said why should you all be punished for the actions of one man," the mayor was rubbing his chin with his right hand. "The judge only talked about Collins leaving. He has nothing on the rest of you."

"So?" Jackson was not following.

"You men don't have to leave," the mayor was bobbing his head with excitement. "Just Collins."

"How's that going to work, mayor?" Andy was trying to catch on.

"Send Collins on a Greyhound back home and you guys stay."

When Jackson returned to the campgrounds, four of his five men were elated. Collins was pissed. "I didn't come all this way to have my ass hauled back to Utah. I want to stay."

"We know how you feel, soldier. We appreciate everything that you've done," Andy Jackson was trying to calm Collins down. "But for the sake of the mission, soldier, you'll have to sit this dance out. There'll be other operations. Maybe back in

Idaho."

Collins nodded, resigned to his fate. One of his mates drove Collins to the Greyhound bus station in downtown Twin Oaks and picked up more supplies. Their campground was only five miles from downtown, just into California territory. Jackson wanted to remain out of the jurisdiction of Chiloquin and the local police.

In the afternoon, Jackson called up Bart Stoker at ICE and apprised them of the new situation.

"We're going to do some local roundups at the schools this week," Stoker told Jackson. "Probably not a good idea if you are around."

"I was thinking that we could drive someplace and park. Divide up and roam the streets," Jackson said. "If we're not in our car, the police can't pull us over for some bull shit ticket!"

"Good idea. And if you break up into teams, they don't have enough resources to track you" Stoker was smiling over the phone. *The reserves have arrived.* "The Marines trained you well. You make us proud."

"Just doing our civic duty."

"By the way, there is a local policeman who is loyal to our cause," Stoker said. "Call him up. Here's his private number."

That night Jackson and Barnes talked on the phone for over an hour. Barnes did not want to meet with Andy because he was afraid somebody might see them.

For the next several days, the five Utah American Freedom members made themselves conspicuous in town. As soon as Chiloquin found out, he assigned one of his officers to patrol the downtown area and keep an eye on of Andy Jackson, the leader.

On Friday, Jackson was standing outside of the police station. Chiloquin decided to grab the bull by horns and walked to the front of the building to confront the out-of-towner.

"Can I help you gentlemen with anything?" the police chief said politely.

"The question, chief, is do you want us to help you? Jackson was cocky.

"Thanks, but don't need your help."

"But, chief, we can't let these wets destroy our country!"

"Watch yourself, my friend."

"Just trying to make America great again."

## Chapter 23 – Say Cheese!

***Wednesday, May 9, 2018***

Corkie had a quick lunch with Holly who had just rushed into town for her routine legal consultations. Holly had missed her prior scheduled visit and had to recalendar her community service date because of another big case back at the Medford office.

"Hey, girlfriend, haven't seen you in a while," Corkie sipped her hot Egyptian licorice tea. She was sitting across a funky wooden table from Holly. Working people were finishing up their soup-and-salad lunches before going back to work.

"Manny took a case involving a U.S. citizen who was held in custody by ICE for three days. No phone calls. They were going to deport him. One of his coworkers saw the green immigration vans pull up at the orchard supply building and they just start herding people away."

"Where?" Corkie's eyes were as big as pies.

"Medford. The Harry and David's storage facility. Right when work was letting out."

"So who is the client?"

"José Garcia," Holly started to explain. "He was born in Brownsville, Texas, and came to Oregon as a migrant farmer worker in the 90's. He got a job at Harry and David's and worked his way up to supervisor."

Harry and David's was one of Corkie's favorite places to

buy holiday gifts, like fruit baskets. The gourmet snacks and specialty items were special treats.

"His family was worried about him," Holly continued. "One of the workers told his wife that he had seen ICE dragging José into custody. Nobody ever contacted the family about José."

"That's b.s." Corkie was angry. "Friggin' Nazis!"

"Hey, are you ready to go to law school and hook up with Manny and me?"

"Hey, do I look that naive?!" Corkie gave Holly a smirk. *I'm too old. I can't imagine sitting in class with a bunch of twenty-year-olds.* "I wouldn't see my husband for three years and then I would still work the same long hours. I don't think so."

"We are fortunate back at the office. Manny has a lot of friends with the American Constitution Society (ACS). They are going to co-counsel with the Oregon Legal Project."

Corkie knew that the ACS was a national progressive legal organization that promoted the values of human dignity, individual rights, equality, and justice. She had once seen the former Oregon Supreme Court Justice, Hans Linde, give a legal presentation at an annual ACS dinner. Her head spun from his legal acumen and abstract analytical skills. Judge Linde was a legal genius on steroids.

"When do you file?" Corkie asked. She was getting the hang of the legal jargon.

"We submitted the papers two days ago. Federal court in Medford."

"Good luck!"

Forty-five minutes later, Holly was doing her routine legal intake at the community center. She had more scheduled cases than usual because she had missed the previously scheduled session. For her first case, she had a mother whose 13-year-old-son was in juvenile court for the third time. The boy kept running away from home. There was no father in the picture.

The next case was a landlord-tenant situation where a single mother failed to pay the rent and the late fee charges. The young woman and her two children were set to be evicted. Holly got a temporary reprieve while the mother borrowed the money for rent. The late fee charges were dropped. Holly knew that the following month would be no different. The cycle would repeat itself. She knew that poor, uneducated women had very few choices in life.

Holly took a break and grabbed some tea from the community center break room. The waiting area was full. She noticed two middle-aged, military-looking guys walking about and staring down people. She went back to her room for her third appointment. David Underwood was from Micronesia and was attending high school on a student visa. He decided that he would drop out of school and explore the Western United States. Immigration had been trying to track him down. He showed Holly a Notice to Appear at the U.S. Citizenship and Immigration Services (USCIS) office on Friday.

The fourth and fifth clients did not answer when called. She went to the bathroom. The two burly, hard looking military guys were still in the waiting room glaring at the people in the waiting room. Holly casually went over to the receptionist, Ayline Rodriguez, and bent over to speak to her in a soft voice.

"Anything going on, Ayline?"

The receptionist turned her head to the left to observe the

waiting room. "I think those two big guys might be giving some of the clients a hard time."

"About what?"

"I don't know," Ayline said nervously. "But some people have left."

*¡Crap! Not on my watch!* "Ayline, I'm going to find out who they are and what they are up to," Holly was trying to figure out how she was going to approach the duo. "If I raise my left hand, please call the police. Tell them our clients are being harassed by some out-of-towners. Do you understand?"

A minute later Holly drew herself up in front of the two military types. They both smiled.

"Can I help you, gentlemen?" Holly said politely.

"Yes, ma'am," said the taller one. "We're looking for a Gloria Queso [mispronouncing Ocaso]. We're trying to send these criminals back home where they belong." The two men laughed.

"This place provides legal services to anyone," Holly stood her ground. "I will not have anyone interfere with that. I am asking you both to leave."

"And what if we don't want to," the shorter one said contemptuously.

"Just a second gentlemen," Holly raised her left hand and pulled out her cell phone with her right. "Say cheese!" the camera feature flashed three times.

"Hey, we have a right to be here," said the taller one. "This is a public place!"

“Not for you. You’re trespassing,” Holly stole a look over to Ayline who gave her a nod.

# Chapter 24 – MAGA Militia

## *Wednesday, May 9, 2018*

It was almost five o'clock that same afternoon when Corkie peeked into the interview room where Holly was sitting with a stack of files in front of her. With her head bent over, Holly was making notes on the intake sheets.

"You driving back tomorrow?" Corkie asked, hanging onto the door knob.

"Yeah, need at least an hour to finish sorting through these." Holly had decided to spent the night at her friends, Ken and Ann's, rather than at Corkie's. She didn't want to wear out her welcome at the Becerras. "Tell the big boy hi. This ought to keep him happy until the next time." She handed Corkie a cloth bag with three bottles of wine, all red.

"Thanks, I'm sure it will," Corkie smiled. "By the way, saw Chiloquin here. Everything's all good." Sometimes Holly called the police to assist her if there was a domestic violence issue or the like.

"Yeah, a couple of those Utah skinheads tried to intimidate the clients. They left before the police got here. Assholes!"

*Must be election season again,* Corkie thought, as she hopped into her metallic green Toyota Corolla and started to make her way home. The evenings were now remaining a little brighter, much later. She needed to check on her strawberries and fruit trees this weekend. She turned the radio on to a soft jazz station. The Becerras lived right at the edge of the city's boundary, about a 15-minutes-drive from the community center.

She looked in her rear view mirror and saw a large vehicle behind her, about 100 yards. She turned on her headlights. At the three mile point she turned right onto a small rural road. Corkie thought that the car behind her did the same thing. Normally, there was not much traffic out her way.

It was now getting dark as she turned onto the gravel road that led to her house. Corkie stopped at a little junction where a half dozen mailboxes were posted. No mail. That meant that Lorenzo was probably home. As she walked back to her car, she noticed that the vehicle had stopped down the road. It looked like a gigantic black SUV.

Lorenzo had a small fire going when she walked in the door. She brought in the wine and gave him a kiss. He opened a bottle and they started to imbibe.

Corkie sat on the couch and closed her eyes. She exhaled. Chispa came over and sat by her.

"You look tired, my dear. How was your day?" Lorenzo scooted over closer to her.

"Same. Had a nice lunch with Holly. She's working on another big case. ICE grabbed a U.S. citizen and locked him up."

"That was sweet of her to send over some wine. Got home early. We ended practice early this afternoon," Lorenzo took another sip of wine. "Some of the kids have midterms tomorrow and need to study."

"Hey, babe, have you talked with Chiloquin lately?"

"No. What's up?

"Well, there were these two rednecks at the community center today. They were hassling the clients and Holly."

"Did someone call the police?" Lorenzo sat up straight on the couch.

"Yes, but they jammed before the police arrived." It was Corkie's turn to take a big swallow. "But I think I may have been followed home. There was this big SUV that stopped short of the mailboxes. Didn't recognize it."

"Do you know what color it was?"

"I think black."

"Do you want me to call the police and have them look around?" Lorenzo wanted to appear calm in front of his wife. He had heard that the Utah militia group was milling around town, trying to intimidate people. He also knew that these guys were driving around in a black Humvee.

Corkie nodded no. She was tired and just wanted to relax. *Need to take my shoes off!*

Lorenzo had reheated some leftover chili and warmed up the cornbread. Chili was always better the second day. Suddenly, Chispa started to bark and darted toward the front door. Corkie and Lorenzo were a half mile from their closest neighbors. They looked at each other. They rarely had visitors, especially unannounced.

"Hon, grab the flashlight!" Lorenzo commanded calmly. Corkie went to the nearby closet and grabbed the gigantic LED headlamp. Lorenzo grabbed the shotgun that was hidden under the sofa. He grabbed some shells from a drawer.

"Should we call the police?" Corkie was calm and collected.

Lorenzo hesitated a moment. "It could just be Holly bringing us more wine," he was trying to make light of the situation. "But let's bring the cell phone with us . . . just in case." Corkie put her shoes back on.

Lorenzo turned on the front yard halogen lights and the three exited the house. Chispa never wore a leash since they lived out in the country. Lorenzo lit the unpaved road with the flashlight. There were woods, open fields, and hedges on both sides of the path. They proceeded on their normal doggy duty walk and twenty minutes later came upon the mailboxes. Nobody was around. They turned around and started back.

Chispa gave a blood-piercing cry and started to bark violently. His nose was pointed straight in front of them, toward their house. Two tall men dressed in camouflage gear suddenly appeared out of the thickets.

Lorenzo walked straight toward the two strangers holding Chispa by the collar. Corkie was fidgeting with the cell phone in her pocket.

"Howdy, hope we didn't scare you," one of them said in a strong, gravelly voice.

Lorenzo kept walking without responding.

"Heard you two are troublemakers in town," the first stranger continued. "Our country doesn't need communists like you. We need to make America great again."

"I will ask you both to leave here," Lorenzo was frightened, but he had to take control of the situation, just like when kids were acting out in class. "You're trespassing on my land."

"And if we don't?" the second stranger said smugly.

"We'll call the police and you can talk to them."

The first stranger started to lunge toward Lorenzo. Chispa sprang forward and quickly had the attacker by the throat, twisting and growling. The second man seemed to be pulling something out from behind him. Instinctively, Lorenzo swung the giant flashlight around and whacked the guy's knee cap. A giant scream rang through the woods.

Corkie calmly called the police.

## Chapter 25 – Free Speech

### *Thursday, May 10, 2018*

"Ms. Squires, there's a Mr. Beckham here to see you," the city hall receptionist said over the intercom late Thursday morning.

"Thank you," the city attorney replied. "Please send him up."

A few minutes later the red-faced Beckham walked into her office. "Marsha, we have a problem. A big one!"

"Please, be seated," Squires said calmly and coldly. "How can we help you?"

"We need to file criminal charges," Beckham was huffing and puffing. "We can't have this savagery in our town!"

"Filed against whom?"

"The Becerras," Beckham asserted, as he nervously rubbed the band on his gold watch. "And that wild dog needs to be put down. Can't have vicious animals around."

"Okay, let's begin with who is filing the charges," Squires took out some forms and a legal pad and began writing.

"Charley Riggs and Gene Simon," Beckham said in a matter of fact manner.

"What are their addresses?"

Squires asked a series of questions and then abruptly

stopped. “These guys seem to be colleagues of our mutual friend Jim Collins. They are all from Utah. Were they all up here together?” *I thought they had left?*

“Yeah. Just came up to enjoy some outdoor activities around our town. No harm in that.”

“What do you want the Becerras charged with?”

“Aggravated murder or at least, attempted murder with a deadly weapon and whatever else you can think of.”

“What’s the deadly weapon?”

“That wolf dog they own. And the baseball bat.”

“Anything else?”

“I’m going to file a civil action against them,” Beckham was pushing out his chest. “We need to teach them a lesson.”

“Well, Alvin, you’re right. Someone needs to be taught a lesson.”

“Damn right,” Beckham said smugly.

“But we have a problem here, Alvin,” she gave him a coy look. “Your boys were trespassing on the Becerra property.”

“It was a road. That’s public, isn’t it?”

“Sometimes it is,” Marsha leaned forward and brought forth some photos. “The police report corroborates the Becerras. It’s their own private road.”

“But the public has some kind of an easement. They can go on that road.”

“That’s a problem, Alvin. Charley and Gene’s Humvee was

parked back in the forest, on private land. No public easement."

"But my clients were injured! Injured bad!" Beckham was becoming agitated again.

"A person has the right to defend his or her property," Squires calmly lectured. "Can even use force."

"Who's going to pay for their medical bills?"

"Maybe the same person who is paying your legal fees and who called in these roughnecks from out-of-state."

"This is outrageous!" Beckham stood up.

"What is outrageous, Alvin, is that someone is trying to intimate our town. They are agitators from Utah."

"No law against Free Speech."

"You're right on that count, Alvin. Your clients can explain their situation to the FBI. I called them this morning. They can explain why they came to town. Divulge who invited them. Their Utah residences will be verified. The feds will run a criminal record check on each of them. Maybe even check out their military discharges."

Ten minutes later Beckham was in his car calling Masters.

"Did you scare her?" the gold mine owner asked.

"She called the feds. They're coming."

"What the f**k, Alvin?! Why am I paying you for this b.s.?"

***

Corkie was finished at work and jumped in her car to drive home. She was exhausted from the traumatic experience the night before. The police had come. They took photos and found tire tracks in the mud. The first order of business was getting back to the house to give Chispa a bath to get rid of all the blood. Corkie wanted to discard the clothes that she and Lorenzo had been wearing, but the police wanted them for evidence. It was after one o'clock in the morning when she and Lorenzo finally collapsed into bed.

She was less than five minutes from home when she thought she saw a black Humvee speeding in the opposite direction. Her senses went on full alert. She immediately called Lorenzo.

He picked up on the third ring.

"Hey, babe, are you on your way home yet?" the husband sounded cheerful.

"Have you seen anyone around the house in the last half hour?" Corkie nervously said.

"No, why?"

"How's Chispa?" Corkie ignored his question.

"Fine," Lorenzo sensed his wife's tension. "He was barking about ten minutes ago. Probably a squirrel."

"Hey, babe, just saw that black Humvee coming from the direction of our home. They were in a hurry!" Her voice stared to panic.

"Just stay calm," Lorenzo said. "Don't . . ."

Bam! Corkie heard an explosion about a half mile in front of her. Bam! Her car shook and she tried to brake. Bam! A third explosion.

## Chapter 26 – Thanks, Cuz

### *Friday, May 11, 2018*

Chiloquin walked back to his office from his meeting with the city manager. *Budget variances are worthless. Who can predict crime or public safety issues?* he thought. He sipped his second cup of coffee that tasted like a cross between battery acid and a tin can. There were more files and telephone messages piled on the rickety wooden desk as he sat down in his office.

His private cell phone rang. He recognized the number.

"Hey, Miles! What's up?" Chiloquin asked enthusiastically. "How's auntie?"

"She's the same as usual. Crabby and demanding," his cousin Miles said, grinning at the other end of the line. "I'm bringing you some smoked trout and elk sausage. Mom made you a berry pie too. Man, she spoils you."

Miles Pearson was Chiloquin's cousin on his mother's side of the family. He and Chiloquin had been raised in Klamath Falls on the reservation during their formative years. Miles was now the supervisor at the tribal Ponderosa Pine Mill. He and his twenty-year-old son, Dennis, were coming up to Twin Oaks to look for some new carbide-tipped saw blades.

A week earlier Miles and Dennis had arranged to stay at Chiloquin's place for a few days. Since Chiloquin was a bachelor, there was no problem. His cousin and son would run their errands and then would hunt or fish in the nearby forests and lakes. Chiloquin was like a godfather to Miles. He had tried to be a big brother to his cousin when the latter's father left them. Yesterday, when Miles called to say that they were on their way, Chiloquin asked for a favor. Miles didn't ask any questions.

"Is it done?" Chiloquin asked vaguely

There was a slight chuckle on Miles's end of the line. "Yup! Saw some gold mine company tow truck with the Humvee on its bed. It was going south on Highway 395 toward Reno."

"Did you see any passengers?" Chiloquin pressed.

"Saw a guy with a bandage over his ear and another guy with crutches," Miles replied. "Saw them all leaving together in the tow truck."

"How many?" Chiloquin couldn't believe that everyone would fit in the tow truck.

"At least four, plus the driver."

"Any other cars or trucks with them?"

"No cuz. I think we scared the living shit out of them," Miles laughed as he described how the previous night he and his son Dennis had driven within a half mile of the California campground where the Utah rednecks were staying. The father and son had night goggles and high-powered hunting rifles. They slowly zigzagged through the lush terrain until they spotted the Humvee parked in front of a canvas-sided cabin. They sat and waited until all the lights of the hut went off. Then at exactly one o'clock in the morning a pair of pops went off. Then two more. The tires on the passenger side of the Humvee exploded with gigantic whooshes. A second later, the headlights were shattered into thousands of pieces.

The lights of the cabin came on. Two flashlights were seen

futilely trying to scan the area. Marty and Dennis retreated and drove back into the woods. They parked their four-wheeler on an offbeat road. In the early morning they came back to their original observation spot. They saw four guys and the gold mine company tow truck driver all gesticulating with their hands and arms. A black Dodge Ram tow truck arrived on the scene. The identity of this driver was difficult to discern because of the tinted windows. One of the Utah American Freedom guys, who looked middle-aged but solidly built, jumped into the passenger side. The truck then kicked up gravel as it peeled out. After the Humvee was loaded onto the truck bed, the other rednecks jumped into the cab.

"Thanks, cuz," Chiloquin said. "I owe you one."

"Not me," Miles replied. "Dennis. That boy can shoot."

***

Mayor Keough was not happy about going over to the downtown office of the Cook Bros. Gold Mine. The place smelled of cigarette smoke and dust. A pretty young thing escorted him into a small conference room where the bald, ruddy-faced Willie Masters was sitting with Randy Miller and Andy Jackson, the sole survivor of the Utah American Freedom militia.

"What is so damn important that I have to come here and hold your hands?" the mayor said in an exasperated tone.

"Your re-election, for one thing," Masters said in a casual tone.

"What's all this have to do with my election?" Keough probed.

"Well, Andy and his men came up to help with the situation.

But it seems that everything has gone sideways. People have been arrested. An SUV was shot up. People were assaulted. This is not a safe community, Mitch." Willie shoved a glass of Jim Beam and ice over to the mayor who instinctively took a large swallow. "Andy is the only one left. We can't let the Mexicans and your police control the city. And then there are these community agitators who are defying the laws! Mitch, we gotta act. Especially if you want to win re-election."

The mayor nodded his head slightly. He was trying to buy time to think of a plan. Normally, Pastor McConnell would be the strategist, but the weekend was upon them and there was no time.

"We can create a little mischief," Andy suggested. "A little diversion here and there. Make the people afraid and come crawling to you."

"What's happening at the schools" Keough ignored Andy's suggestion. "How come we can't get any traction there?"

"Chiloquin and the school principal," Masters poured himself another drink.

"I thought that police guy Barnes was going to help us?"

Masters and Miller had blank expressions on their faces. There was silence.

"Let me call B.B.," Randy offered. He hadn't really said much, but then he was only a goon for Keough.

Keough nodded his head slightly. "By the way, Willie, Andy needs to stay with you for a while." Masters' head jerked back. He didn't like what the mayor was saying.

Randy left the conference room and went to the bathroom.

He dialed police officer Barnes.

"What's shaking, B.B.?" Randy said in homeboy fashion.

They talked for a few minutes before Miller walked back into the conference room.

"Don't know if this is helpful, but I just found out that there is some kind of problem at the Armadale United Methodist Church," Randy said. He didn't really like the pastor there.

"What kind of problem?"

"Some Mexicans or Guatemalans want asylum," Randy continued. "ICE wants to arrest them and the police chief is saying no."

## Chapter 27 – The Starmonts

### *Friday, May 11, 2018*

There were two white Twin Oaks police vehicles with their blue and red lights flashing in the pitted Armadale United Methodist Church parking lot. On the street there was a light green windowless van with the logo “ICE” on its doors.

“I suggest that you drive away, Bart,” the police chief addressed the immigration officer in an authoritarian manner.

“You know, chief, these people are illegals,” the ICE agent grinned at his own cleverness for using a double entendre. Chiloquin was both Native American and the police chief. There was no love lost between these two. Bart Stoker was equally determined to assume control of the situation and apprehend the Guatemalans who were locked up in Sandra Starmont’s car. “I plan to arrest them.”

“Do you have an arrest warrant?” Chiloquin countered.

“Don’t need one,” Stoker’s face was smug. “They don’t have any proper identification. They look awful suspicious.”

“How do you know that, Bart?” frowned the police chief.

“Your deputy here,” Stoker turned his head toward police officer Branson “B.B.” Barnes, who was about thirty feet away next to the car in question. “He discovered their immigration status during a routine traffic stop. We have reasonable suspicion to question them.” Stoker was probing for a weak spot. He wanted to back Chiloquin into a corner.

"They're on church property now," Chiloquin continued. "And without a warrant, you have no business interrogating them against their will."

"Oh, chief, we can get a warrant," Stoker bluffed. "Or we can wait this out. Catch them when they leave the premises. But, chief, we don't want to play that way. Why don't you save us some time? Let us question them. We're going to get them sooner or later."

***

An hour earlier the Twin Oaks Police Chief, Marty Chiloquin, had received a frantic phone call from the Reverend Dell Starmont. He related to the police chief that his wife Sandra and the parishioner, Margaret Fisher, were just about to pull into the church parking lot, when they were stopped by a police officer for a broken taillight. Sandra said that the police officer questioned her about what she was doing and then started to question the passengers. Dell said that his wife and the parishioner were trying to help a Guatemalan couple get medical assistance for their seven-year-old son who had a rare form of bone cancer. They were just coming back from the hospital when they were pulled over. The police officer asked for the identification of all the passengers. The Guatemalan couple were petrified. They had no ID.

The policeman then asked everyone to remain in the car. Sandra protested because they were just feet away from their parsonage. The officer refused to let them go and walked away. She saw him pull out his cell phone and make a call. It lasted about two minutes with the officer's head bobbing up and down. Sandra took the opportunity to text her husband who within minutes rushed outside the parsonage to confront the officer. The policeman identified himself as B.B. Barnes and notified

Reverend Starmont that they were waiting for ICE.

The Reverend argued that there was no reason to detain his wife.

Barnes said that she was harboring illegal aliens. He wouldn't budge.

The Reverend ran back into the parsonage and called the police chief. Within ten minutes Chiloquin arrived and was just about to order Barnes to release everyone when Stoker arrived in the ICE van. That's when the standoff began.

By eight o'clock Stoker realized that Chiloquin could wait him out. He would just have to try again another day.

Sandra took the Guatemalan family into the church. Poor Margaret Fisher, the parishioner, had to drive home alone. Reverend Starmont was upset by the turn of events. After the Starmonts went into the church, Barnes was ready to go home. He had had a long day.

"B.B., take a walk with me," Chiloquin said, not asking.

Barnes was hungry and just wanted to leave. He was hang dog.

"Didn't you and I have a discussion about us not doing grunt work for the Immigration Service?"

"Yeah, but this was a traffic violation," Barnes was trying to explain. "I just found out the information about the illegals during the stop."

"When did you first notice the broken tail light? In town?"

Barnes wanted to lie, but wasn't swift enough to come up with one. "Well, I saw the vehicle with the broken tail light in town and followed it. I called in the vehicle's license number and found out that it belonged to Wendell and Sandra Starmont. I knew that it was that Methodist preacher's car."

"Did you first see the car at the Emergency Room entrance or at the front door of the hospital?"

"The ER . . ." Barnes tried to stop, but he had already blurted out the fact that he was tracking Starmont's vehicle.

"Why were you tailing the Reverend's vehicle?"

"Well, everybody knows that they are harboring illegals in their church."

"But that's none of our business."

"But they are breaking the law," Barnes argued righteously.

"But we have no authority to enforcement federal immigration law," Chiloquin said matter of factly. "I have already told you that. State law prohibits it."

"But the state law is wrong!"

"Barnes, do you realized that you detained two U.S. citizens? Mrs. Starmont and Mrs. Fisher?" Chiloquin shook his head and blew out a breath. "They could sue us. And you, personally."

"Let them try. There are people in town who would have a field day with this," Barnes spoke with bravado.

"Well, Barnes, you give me no choice," Chiloquin. "As of this moment, you are officially suspended from duty without pay for the next three days for violating the state sanctuary law."

# Chapter 28 – Suspension

## *Saturday, May 12, 2018*

Barnes woke up early Saturday morning with a hangover and a bad case of cotton mouth. The night before had been disastrous. He had closed down the local watering hole where gold mine workers and lumberjacks always threw back a few brewskies after work. Maybe they hoped that the dust and dirt encrusted on their bodies would simply be washed away.

B.B. was pissed. *How could that holier-than-thou police chief suspend him?* B.B. was just doing his job. Keeping the peace. Keeping the town safe.

Barnes had called Stoker after his conversation with Chiloquin the night before. He needed to vent. The ICE agent tried to console B.B.

"This country is going to sh*t," the ICE agent lamented. "Too many liberals and commies pampering the criminal element."

"What I really don't understand is why all this bull shit matters to Chiloquin," B.B. fretted. "It shouldn't be any big deal to him. We get paid just the same. We're just doing our job. Nothing else."

"I know that some of your brother officers are not happy with him," Stoker grinned. "Maybe you should run against him come election time. I know that you would have a lot of support. Never too early to start thinking about it."

Barnes' eyes blinked. He was trying to think over what

Stoker just said. "I think that the police chief is appointed by the city manager and approved by the city council." There was no election for the position.

Stoker knew that Mayor Keough usually had three of the votes on the city council. The mayor could get rid of Chiloquin in a heartbeat if he really wanted to. Stoker had to terminate the phone call, because cell reception was getting spotty. He was driving through the mountains going back to Portland.

Barnes was still fuming. He didn't want to go home just yet. Instead he swung over to the Round Rock Tavern on the outskirts of town. It was hangout for locals. He took a seat at the bar. He was still in uniform, so the patrons gave him wide berth. Most of the time, Barnes did not make social calls to this particular establishment. But tonight was different. He wanted to forget.

The bartender served him up a Deschutes Brewery draft IPA. That was gone in less than a minute. B.B. was in the middle of his second brew when the local troublemaker, Randy Miller, pulled up a stool next to him.

"Well, look what the cat dragged in!" Randy teased with a cowboy drawl. "What brings you in to hang out with us common folk?" He laughed.

Barnes kept silent and just stared straight ahead. If he got any more upset, he was going to shoot this son of a bitch.

"Rumor has it that you've been grounded," Miller asserted. "Life's a bitch, friend."

"How'd you know?" B.B. turned to face Randy.

"News spreads like wild fire. But half of the town is on your side. We just keep letting the riff-raff take over," Miller asserted.

The pair kept chugging down more beers until the tavern closed down. It was past two in the morning when Barnes drove home, more than half-drunk.

***

B.B. woke with a start. Now, it was Saturday morning. He had never slept in on the weekends. He was always on the job early. He poured himself a cup of stale coffee. He longed for a cigarette, but he had quit. Barnes ate two pieces of toast with his favorite boysenberry jam. This was his comfort food. What was he going to do with a day off? Well, actually, three days off. What did he want to do? He couldn't think of anything.

*This being a cop gig was getting old*, he thought. *Can't just do your job. Have to follow all the rules.* Stoker had suggested that there might be some openings in ICE coming up. *Probably even pays better.*

B.B. figured that he could move out of state. He liked Idaho or maybe even eastern Washington. Barnes did a cursory cleanup of his apartment. He had been married once, but that didn't last long. Part of the breakup was due to the fact that while B.B. tended to be a neatnik, his wife was a slob.

Barnes ran over to the grocery store and stacked up on provisions. A couple of frozen pizzas, two loaves of white bread, pretzels, and a pound of assorted lunch meat. He was good to go.

Barnes took a nap in the afternoon. Afterwards, he avoided the temptation of going back to the bar. He microwaved a cheese and sausage pizza and watched his big screen TV for the remainder of the evening. He ended by watching the news.

Sunday morning arrived. He showered and shaved. He put on some nice civilian clothes and drove over to Pastor

McConnell's Christian Apostolic Congregation. He ran into several members of the church with whom he briefly chatted. A few said they were sorry that he had been mistreated by the police chief. The church service lasted over two hours. Afterwards, Pastor McConnell walked over to B.B. and shook his hand. Barnes was surprised. The pastor had never paid much attention to him before.

"Patience, my son," the pastor put his right hand on Barnes' shoulder. "This too shall pass."

Tears started to well in B.B.'s eyes. "Pastor, I didn't do anything wrong! Why is this happening to me?"

"I know, my son," the pastor moved closer to him. "The Lord says we must love our neighbor. But that doesn't mean letting them take advantage of us. We just want to pray in our own way."

Barnes' head was nodding in agreement.

"Some of these people are criminals," the pastor continued. "They are criminal aliens. They are not like us."

"Well, what should we do, Pastor?"

"B.B., how would you like to work on the mayor's re-election campaign? They need a devoted person like you."

# Chapter 29 – Jesús

## *Thursday, May 17, 2018*

The wind was howling as the warm Spring precipitation fell sideways onto the Twin Oaks civic buildings. The May flowers savored the rainwater. Corkie sat in a little office that was one step above a cubicle. She had Sandra Starmont, the Methodist preacher's wife, and María Bautista squeezed tightly in front of her. They were preparing for a 2 o'clock appointment with Holly Acevedo who was doing her biweekly legal intake at the community center.

Earlier in the week, Sandra Starmont had called Corkie on behalf of the Guatemalan family that was being given sanctuary at the Armadale United Methodist Church. The preacher's wife was very emotional as she described the hostile confrontation between Police Chief Chiloquin and the aggressive ICE agent who was trying to arrest the Guatemalan family, the Bautistas. She didn't understand how a traffic stop could result in a major skirmish with the feds.

"It was almost like that cop was working for ICE," Sandra blurted out in anger. "And not for us!"

Corkie was taking copious notes. She didn't know where to begin. Chronological order probably worked best.

Sandra went on to explain that the mother, María Bautista, and her husband, Josué, had come to the States to flee from the dangers and violence in Guatemala. Their seven-year-old son, Jesús, had been diagnosed with bone cancer and needed proper medical treatment. María explained that at first, life was better when the family lived in Tucson. Then, the symptoms of Jesús seemed to worsen. He was coughing up blood and looked jaundiced. The parents tried to take him to the hospital, but ICE agents were stationed there. Additionally, the hospitals were turning away patients if they didn't have insurance.

Some church parishioners had recommended moving to Oregon. Josué and María decided to take a chance for the sake of Jesús and go. They made the long bus ride from Tucson to Twin Oaks. They had been advised to seek assistance from the Armadale United Methodist Church which was reputed to have a true Christian approach to immigration. The church had six small cottages that afforded temporary refuge to unfortunate victims. The Baustistas moved into a unit, and less than a week later Jesús started running a fever and had diarrhea. The boy was constantly wailing from pain.

María hurried over to the parsonage and begged for assistance from Mrs. Starmont. Sandra and a local parishioner volunteer, Margaret Fisher, drove the family to the emergency room of the local hospital. The doctor gave the child a general examination, but wanted to run some tests. The doctor also wanted to call in a pediatrician specialist for a consultation. The entourage finally left the hospital. On the way back to the parsonage, there were stopped by Officer Barnes.

Corkie asked Señora Bautista some clarifying questions in Spanish. After listening to both ladies, Corkie concluded that the boy, Jesús, definitely needed more medical testing. At 1:50, the trio left the cubicle and everyone made potty stops before their meeting with Holly.

Holly was in a good mood as she warmly greeted the trio of women. She took a swig of her tepid coffee and began, "So the local police are working with ICE?" Holly had heard the rumors.

Sandra wanted to be low key. Her husband had been livid when she told him the details about last Friday's confrontation. But Dell was a preacher and had to set a good example for his parishioners. He would let Sandra handle this on her own.

"Holly, we just want to get little Jesús the proper medical care," Sandra stated humbly. "Their immigration status is secondary."

Holly looked at the preacher's wife. She had a sad look on her face. "Unfortunately, Sandra, the two things are tied together," the attorney said in a soft tone. "Historically, humanitarian assistance has almost always been granted to people who have grievous injuries or medical conditions. But with this new administration, there is no heart or soul. The practices have become cruel and inhumane."

For the next hour the group strategized. It was finally decided that Corkie would seek out a friendly local doctor to care for Jesús. Sandra would safeguard the family on the parsonage premises and arrange transportation to and from the hospital and medical offices. And Holly would start the legal process for asylum.

They coordinated around Jesús's next medical appointment with the pediatrician that was scheduled for Friday. Sandra would arrange for her faithful friend Margaret Fisher to give the Bautista family a ride since Sandra had not fixed the broken taillight yet.

It was almost five o'clock when Sandra and María arrived back at the Armadale parsonage. They entered the main house. The lights were on. María excused herself and went to her cottage to check on her son.

"How did it go?" Dell asked. He was sitting in an old

wooden rocking chair with his shoes off. He had been reading the newspaper.

"Whew! I have a lot to report." Sandra summarized the day's events.

"I don't think our church should get political," he measured his words. "But we have to take a moral stand against inhumane treatment of other human beings. We can't call ourselves good Christians if we look the other way."

Sandra nodded.

***

About two blocks away, within sight of the Armadale church, a police car was stealthily parked under a big weeping willow tree. The police officer tried to adjust his binoculars, but to no avail. He really needed night vision goggles, but was out of luck. He reached into his pocket and pulled out his cellphone.

"They're back," Barnes reported.

Words were communicated back and forth.

"Okay, you're on for tomorrow morning," B.B. finally said. He was ready to go home.

## Chapter 30 – Whoops!

***Friday, May 18, 2018***

Dark grey skies attacked the Twin Oaks valley. Every twenty minutes there would be pouring rain, then it would stop. Visibility was on again, off again. The air was perfumed with spring florals, but the streets were flooded with water.

A black Jeep SUV drove out slowly from the back of the Armadale United Methodist parsonage with its windshield wipers rapidly swooshing back and forth and its headlights on. It was about 8:40 a.m. on Friday morning. The rush hour traffic had subsided for the commuters.

Another car was parked clandestinely a short distance away. There was movement inside the car. A tall, muscular driver put down his binoculars and called police officer Barnes. "B.B., they just left."

"How many, Randy?" Barnes was back on duty working the downtown area after his three-day suspension. During his "timeout," Barnes had agreed to assist Mayor Keough in his re-election bid. Barnes was put in charge of keeping illegals out of Twin Oaks. He was assigned to work with Randy Miller, the mayor's minion, in order to avoid direct contact with Stoker or ICE. He would have plausible deniability if anything went sideways with Chiloquin, whose days seemed numbered.

"Three!" Randy shouted over the phone. "I see two women and a kid."

"Good work! Give ICE a head's up to meet us at the hospital," Barnes directed, as he turned his vehicle around. He would get those liberal Starmonts for harboring illegals.

Fifteen minutes later the Jeep came to a stop and then turned left into the hospital parking lot. A vacant parking slot was readily available. The driver was just opening up the door, when flashing lights appeared behind her. Despite the torrential rain, the police officer flew out of his vehicle and rushed toward the woman.

"Ma'am, please get back into the car!" the police officer said gruffly. "I need your driver's license and vehicle registration."

"Officer, what have I done? These people have a doctor's appointment," the woman said excitedly. "It's an emergency!"

"Ma'am, back into the car!"

Two minutes later the police officer was citing the driver for not coming to a full stop at a stop sign. Then suddenly a green van with an ICE logo pulled up behind both vehicles blocking all possible egress. An ICE officer approached the stopped vehicle.

"I need to see everyone's ID!" he shouted.

The back passenger door suddenly opened and a youngster tried to run away. Barnes dropped his citation book onto to the wet pavement and sprinted after the fugitive. The youth was quick, but Barnes was stronger. The officer tackled the child who smashed into a concrete bench. The kid let out a blood curdling scream.

An hour later the trio from the Jeep SUV had been taken by Immigration and placed under an ICE detainer at the local jail. Local jurisdictions had informal arrangements that allowed ICE to hold suspected undocumented immigrants in their jails for short periods of time. The child was not afforded any medical attention and sobbed in his mother's arms.

***

"Good work, B.B.!" Masters had received a phone call at his office at the Cook Bros. Gold Mine. He praised the police officer who had just informed him of the apprehension of illegals. "With you on the team, the mayor is a shoe-in for re-election."

B.B. wanted to share the credit with Randy who had been staking out the Starmont place, but he changed his mind.

***

"Bart, mission accomplished!" ICE agent Johnson had called his supervisor who was stuck in Medford in a meeting with the U.S. Attorney.

"Any problems?" Stoker was antsy. He didn't want to go back to his meeting. More bureaucratic bullshit.

"Naw!" Lonny said.

***

The ICE agent, Lonny Johnson, was still in the police station waiting room when his cellphone buzzed. The text identifier seemed to be from B.B. Barnes. Barnes had specifically told him that he couldn't be in direct contact with him. So Johnson wondered, *Why the text?*

Five seconds later, he knew why.

The text read: **"It's not them!"**

Johnson texted back. **"Not who?"** *What was B.B. saying?*

A minute later, another text from Barnes popped up.

**"Not Mrs. Starmont and her illegals. Bad**

**bust!"**

Johnson was confused. He texted back.

**"Who are these people, then?"**

**"Puerto Rican parishioners."**

*Holy f*ck!* Johnson thought. *This clown can't get anything right. It was a simple operation.*

**"Your intelligence had me believe that they were Mrs. Starmont and the illegals. This shit is not going to fall on us!"**

**"Sorry, man,"** Barnes felt like a fool. **"Bad info."**

**"You know I have to release them now. They're frigging U.S. citizens!"** the ICE agent texted. **"This is not going to look good. Don't think we can cover for you."**

**"Hey, it was an honest mistake!"** Barnes was nervous. His stomach was churning. **"They looked Mexican!"** If Chiloquin found out, he was totally screwed.

**"If I were you, I would make sure that the injured kid is taken to the E.R."**

***

Margaret Fisher finally arrived back at the parsonage, visibly shaken. She had been sobbing and her wrists were bruised from the tightly-administered handcuffs that ICE had used on her. The other woman was mouthing silent prayers with her eyes closed. Her daughter, who was suffering from bronchitis, had sustained a sprained ankle and a concussion as a result of the tackle by Officer Barnes. For a split second, Margaret wondered whether she should continue assisting the Starmonts.

The reverend's wife, Sandra, was livid when she heard what happened. She wanted to confront Barnes. By the time the reverend came home, Margaret had left and Sandra was on her second Jameson's.

Reverend Starmont was even more livid. He called Chiloquin. They set up a face-to-face meeting for the next day. Sandra called Corkie who spewed out a litany of cuss words.

"Those mother f*ckers will pay!"

## Chapter 31 – Proposition 105

***Sunday, May 20, 2018***

The phone rang at the dismal hour of six a.m. Mayor Mitch Keough was not happy when his beauty sleep was interrupted after a night of heavy imbibing.

"Be at my church by eleven!" the voice at the other end of the line commanded.

"Hey, Pastor, you know I don't go to church," the mayor squirmed.

"Be there!" Pastor McConnell barked. He wasn't taking any pushback. "You need the exposure with my congregation for your re-election!"

After the phone call ended, Keough tried to go back to sleep, but tossed and turned restlessly. Finally, he got up, showered, and shaved. At the evangelical church, he ran into supportive parishioners with whom he shook hands and whose babies he kissed. The ten o'clock services had just let out. He saw William Masters from the Cook Bros. Gold Mine, who approached him.

"That was a total cluster f**k the other day!" Masters exploded into Keough's face as they stood near the entrance to the parsonage. Andy Jackson was with him.

"Where did you get those guys? They're friggin' idiots!" Willie continued. Andy was trying to suppress a grin. *Why are they trying to get this guy re-elected?* he thought. *The mayor is a fool!*

"It was an innocent mistake," the mayor backpedaled. "It was raining hard. Nobody could see nobody."

"But that huckleberry cop should have figured it out!" Masters continued to berate the mayor. "This is a total sh*t sandwich."

At just past eleven they were meeting in Pastor Paul McConnell's office.

"Thank you all for being here," he said cordially. B.B. Barnes and Randy had not been invited. Keough, Jackson, and Masters politely nodded. "I think, gentlemen, that we need to regroup. That police officer got a little ambitious about wanting the police chief's job and exercised poor judgment."

There was some muttering by Keough and Masters.

"We have to up our game. The anti-illegals campaign should be a winner for us. We just have to play smarter," everybody was listening. "It will get Mayor Keough re-elected."

"Well, for sure, we have to get rid of the police chief!" interrupted Keough.

The pastor held up his hand and stopped the mayor before he could continue. "There is a statewide ballot measure set for November. If it passes, Chiloquin's hands will be tied. We'll have him right where we want him."

At that moment, there was a tapping at the conference room door. "Come on in!" yelled Pastor McConnell. "Right on time!"

A short, pasty-white, plump middle-aged man walked into the room nonchalantly like he owned the place. He was sporting a reddish-brown comb-over and wore a cheap grey shirt with a U.S. flag tie. He plopped his thick, worn out black leather briefcase on the conference table with a thud.

"Gentlemen, this is Boris Jones. He is here to help us with the re-election of Mayor Keough and the passage of Proposition 105."

Jones explained that one of McConnell's Republican parishioners was a big RNC (Republican) donor, who had strong ties with FAIR (the Federation for American Immigration Reform). This group was one of the sponsors for Proposition 105, an initiative that was slated for the November 2018 ballot. This Proposition 105 measure would repeal the Oregon Sanctuary Law and allow local government and police to enforce federal immigration laws.

"How is this going to help get me re-elected?" Keough blurted out.

"I'll take questions at the end," Jones took command of the meeting. "Let's begin with some basics. We're all on the same page about getting rid of the illegals. But we have different approaches. The old ways of intimidation no longer work." Jones stared directly into Jackson's eyes. "There is too much media coverage. It might work in the short run, but the public doesn't like to see it. We have to be smarter. Let's begin at the beginning."

Jones gave a very brief summary of the 1987 Oregon Sanctuary Law. It had been a bipartisan bill with almost no opposition. It had been supported by the growers and most law enforcement agencies. The others at the table had their jaws dropping in surprise.

"But now, all of us here want to repeal the Oregon State Sanctuary Law," Jones continued. "That's what Proposition 105 does." He explained further that anti-immigrant groups, following the president's agenda, wanted to oppose sanctuary states and cities. The president even wanted to withhold federal funding from sanctuary states. The Oregon Republican Party and some rural county sheriffs supported the measure.

That was good enough for the pastor. "I'm all in," Pastor McConnell shouted out.

Keough agreed, "Oregon shouldn't give shelter to foreigners here illegally! We need to protect Oregonians from those criminals!"

"We need to take down the barriers between the police and ICE," added Masters.

They continued the discussion. "Who is going to oppose this kind of logic?" Keough blurted out.

"The governor and the Democrats to begin with," Pastor McConnell answered.

"It's those friggin' Communist Democrats!" cried out Keough as he pounded on the table. "They should all be deported back to Russia!"

"We're not going to attack the opponents," Jones continued. "We are going to motivate the base that is in favor of immigration reform and the Republican party. We are going to get the churches involved. Pastor McConnell has been a tremendous help in the past. He will deliver again come November."

Jones took some handouts out of his briefcase and passed them to the other four men. There were responsibilities assigned and timelines to follow.

"Any questions?" the political strategist asked.

"Yeah, again, how is this going to help my re-election?" Keough pushed. "This is an anti-illegal campaign, not a re-election campaign!"

Jones was smooth. He had several political campaigns under his belt. The Oregon Republican Party really liked him. He could handle these dolts who acted like spoiled children. "It's both. Your campaign will take a pro-Proposition 105 stance. The voters will applaud your advocacy on this issue."

"How can I be sure?" the mayor asked.

"Because I am your new campaign manager, courtesy of FAIR and the Republican Party."

More questions popped up and Jones handled them deftly.

"What about Randy Miller and B.B. Barnes?" Andy Jackson asked. He thought how the mayor's toadies had screwed up with the recent immigration stop.

"They're out!" Jones said abruptly. "No screw-ups on my watch." Keough said nothing about his two gofers who had just been let go.

"Andy, can you recruit some volunteers from Utah? Some clean-cut types," Jones stared at the paramilitary skinhead without blinking an eye. "No more survivalist types."

"Sure, no problem."

The meeting ended and everybody seemed satisfied with the new direction. Jackson got into a rental car and started to drive off. He picked up his cell phone and dialed a number.

"Reich!" the other side answered.

"We're back in business!" Jackson said smiling. "Send me

twelve trained guys, fully-armed, and three Humvees."

"Done, sir."

"Make sure each one packs a suit and tie."

"What?!"

# Chapter 32 – Termination

## *Monday, May 21, 2018*

It was a beautiful Monday afternoon and sunshine lit up the blue sky. Corkie was planning to cook a healthy dinner. She was carrying a small straw decorative shopping basket as she strolled down the aisles of the Two Daughters Country Grocery Store. The sibling owners were in their eighties, and their store was the go-to place for the locals. The store carried everything from goji berries to Sriracha salsa. Today Corkie was looking for some firm tofu. She and Lorenzo were not vegetarians, but they preferred alternatives to red meat for their protein.

"You all kicked some ass a few weeks ago," a gruff voice sounded. Corkie had smelled the sour tobacco odor before she heard the words. "You sent those tough Utah boys home with their tails between their legs." He laughed derisively.

Corkie knew Randy Miller. He was the 45-year-old ex-Marine who worked for the mayor. She stared at him expressionlessly.

"If I were your friend, I'd being looking over my shoulder," Miller warned. "They're watching her."

*Who was he talking about?* She wondered. She didn't want to engage him in conversation, but she had to know.

"Who do you mean, Randy?"

The skinhead grinned and paused a moment before answering. "That miss goody two shoes preacher's wife." Randy was still smarting about B.B. and him being dropped from the mayor's inner circle. He was pissed that the outsiders from Utah had just waltzed in and taken over their spots. *So much for friggin' loyalty,* he thought. He walked away.

An hour later when she arrived home, Corkie shared her unpleasant experience with her husband. Neither of them were hungry for dinner after that. They debated about whether to call the Starmonts to warn them.

"Why would Randy talk to me?" Corkie had a puzzled look on her face.

"Don't know," Lorenzo's brow was furrowed. "I don't trust Randy, but something is going on in town. I can sense it"

Finally, Lorenzo called Chiloquin and relayed the incident.

"Should we let Dell and Sandra know?" asked Lorenzo.

The police chief thought about it for a brief moment and replied. "Let me do it. I should pay them a visit. I'll have a deputy check out the premises." *This used to be such a small, quiet town,* Chiloquin thought

"Thanks, chief," Lorenzo said.

"You heard that I was forced to fire Barnes, didn't you," Chiloquin was tired of all the high drama of local politics. "He was getting too cozy with the feds."

Lorenzo had heard rumors that Barnes wanted to be police chief. Probably with the mayor's encouragement.

***

Mayor Keough had been going over to the downtown office of the Cook Bros. Gold Mine at least twice a day. Boris Jones had set up the unofficial campaign headquarters there.

Boris had different colored charts taped to all the walls. There were three computers in the middle of the room. One of Masters' trusted secretaries, Darla Bennett, staffed the office. In addition to Masters, only Boris Jones, Mitch Keough, and Andy Jackson had access to this war room.

There was an empty coffee pot in the corner of the room that looked like it hadn't been scrubbed for years. Boris was a strict non-smoker so he made sure that the place smelled clean and fresh.

"Hey, did you hear that Barnes was fired?" Keough spurted out as he rushed to sit down.

"That was to be expected," stated Jones. "He was a liability to us anyhow. Just like your boy Miller."

Keough wanted to protest, but Jones had him on a short leash.

"But, Mitch, we have good news," Boris began confidently. "We have canvassed over two thirds of the city's precincts, just doing R's and I's (Republicans and Independents). Hope to finish the remainder by Friday."

"Sounds good," the mayor gave an ingenuous grin.

"We will start phase II of the campaign this weekend," Boris walked over to some precinct maps and charts. "We'll do a heavy GOTV (get out the vote) push this weekend. The primary is a week from tomorrow. You're looking good, but we can't take anything for granted."

"Do I still need to do the town halls and coffees?" Keough was a politician who hated schmoozing.

"Hey, you're doing great in the gated communities. They

love you," Boris was trying to stroke his candidate. "Just keep pounding our message: This sales tax puts a financial burden on all of us. Vote No on Measure A next Tuesday. Measure A is a one-cent sales tax for emergency city health services sponsored by the liberal Twin Oaks Health Coalition. And sign up to support Proposition 105 and help prevent us taxpayers from paying the medical bills for illegal aliens."

"Pastor McConnell wants me to go to his church on Sunday," Keough said weakly.

"That's a no-brainer," Jones sighed. "Go! We'll get a staffer to drive you and collect volunteer cards."

"How about Barnes or Miller?" Keough threw out.

"Not a great idea," Jones responded. *Are you friggin' kidding me with those Neanderthals?!* "I'll find someone." *Maybe one of Andy Jackson's boys.*

Keough left and Jones called Masters. "We're looking good. Ready for Phase II."

## Chapter 33 – Un-Oregonian

***Tuesday, May 29, 2018***

It was primary election day and the enthusiasm in town was underwhelming. The No on Measure A campaign had been doing a full court press, relying on Republicans, conservatives, and religious fundamentalists to oppose the measure. The proponents of Measure A were outgunned and very naïve. People don't normally vote for what is good for society; they vote for self-interest. Why would anyone want to pay for someone else's medical bills? It was difficult enough paying for one's own. But what made it worse was that it was sales tax! That's un-Oregonian! It was part of every Oregonian's genetic makeup to be opposed to any sales tax! The only thing worse would be to try to repeal Oregon's Bottle Bill.

Corkie and Lorenzo had walked some precincts the prior two weekends. Chispa loved exploring new neighborhoods and making new friends. But, the Becerras found out that there wasn't much support for the ballot measure. The opponents had painted Measure A as free medical care for illegals.

***

Holly was still in her Medford office trying to finish up her work so that she could rush home to watch the election results. She took a quick break and called Corkie in Twin Oaks. "Hey, how is the Measure A campaign going?"

"We're getting our asses kicked!" Corkie lamented. "The other side is better organized and better funded. We're like amateurs."

They talked about trivial stuff before Holly asked Corkie about the chances of doing some fundraisers for Gloria's expenses. She knew that Corkie was a decent person and would want to help. Corkie gave Holly an update on Gloria's living situation and the bureaucratic bullshit of trying to locate her daughter.

Holly had been working frantically for weeks trying to get additional legal assistance for Gloria Ocaso. Gloria was out on bail, but the deportation order hung over her head. Soon her job as a cafeteria worker at the local middle school would be over for the summer recess. She would have no job. She would have no money. There still was no word as to the location of Yesenia. Misinformation by the federal government was rampant. There were several national organizations trying to locate these victimized children. A few members of the U.S. Congress tried to visit some of the detention centers, but were met with bureaucratic resistance. The U.S. president said that it wasn't his problem.

On the other hand, a federal judge had been gracious enough to allow Holly to re-file an application for asylum in California. The most likely forum looked like Sacramento. She contacted Mason Grossman of the Northern California ACLU. She had met him once before at a legal conference in San Francisco. Grossman was willing to do the paperwork, but insisted that Holly would have to make the court appearance. This was going to cost money. Manny had said no to out-of-state travel.

"We could do a pot luck at the community center and ask some of the Latinos to contribute," Corkie was now brainstorming with Holly. "But judging by the lack of attendance at the Cinco de Mayo festivities in the city, the chances are slim for raising a lot of money."

Holly knew that Corkie was probably right. The two talked some more and came to the conclusion that the Latinos in Twin Oaks had gone underground. Nobody wanted to be identified as Hispanic. They didn't want any harassment from the mayor and the locals. They had to reside there and make a living.

"Well, the good news is that Gloria is at least allowed to remain here temporarily," Holly tried to put a positive spin on their conversation.

"Hey, Holly, how much are you up on this Proposition 105?" Corkie posed the question. "The mayor has been supporting it. It's part of his re-election platform."

"What I know is that it would repeal the Oregon Sanctuary Law," remarked Holly. "That would be really bad news, especially for people of color. I'll find out more about it and let you know."

"So that's his play. I think the mayor has the Republicans and fundamentalist Christians on his side on that issue. He's making it sound like a law and order initiative."

"Crap! All we need now is for the Fascist feds to take over our cities," Holly emoted. "How much Kool-Aid can they force us to drink?"

They talked about the possibility of Lorenzo and Corkie spending a long weekend at Holly's place in Jacksonville during the summer. A little wine tasting and some Ashland theater performances would be a well-deserved vacation. Tasting some different ethnic cuisines would be good also.

"Hey, Holly, I have a dumb question," Corkie hesitated in asking. "You said Gloria's request for asylum was denied because she lived on the California side of Twin Oaks. Yes?"

"Yeah. The judge threw it out on jurisdictional grounds."

"I'm thinking that when Gloria has no job and no money, she'll probably have to move."

"Okay. I'm listening."

"What if she moved to the Oregon side of town?"

Holly's wheels were spinning on the other end of the phone. "We could then refile an amended application for asylum here! We wouldn't need to go to California!"

"I'll get right on it," Corkie smiled.

"That would save so much time and money. Manny is going to be so happy!" Holly was exuberant. "I see a case of wine in your future, girlfriend."

## Chapter 34 – Caged

***Wednesday, May 30, 2018***

It was the day after the primary election. Measure A was soundly defeated. Corkie was at the La Causa office for a debriefing on the election results.

"We worked hard on Measure A. Thank you for all of your hard work," Corkie was talking to the staff. "But now the real effort begins. We worked hard, but now we have to work smarter. We need to go after the middle-of-the-roaders, the undecided, the real thinkers. We have just over five months to get our message across. No on Proposition 105!"

"No on Proposition 105" was loudly echoed by the staff and supporters.

Afterwards, they talked over other La Causa business.

After the session, Corkie went back into her office and checked her email. There were some recent newspapers articles sent from Holly regarding the horrific living conditions that alien minors had to suffer in ICE detention facilities. Corkie automatically thought of Gloria's missing daughter, Yesenia.

She started reading the BBC and The Guardian articles:

> **Trump migrant separation policy: Children 'in cages' in Texas**
>
> ***Former First Lady Laura Bush has compared it to the internment camps used for Japanese-Americans during World War Two. A Democratic congressman***

***who visited the site said it was "nothing short of a prison". The Texas facility is known as Ursula, though immigrants are reportedly calling it La Perrera - dog kennel in Spanish. . ."***

**Separation at the border: children wait in cages at south Texas**

***Inside an old warehouse in south Texas, hundreds of children wait away from their parents in a series of cages created by metal fencing . . .***

***One cage had 20 children inside. Scattered about are bottles of water, bags of chips and large foil sheets intended to serve as blankets . . .***

***Criticism and protests over the Trump administration's "zero tolerance" policy and resulting separation of families. . .***

***Nearly 2,000 children have been taken from their parents since the attorney general, Jeff Sessions, announced the policy, which directs homeland security officials to refer all cases of illegal entry into the US for prosecution . . .***

***Church groups and human rights advocates have sharply criticized the policy, calling it inhumane . . .***

Tears rolled down Corkie's cheeks. Such savagery. What a friggin' evil president there is in D.C.!

Corkie left her office crying.

***

Meanwhile, Andy Jackson was standing in front of Willie

Masters and Boris Jones in the downtown Cook Bros. Gold Mine office. Andy's half-brother Seth was with them.

"Your men have been doing a great job," Boris congratulated the Jackson brothers. He was glad that primary election was over. "That's what campaigns are all about. Good people committed to the cause." Boris reached out and shook their hands. "Good luck!"

Boris turned to Willie Masters and said, "this is goodbye. Thank you for everything."

"Will you be back to run the mayor's campaign?" Masters didn't understand why Jones was leaving with the general election so soon.

"No, they have me going to Burns, Oregon, to run the Yes on Proposition 105 campaign," Jones said nonchalantly.

"But what about Keough's campaign?" Masters asked with a concerned tone. The general election was less than six months away.

"You guys already have a game plan," Boris said. *I don't know how much more I can take being around these small town dunces,* Boris thought. "Just canvas the Republicans, Independents, and fundamentalists. The numbers are on your side. But make sure that the mayor's platform is the repeal of the state Sanctuary Law."

Boris picked up his briefcase and left the office.

"Well, boys, sad you're leaving also," Willie added, looking at Andy and Seth. After they left, he would have to make peace with Randy Miller and B.B. Barnes. He opened his middle desk drawer and handed Andy a thick envelope. "Just a little token of appreciation for your hard work."

Andy was tempted to open the envelope, but he knew better. He knew it was cash. That's how things always worked, especially if one wanted to hide certain things. He would keep 50% and give the remainder to Seth and his two teammates who had run a clandestine voter repression campaign in town. This group had printed some red postcard-sized flyers that stated that it was illegal for persons to vote in elections if they did not have proper identification. The warnings were both in Spanish and English. They had been drafted by Andy who was fluent in Spanish since he had been raised in a small Mormon community in Mexico.

With Jones out of the picture, Masters was wondering who would run the mayor's campaign. It had to be him. He couldn't trust anyone else.

"Andy, would you be interested in coming back to help with the campaign?" Willie threw out the offer.

"Don't know," Jackson knew that he was in the driver's seat. Masters was not a strategist. He was just a money guy. "What do you have in mind?"

"Oh, I don't know yet," Masters was still thinking. "But it would be a paid position, of course."

"When would we start?"

"I think right around Labor Day," Masters was winging it. He wanted to keep Jackson interested. "Nobody does anything during the summer. Everybody's on vacation."

"We'll see," Jackson was non-committal. "Where does Pastor McConnell fit in all of this?" He knew that the pastor was a competitor for Mayor Keough's attention. Jackson was leery of McConnell's undue influence over the mayor.

"Don't know yet," Masters was also being non-committal. "This is still a work in progress. Let's keep in touch."

***

Manny and Holly had papers spread out all over the conference room table at their Medford office. On the walls were newsprint charts with several legal issues involving the stop, arrest, and incarceration of Margaret Fisher and the Martinez family on May 18.

"Have you read the legal memoranda that Monica drafted?" Manny asked. Monica Rizal was a third year law student from Willamette University in Salem, Oregon. She was doing an American Constitution Society summer internship with them. Monica was a Filipina-American whose family had had immigration problems coming to the United States after World War II. *Promises made, promises broken.*

"Yes," Holly said. "She is awesome!" Monica was staying with Holly and her two roommates for the summer. Free lodging was a great perk for the young student. Holly's roommate, Carlos, was only too willing to give Monica a personal tour of the Red Sage Winery. She had given him a conditional "maybe."

Monica had come aboard two weeks before and was being treated as an equal participant on the legal team. Manny took on the task of trying to find and research all the causes of action for the plaintiffs: Margaret Fisher, and Marta and Samantha Martinez. Illegal arrest? Illegal incarceration? Violation of the Oregon Sanctuary Law? Assault and Battery?

Holly was in charge of the jurisdictional issues on the case. After the Gloria Ocaso fiasco, Holly made it a point to master the criteria for jurisdiction. What causes of action could be brought in federal court? In state court? Was there concurrent jurisdiction? What were the advantages and disadvantages of each? What were the remedies?

The question of where the litigation would take place was a key decision. Medford, Portland, or Twin Oaks? Was it going to be a jury trial, and if so, who would be in the jury pool? Was there a problem with jurisdictional damage amounts? How about restrictions on punitive damages?

Monica was a favorite student of Willamette Law School Professor, Gilberto Blas, who was an expert in Civil Rights law. He had worked as an Assistant U.S. Attorney under Presidents George W. Bush and Obama. Monica's initial research concluded that a federal case was too time consuming and expensive. The case law favored warrantless ICE stops. The feds would mount a formidable defense of ICE. She recommended that their legal strategy should be a double pronged attack. A state civil action for damages and a separate state case for violation of the Oregon Sanctuary law. The advantage of this was that a private attorney could represent Fisher and the Martinez family. That would take some of the burden off the Oregon Legal Project.

"What do you think, Manny?" Holly asked after Monica explained her recommendations.

"I think she is spot on."

## Chapter 35 – R & R

***Ashland***
***Friday, June 1, 2018***

Corkie was driving Lorenzo to Ashland for the weekend. He was exhausted from grading the senior class final exams. The official school year had ended the week before, and the high school graduation took place last night. Lorenzo had been working diligently making sure to get his grades in by the Thirtieth. He was exhausted. The weather was dry and beautiful. They stopped for a snack breakfast just before crossing the mountains. Corkie was depressed about the dire conditions that alien minors, like Yesenia, were suffering. They both needed a well-deserved break. They would leave all negativity back in Twin Oaks. Now for Ashland! Home of the Shakespearean Festival!

Holly had offered to let Corkie and Lorenzo stay at her place, even though it was crowded now that Monica was staying there. Corkie had graciously declined. She wanted at least part of her weekend to be romantic. The good news was that Holly had scored tickets for them for two performances. For sure they would be able to see "Othello" and a new production called "Manahatta." The latter was the one that Corkie really wanted to see. It was supposed to be about a Native American stockbroker from New York City who returns to her forbearers' lands in Oklahoma. It was a story of cultural eradication and the Native American struggle to keep their language and lands. Jonathan, Holly's roommate, was the costume designer for both performances.

It was just past noon when Lorenzo and Corkie pulled into

Juliet's Lair, their Ashland B&B. Lorenzo grabbed a cup of black coffee to get energized, plus two oatmeal cookies from a small table by the receptionist's counter. Their cozy room had an old-fashioned canopy bed with a quilted cover. The furniture looked very antique. The wallpaper was a flowered rose-pattern. The smell of the room was a combination of floral and wood. The pair were now ready for lunch. They walked six blocks to downtown Ashland and found a healthy eatery that had Middle Eastern food. They shared a pita bread appetizer with hummus and baba ganoush, and split a Greek salad and a chicken kabob. This type of food was never available in Twin Oaks, so they were pleased. On their walk back to the B&B, they carefully avoiding an ice cream parlor.

After unpacking, they got back in their car and drove up to Medford. About a twenty-minute ride. At just before three o'clock they arrived at Holly and Manny's office in an old two story brick building. Holly had arranged for an afternoon meeting at her office to discuss the No on Proposition 105 campaign. They assembled in a shared conference room. Holly introduced her office mate Manny to Lorenzo whom he not yet met. Also present were Ramona Ruiz from La Voz, Ken Weinstein from the National Lawyer Guild, and the new legal intern, Monica Rizal.

Ramona represented the statewide anti-Proposition 105 coalition, Oregon First. She began the briefing with a short background and sketch of the campaign plan. Ramona was about 4'10", young, and skinny, but she was a force to reckoned with. She had six older brothers, some of whom had been in the Marines. They stayed away from her when she was on a mission. She took no prisoners.

"We have the Willamette Valley fairly well covered," Ramona said seriously. "Ashland is looking good, but Medford still is a problem." She pointed to printed maps. She talked for about ten minutes more. Lots of information.

"When will you start the campaign?" Corkie asked innocently.

"It's already started," Ramona said. "We have been doing coalition building. Governor Kate Brown and the Democrats are supporting us. Labor, mainline Christian, Muslim, and Jewish groups, environmentalists, health professionals, and civil rights groups are all on our side."

Lorenzo and Corkie were wide-eyed. "That sounds like everybody."

"Well, that's where you come in," Ramona continued. "The rural areas and Eastern Oregon are tough nuts to crack. So are the Republican and fundamentalist Christian strongholds. Right now the polling is showing this to be a very close race. We need to shave off some points in the conservative areas."

"How can we help?" Corkie naively asked.

"First, you can be the point person for the Oregon First campaign in Twin Oaks," Ramona was not shy about asking.

"But I work for a local government agency," Corkie was trying to back away. "I can't be involved in a political campaign."

The conversation lasted another half hour. Ken was there as a legal resource to the campaign to help guard against voter repression and intimidation, and other Republican dirty tricks. He cited that since Oregon was a vote-by-mail state, there had been a few incidents where the ballots of entire precincts went missing.

It was just after five when the meeting adjourned. Corkie and Lorenzo had tons of literature and a list of contacts for the No on Proposition 105 campaign. Holly, Manny, Monica, Lorenzo, and Corkie walked over to a Happy Hour at Vito's Pizzeria for a couple pitchers of Caldera Brewery lager beer. Some fried calamari and pizzas rounded out the fare. When they finished eating and drinking, Manny excused himself.

"Very impressive," Holly stated. "That Ramona is a tough cookie."

"I just don't know how much time we can devote to the campaign," Corkie was saying. "I've never done anything like this before. So, I don't know what to expect in terms of a time commitment."

"Twice as much as you think," Holly was trying to be honest. They debriefed for a few more minutes. Then Holly reached into her leather bag and pulled out two ticket envelopes and handed them to Corkie.

"Thank you," Corkie said.

"You need to thank Jonathan for both performances. He did the costume design for both and scored the free tickets," Holly said. "The bad news is that we couldn't get you tickets to 'Oklahoma.' Completely sold out."

"That's okay," Corkie said softly. "We appreciate everything that you did for us."

"But we're going to make it up to you," Holly had a devilish grin on her face. "Since you don't have a performance on Sunday, you are coming over to our place for a homemade Filipino dinner!" Holly turned her head toward Monica. Holly's other roommate, Carlos, had taken an interest in Monica. They were like two high school kids. Carlos had taken Monica wine tasting the prior Saturday. They fell into a conversation about wine pairings with Mexican food, Asian food, and Filipino food. They decided to have a contest with Holly and Jonathan being the judges. On Sunday Carlos had made tri-tip with camote. He poured a local pinot noir with it. It was tasty. The coconut cajeta and chocolate brownies were to die for.

This Sunday, Monica was prepared to cook up some lumpias, pork adobo, shrimp pancit, and ube putos. She asked Holly to help her pick the compatible wines. Holly's retort was, "I thought beer went with Filipino food."

Holly knew how young and innocent Monica was. Holly believed that Carlos wouldn't hurt her intentionally, but Monica was very naïve. As Holly looked over at Corkie and Lorenzo, they seemed to be the perfect couple. Loving. Working as a team. *Maybe I'm just a little jealous,* she thought. She was a smart professional woman. Her previous relationships with a carpenter, a doctoral student, and a court reporter had not lasted very long. After the sexual attraction waned, the relationship became a burden. *But still, I would like to find someone.*

## Chapter 36 – Protecting All Oregonians

***Wednesday, June 6, 2018***

Mayor Mitch Keough was picking his teeth after his Reuben sandwich and two Jack Daniels lunch with City Councilmember David Baumgartner. They had a good ol' boy conversation about a building project at the north end of town. Maybe they could even make a few bucks from it. The takeaway was that they both officially endorsed each other in their re-election efforts. The mayor was feeling good. He had to remember to have Masters get him a booth at the July 4$^{th}$ Fair.

When he came back to his office his secretary, Yolanda, informed him, "Marsha needs to see you. And the Animal Shelter guy is here for your two o'clock."

The mayor's eyes rolled up. He just wanted to take a little nap on his office couch. "Can it wait, Yoli? Reschedule the animal guy. Better yet have the guy send me a memo."

"He already has. The memo has been on your desk for weeks."

"Just get rid of him," Keough was exasperated. *What is this guy bothering me? Doesn't he know I'm busy.*

"Marsha says it's really important."

"Okay, okay, call her in." *Why me? Why can't they figure this stuff out on their own?*

Minutes later, City Attorney Marsha Squires walked into his office. But before she could sit down, Keough snapped,

"Marsha, what is so dang important?"

She took her time and sat down. She handed over a twenty-page document to the mayor.

"What's this?!" the mayor replied. *I don't have time to read this crap!!*

"This a civil lawsuit against the City, the police, and you."

"You're kidding!" he let out a weak laugh. "What for?"

"Do you remember the incident a few weeks ago when two women and a kid were pulled over by a police officer and then detained by ICE?"

He shrugged. "So what does it have to do with me?"

"The lawsuit is alleging false arrest, assault and battery . . ."

*So how in the hell am I involved?* he grimaced.

"Just make the damn thing go away, Marsha!" Keough didn't want to be bothered. He waved his right hand dismissively.

"Mayor, first of all we have to file an answer to the complaint," Squires stated affirmatively. "Second, you will in all probability be deposed."

"For what?!" Keough was really getting pissed.

"For any role you may have played in the incident."

"I didn't do anything!" Keough was choking. "I deny everything. Why are they going after me? Just take care of everything."

Squires leaned forward and spoke, "I think you have a bigger problem."

"What's that?"

"You are being sued both in your official capacity and as an individual."

"What in hell does that mean?"

"In simple terms, it means that you need to hire your own attorney as part of your defense," Squires explained. "I can only defend you for official actions and policies."

"Who is suing me?"

"The Oregon Legal Project and a local attorney."

"Those f*cking illegals are the cause of this!"

***

"¡Felicidades!" Holly tipped her glass to Corkie as they sat in the Becerra living waiting for Lorenzo to come home. "When do you start?"

Lorenzo and Corkie had a marriage that was based on mutual respect. On the drive back from Ashland the couple discussed what they were going to do to help defeat Proposition 105. Raising money was not going to be enough. Neighborhood canvassing was also a critical component that had to be managed. There was a lot involved in conducting an effective campaign.

"Let's do our force-field analysis," Lorenzo had suggested. When the married couple had hard problems that had difficult ramifications, they would try to list various scenarios, each with its respective advantages and disadvantages. Some options had both positives and negatives; others had no advantages.

"You, first," Lorenzo put his wife on the spot. "What are the advantages of getting involved?"

"Protecting all Oregonians."

"Protecting local police."

"Protecting aliens."

"Protecting cities and counties."

They sputtered on for five minutes. Sometimes throwing out silly answers. That was part of intrigue and fun of doing this exercise.

"Okay, disadvantages," Corkie smiled. "Your turn."

"Will take a lot of time."

"Lots of work."

"Ruin my summer plans," they laughed. They both knew that Lorenzo was committed to teaching summer school.

"It will definitely hurt our budget," they both nodded.

"It will take my time away from the community center and leave it without adequate resources. Some people may not be served."

They weighed all the options and finally made a decision. Corkie would ask for a leave of absence from her place of employment when they arrived back home.

The next day Corkie met with her immediate supervisor at the community center. They talked it over and decided that it was doable. Somebody would have to step in to do her work. The supervisor suggested that this would be an ideal summer job for someone. It was decided that Friday, June 8, would be her last day at the community center. She would come back to work after the November 6 election. *Rats! That seems like an eternity,* she thought.

Corkie then met with La Causa in Twin Oaks to set up the anti-Proposition 105 campaign. She would begin there the following Monday.

***

"June 11," Corkie told Holly.

They continued to chat until Lorenzo arrived home.

"Did you ladies leave me any wine?" Lorenzo teased.

The two women laughed.

"Oh, one more thing, Holly!" Corkie perked up. "Good news! Gloria Ocaso moved in with Señora Sanchez who just lost her husband. Gloria will be her live-in caretaker . . . and she lives on the Oregon side of the city!"

## Chapter 37 – The Deposition

***Medford***
***Friday, June 22, 2018***

Lonny Johnson sat at the head of the conference table in Holly's office. There was a pot of coffee and pastries in the middle of the table that no one had touched. Lonny was dressed in his formal dark olive green Immigration Service uniform with gold buttons. To his right was Assistant U.S. Attorney Dennis Milbanks, and to his left was the court reporter, Karen Rivers. Holly Acevedo from the Oregon Legal Project sat facing him.

"Thank you, Officer Johnson, for agreeing to speak with us about the May 18, 2018 incident." Holly began.

Johnson nodded as to agree.

"If you have a question or need something clarified, do not hesitate to ask," Holly was trying to appear accommodating. "You are represented by legal counsel. Mr. Milbanks. We can stop at any time."

Again, Johnson nodded.

"Are you ready to begin?"

Johnson nodded for the third time.

"Just for the record, you will need to speak your answers out loud," Holly gently admonished him. "The court reporter will not record head nods. Are you ready to begin?"

"Yes." Milbanks had prepped his client on several occasions to just answer "yes," "no," or "I don't know." As a law enforcement officer, he had been trained to answer "I don't recall" as a default response.

After the matronly, middle-aged court reporter, Karen Rivers, swore him in, Holly began the interview.

"Would you state your name for the record.?

"Lonny Johnson."

"What is your occupation?"

"I am an ICE agent."

Holly went through her preliminary checklist of Johnson's background. She did this at a superficial level. There was no real need to delve into Lonny's early background. If she had, Holly would have found out that his grandparents were traditional Portuguese from the Azores who had migrated to Tracy, California, to set up a dairy. They had a precocious daughter, Lonny's mother, who rejected her ethnic heritage and married an Anglo from Sacramento. The married couple moved to Medford, Oregon, when her husband's mother had to be placed in a rest home. Lonny grew up in Medford and did not do well in school. He couldn't qualify for a job in emergency medical services, firefighting, or police work. After four years in the U.S. Army, he became an ICE agent.

"Are you are here voluntarily?"

"Yes."

***

Two weeks prior, Assistant U.S. Attorney Dennis Milbanks received an unusual phone call. It was from Holly Acevedo.

"Ms. Acevedo, to what do I owe the pleasure of this call?"

he was cautious. Nobody ever called without an agenda.

"Well, the last time we met, you sent me behind the woodshed," they both knew that she was blowing smoke. "I'm getting ready to file a lawsuit regarding that terrible May 18 incident in Twin Oaks. And I was thinking of naming the Immigration Service as a party."

Milbanks was a wise and experienced attorney. He kept silent. He wished all his clients could maintain self-restraint.

"I would probably lose though. You guys have the courts in your pocket," Holly was sugar-coating it. "You would probably have to drive over to Twin Oaks for a couple of court appearances. And maybe a few more times for depositions and the like." She paused and waited.

Milbanks knew that she was playing him. "Okay, I'll bite. What do you want?"

"Well, if we could depose the ICE agent who made the arrest and find out what really happen, we might be willing to forgo suing the feds."

"First of all, no deposition," Milbanks wanted to get this over quickly. The four-hour drive over the mountains to Twin Oaks was brutal. He could be hanging out at home. "And I assume, there are other conditions."

They haggled for a few minutes and agreed to a sworn deposition at Holly's office with Milbank present. If the testimony was truthful and the ICE agent had acted in good faith, Holly promised to leave the feds out of the lawsuit.

They agreed. Milbanks smiled. That young woman is learning fast. On her end of the phone, Holly was thinking, *I dodged a bullet. We have no money to fight the feds.*

***

Since this was not a court of law and the rules of evidence did not really apply, Holly began with open-ended questions. She knew that Milbanks wouldn't object.

"Mr. Johnson, ICE was working in the Twin Oaks area on or about Friday, May 18 of this year?"

"Yes."

"And you were on duty?"

"Yes."

"Can you please describe what happened that day."

"We received a phone call that some illegals were leaving the Armadale church. We had made arrangement beforehand to stop and question these people after they left the church grounds."

Johnson went on to describe his arrival at the hospital. A Twin Oaks police officer had detained two women and a child near the hospital parking lot. He later took over and arrested the trio when the driver and the two passengers couldn't prove they were U.S. citizens. He transported all three to the city jail and put an ICE detainer on them.

Holly peppered him with clarifying questions.

"Did you see the police officer pursue the child?"

"Yes."

"Did you see the police officer tackle the child?"

"Yes." Johnson's face got redder and redder.

"Did you personally render medical assistance to the injured child?"

"No."

"Who was the police officer who initially stopped Mrs. Fisher and the Martinez family?"

"Officer B.B. Barnes."

"Was it he who called you about the people leaving the Armadale church?"

"No, it was Randy Miller."

Holly was surprised to hear the mayor's flunky's name. She hadn't seen that coming.

## Chapter 38 – Holy Frijole

***Monday, June 25, 2018***

La Causa Community Action complex consisted of three stand-alone, white wooden buildings located on the outskirts of town. The location had previously been a religious retreat center. The Si Se Puede Learning Center occupied one building and offered a few classes ranging from English as a Second Language to Zumba. Adelante Por Los Niños was situated in the second building and ran a day care center for 3-9 year-olds. The third building that housed the main La Causa office was a bilingual social services referral agency. Oregon First was subletting a portion of the space as regional campaign headquarters. The only problem with trying to run a campaign at this location was the fact that Señora Gracia Nava made a pot of beans (with bacon, onions, and cumin) every day for the children. This maddening aroma coupled with that of fresh handmade corn tortillas drove everyone crazy. The adults were always scavenging for any sobras (leftovers).

Corkie was on a steep learning curve. *Running a citywide campaign is crazy! Not enough time or resources! Glad I have Lorenzo,* Corkie sighed. She watched as three young boys brought in boxes of campaign materials and stacked them against the wall. One dark-skinned Latino kid wore a white Twin Oaks High School tee shirt. The tall blonde kid had a black Stars Wars shirt, and the short curly haired one just wore a faded brown shirt. These were her strongest volunteers.

The chairs in the room were arranged in a circle. Corkie was having her first real coordinated campaign meeting. She was on her second three-ring binder, writing down names and taking notes, since starting the campaign. She felt bad about using so much paper. *By the end of the campaign, I will have demolished a forest! Maybe I should use my own laptop. Can't use La Causa's. This is costing me a small fortune!*

Ramona Ruiz from the state campaign organization was there to introduce Corkie as the new local campaign coordinator and to explain the statewide objectives and goals. When most people arrived and were seated, the self-introductions began. Andrea Fuentes also welcomed everyone to La Causa; she was its executive director. Also, participating in the Oregon First meeting were:

Rolando Fernandez, pres., Twin Oaks HS MECHA
Reynalda Pico, volunteer coordinator
Armando "Mando" Nuñez, lawn sign coordinator
Patricio Ortiz, event coordinator
Ysaac "Ike" Buenaventura, telephone/email coordinator
Jennifer Hill, NCAAP, coalition coordinator
Deke Silverstone, fundraiser coordinator

For the next hour they discussed the canvassing strategy for the No on Proposition 105 campaign. Person-to-person contact was important because voting was by mail ballot.

"We need to talk to everyone," said one of the young participants.

"But we have limited resources," said an older one. "The Republicans are going to vote Yes. Why waste time and effort on them?"

"Is it worth the extra effort to try reaching out to Republicans or Far Right Christians?" Jonathan posed.

"I think ideally, that's a great goal," Reynalda said in a

tough, but tactful tone. "But we really need to be smart in this campaign. We need to prioritize."

Finally, the group decided to focus on door-to-door canvassing of Democrats and Independents. For the Republicans, they simply would drop off materials. If they completed the first cycle, they would repeat the process over again.

They took a fifteen-minute break. By good fortune, Señora Nava had brought some freshly made churros that disappeared in about nine nanoseconds.

The next order of business was a status report on the Oregon First rally at the city park, scheduled for the Wednesday, July 4$^{th}$. This would be the official kickoff of the local anti-Proposition 105 campaign. Ramona explained that they had invited two very powerful and committed Oregon legislators to be keynote speakers at the event, Diego Hernandez and Teresa Alonso Leon.

"Do we need a permit?" someone shouted out.

"Fortunately not."

"How about bathrooms?" there was a slight snickering.

"There are public bathrooms throughout the park. They are open during the day."

"How about security?"

"The police will be doing a normal crowd control patrol. Shouldn't be a problem."

It was past noon when the staff meeting ended. Corkie was hungry, but she still needed to put up the newsprint on the walls of her little office. Schedules, timelines, responsibilities. contact information, and things to do.

*What did I get myself into?* Corkie's head was spinning.

***

At same time, former Twin Oaks police officer B.B. Barnes was paying a visit to Mayor Keough. The mayor reluctantly invited him into his office.

"B.B., long time, no see," Keough gave him a sh*t eating grin.

"Well, mayor, I'll get right to the point. I need an attorney" Barnes was desperate. He was a named party in the Oregon Legal Project litigation.

"Those bleeding heart liberals and Communists have stuck it to us, B.B." Keough was oiling his tongue. "You and I are in the same boat."

"What duh you mean?"

"You and I are being sued not only as official city employees, but also as poor individual slobs," Keough said. "What's more, the city attorney says that she only has to represent the City. We have to get our own attorneys. The City will not pay for our legal representation as individuals. That's what I've been told."

"That's f*cked up," Barnes was on the verge of tears. He had no money. After B.B. had been terminated, Masters had given him a graveyard shift security guard job at Cook Bros. *What was he going to do?*

## Chapter 39 – The Kickoff

### *Wednesday, July 4, 2018*

Corkie was up by six o'clock. It was the Fourth of the July! She had to help set up the Oregon First's booth at the park. She had volunteers signed up, but most were kids. Not exactly reliable. Fortunately, she always had her best helper, Lorenzo. At the moment, he was making coffee for her. She wanted to wear blue jeans, but wanted to create a good impression at the No on Proposition 105 stall. Corkie found some navy slacks that seemed a little dressy, but what the heck. Her compromise was a casual white top with a U.S. flag design with gold glittered stars. She wore her white swooshed Nikes.

Lorenzo drove them to the park in his Dodge pickup and started unloading the boxes. There were small American flags fluttering all over the park. For the campaign, someone else was in charge of signs and posters. Lorenzo didn't mind doing the grunt work because in the end he would be rewarded. For most of the year he and Corkie ate very healthily, but today was special. They took reprieves from the regimented diets. Hot dogs, ribs, and corn on the cob were on today's menu. Strawberries and ice cream for dessert.

The staff and volunteers started to arrive. By ten o'clock everything was set up and running smoothly. The early risers came by and asked a few questions. A few took "Keep Oregon Values, No on 105" buttons, and others signed the ad hoc petition against the ballot measure. At noon a new shift of volunteers exchanged places. A handful of visitors signed up to be volunteers.

Meanwhile, Mayor Keough had his re-election campaign booth on the other side of the park, next to the other two city council candidates, David Baumgartner and Milt Warden. The latter two had dozens of little red, white, and blue streamers covering their stalls.

The mayor was smiling, shaking hands and kissing babies.

"Mayor, my street has a lot of potholes," said one old grizzled gentleman. "What are you going to do about it?"

"Like I keep saying, we have too many illegals here," Keough was waving his finger. "They tear up our roads. Gotta get rid of them."

The mayor was getting hungry and asked one of the volunteers to fetch him a couple of hot dogs. And then added a lemonade. The pimply-faced youngster who wore a tee shirt depicting a mallard duck came back with the food.

"Mr. Mayor, aren't you one of main guys for that Prop. 105?"

"Yes I am, young man," the mayor said giving him a big smile in appreciation of the compliment.

"Well, sir, there is a 'No on 105' booth on the other side of the park," the youngster swallowed.

Keough took off without taking a bite of his food. He waddled down several rows of stalls until he saw it. There were people congregated in front of Corkie and her people. *What the f*ck! How did this happen? Why wasn't I told.* He wanted to get a better look, but did not want to get caught. He decided to walk back. Then he pulled out his cell phone and tried to call Masters. There was no answer. *I could call Randy, but what good would that do? And B.B. is definitely out of the picture.*

After a half hour of stewing, the mayor decided to call McConnell. “Hello, Pastor,” Keough spoke deferentially. “It seems we have a problem.”

The two discussed the matter. “There is very little I can do, Mitch,” the pastor was wondering why the mayor was bothering him on the Fourth of July. “I am here with my family. Our son came in from Nashville with the grandkids. We’re all going to watch the fireworks tonight. What about your boy Randy?”

“He’s busy,” the mayor lied. “Do you still have the phone number of those Utah guys . . .  Andy and his brother?’

“Give me a second,” the pastor would do anything to end this conversation. He went to his office and looked up the number on his old Rolodex. He was not computer savvy. “Do you have a pen. Here it is . . .”

Back at the Oregon First booth, the mood was relatively friendly, and even supportive. The high school student volunteers were waving some No on Proposition 105 posters. They had wanted to chant, but Corkie cut that off. She wanted everything to be peaceful. She didn’t want to overtly antagonize anyone.

Lorenzo was in hog heaven. He had two hot dogs and was contemplating a third. He and Corkie were planning to see the fireworks that night, but he knew that Corkie would be exhausted. Besides, Chispa had been left alone all day and needed some attention. The fireworks really frightened the poor thing. Lorenzo walked around and saw the craftwork. Pens and bowls made from Oregon myrtle wood, necklaces and earrings made from agates, and dozens of medicinal herbal and hemp products.

The No on Prop. 105 students were now marching in a

straight line throughout the park. They were pumping their signs up and down. Most people just watched them go by. But then the group passed Keough's stall. The mayor saw the youngsters. Half of them had dark skin. *Probably all illegals.* He was furious.

Keough saw two young boys at Warden's booth. He walked over. Milt was talking to some constituents. The mayor approached the two boys.

"Hey, guys, it's kinda hot today," Keough gave a fake smile.

The two boys nodded politely.

"How would you two like to make a few easy bucks?" he threw out the bait.

The boys looked at each other. *What boy wouldn't?*

"What do we gotta do?"

"Not much."

Fifteen minutes later the No on Prop. 105 parade was back at their booth. The kids were hungry and thirsty. Corkie had promised them food. There were platters of potato salad, macaroni salad, and barbequed chicken waiting for them. But before they could start to eat, they began to be heckled by a few outsiders.

"Go home!" someone shouted.

"We don't want illegals here!" another shouted.

A few more people joined in the protesting.

Two of Corkie's volunteers wanted to confront the hecklers, but Corkie had schooled them in non-violence tactics.

The chants were getting louder.

Lorenzo was finishing up his ice cream, when he heard the commotion coming from Corkie's booth. He knew that something was wrong and hurried to the Oregon First area. He saw what was going on and then he saw the two boys.

"Hey, I know you two," he pointed at them. "You go to my high school."

A moment later the commotion stopped abruptly.

***

"Thanks for calling, Mr. Mayor," Andy Jackson, the head of the Utah American Freedom militia responded. After a minute, he hung up and shouted out, "We got a call from Twin Oaks. They want us back!"

"When?" asked his half-brother.

"Now!" Andy smiled. "And do you know what the best part is?"

"No."

"We're gonna get paid! Whoa!" Andy was excited. "Let's get packed up . . . and don't forget the bang bangs."

## Chapter 40 – Fireworks

### *Friday, July 6, 2018*

The law office of Thaddeus Schiffman was dated, and reeked of old cigarette smoke. This seasoned legal veteran of the community was a defender of the indigent and the disadvantaged. He was short in stature with yellowed teeth, a scraggly beard, and a short deformed right arm due to Amelia disease, at birth. Holly had solicited him to be to be part of the Oregon Legal Project's legal team against the Twin Oaks principal defendants, regarding the May 18, 2018 arrest and incarceration incident. Holly liked his familiarity with the local bar and court and his folksy style. He spoke slowly and seemed to be unfocused, but he was smart as a fox.

"Let's strike while the iron is hot!" Thaddeus told Holly after her successful ploy to get ICE agent Johnson's sworn deposition. Schiffman contacted the City Attorney, Marsha Squires, and made a similar offer to drop the Twin Oaks Police Department from the lawsuit if Chief Marty Chiloquin testified. Holly's legal strategy was to try to eliminate as many City defendants as possible.

Holly, Schiffman, Chiloquin, and a court reporter were gathered together in a common makeshift kitchen that Thaddeus shared with two other attorneys. Barnes had been given notice of Chiloquin's deposition, but he did not appear. The group sat on yellow vinyl dining room chairs that looked like they were left over from the 50's.

The ancient court recorder Phyliss Weir swore in the police chief. Thaddeus began the interview.

"Please state your name for the record."

The first five minutes were spent on Chiloquin's personal information, background, and training. Next the interrogation transitioned to the organizational structure of the police department.

"Can you speak up a little bit, Marty," Thaddeus requested. He was hard of hearing and was supposed to wear hearing aids, but often didn't.

Chiloquin nodded yes.

The questioning finally narrowed down to focus on former Twin Oaks police officer B.B. Barnes. Marty was questioned about Barnes' personnel file.

"What led to the termination of officer Barnes?" Thaddeus probed.

"Well, there were several incidents in which he showed bad judgement and inappropriate conduct," Chiloquin proceeded to describe the private reprimand, the three-day suspension, and finally, the termination.

"And what, to your knowledge, happened on May 18, 2018," Thaddeus asked. The police chief described what he had learned about the incident second hand.

"Was Officer Barnes within his legal rights and duties in stopping the Fisher vehicle?" Schiffman asked.

"Yes, normally failing to completely stop at a stop sign is reason to pull a driver over."

"Was that the case here?"

"No."

"Can you elaborate, please," Thaddeus continued.

"Officer Barnes colluded with ICE to stop the vehicle."

"And what was wrong with that?"

"It is against department policy. It was against a specific directive that I issued to Officer Barnes. And it is against state law."

"And as a result of his behavior, Officer Barnes was terminated for the May 18, 2018 incident?"

"Yes, we had been following progressive discipline procedures."

"In terms of his behavior, was Officer Barnes acting outside of his legal authority and solely as an individual?"

"Definitely."

***

Mayor Keough had been in a bad mood since the July 4 park festival. *Those friggin' illegals hijacked the Fourth of July 4th event!* On Friday morning he drove to Masters' office. He was irate that the No on 105 booth had gotten bigger crowds than his own campaign rally. Heads needed to roll. He wouldn't be embarrassed by those illegal alien lovers!

"Where in the hell have you been?"

Masters sputtered out an explanation about family commitments.

"How come I didn't know about the that illegal alien campaign booth at the park?"

"Well, we're just starting your re-election effort," *I don't like this guy! He's such a whiner!* Masters thought.

Keough kept venting. Masters said he was still forming Keough's re-election team.

"Keep Barnes away!" the mayor warned. "He's bad luck." Masters did not mention that he had hired Barnes at the Cook Bros. Gold Mine as a security guard or that he was helping with Barnes legal fees.

"How about Randy Miller?" Masters asked.

"Haven't seen him in a while," Keough responded. "Don't worry though, I have the Utah boys coming in."

"When?!" *Holy crap! More trouble!* Masters shook his head.

"Soon."

***

There was a lot of buzzing in the city council chambers. The mayor had called an emergency session for a special resolution to promulgate a new city ordinance. Against the advice of the city manager and the city attorney, Keough wanted to prohibit parades, rallies, and protests on city properties.

"Such an ordinance would go against Freedom of Speech and Freedom of Assembly," Marsha Squires warned.

"We can't just let illegals take over our city!"

Because of the late notice, only one member of the press was present.

The mayor called the special meeting to order, and shortly thereafter proposed the new city ordinance.

There was discussion and questions.

"When would this become effective?" Councilmember Foster Grey asked.

"Right now, of course," the mayor responded.

There was more debate. Finally, the city clerk called for the vote to adopt the new regulation.

Keough and his two supporters on the council, Baumgartner and Warden, voted aye. Councilmembers Williams and Grey vote no.

Kirby had not voted yet. While he supported the regulation in concept, why should he support Keough? If Keough didn't get re-elected, he had a shot at becoming mayor himself.

"Mr. Kirby?"

"No!"

"The vote is 3-3," voiced the city clerk. "Motion fails."

## Chapter 41 – Vandalism

***Sunday, July 15, 2018***

"Great job, mi amor!" Lorenzo told his wife as they drove home. He was grateful that the weekend canvassing was going smoothly.

Corkie set the passenger seat back and closed her eyes. "Another day gone. Whose bright idea was it to get involved in this campaign?" They both laughed.

They arrived home and were happily greeted by Chispa. Lorenzo was hungry, but Corkie was not. She chose to take a short nap. Lorenzo made himself a quick grilled Tillamook cheese sandwich and then took Chispa for a walk. Because it was so hot out, the pair cut it short. Chispa ran into the kitchen and lapped up a gallon of water.

Corkie woke up from her siesta and took a shower. Lorenzo was watching professional baseball on TV, when she entered the living room.

"Do you want to go out for dinner?" he asked. He knew that she was probably starving because she hadn't had lunch.

She thought about it for a moment. "No, how about I make a kale salad with some of the leftover chicken?"

"Sure," Lorenzo was easy. "Sounds good to me."

"I think we need some intimacy time tonight," she continued. "Maybe you could rub my back and shoulders."

Lorenzo nodded in agreement.

"But first we need to drink one of Holly's bottles of wine."

***

Lorenzo had his right arm over Corkie as they slept. Suddenly he jumped up when the mockingbird ring tone went off. At first, he thought it was the clock radio that displayed neon-type blue numbers, 11:45. But it was Corkie's cell phone. She also woke up.

"Hello," she said groggily. She listened and started to get out of bed. She was looking for her clothes as she held the phone. Lorenzo watched her.

Fifteen minutes later they were driving over to the La Causa offices. At the site they were met by Andrea Montez of La Causa, the person who had called Corkie. She was crying. There was a fire truck on the scene. Chiloquin approached them. He looked tired.

"What happened, Marty?" asked Lorenzo.

"It looks like someone vandalized the center," the police chief said. "Maybe two or three people."

"Were they kids?" Lorenzo asked. *Please, God, don't let it be any of my students. I have enough problems with them as it is.*

"No," Marty said slowly. "This was planned out. It was intended to shut this place down. They systematically poured automobile oil on the playground equipment. Easy to buy. Not dangerous. Just impossible to clean up."

"Well, that would have been easy for kids to do."

"Lorenzo, come with me," the police chief gestured. They left Corkie and Andrea trying to console each other. *What would they do for day care? How about the staff? They had no money to fix up the place.*

The two men walked over to the back of the learning center. Painted on the wall in big black letters were the words:

"Go Home! We don't want illegals here!"

"Still could have been kids, Marty," Lorenzo argued.

Then Marty motioned and pointed to the ground. There were two sets of boot prints, size 14 or larger.

***

Barnes was in the middle of his graveyard shift, making his rounds as a security guard at Cook Bros. Gold Mine. He noticed two black Humvees parked in front of the mineworkers temporary lodging building. They had out-of-state license plates.

He took out his cell phone and texted Randy Miller:

"It looks like someone brought the Utah boys back."

***

The staff of La Causa, Lorenzo and Corkie, and Oregon First volunteers spent the next few days cleaning up after the July 15th vandalism. Boxes of baking soda and quarts of acetone and solvents were used under the supervision a lead firefighter. The volunteers wore gloves, masks, and eye protection. Sandra Starmont had offered the Armadale parish facilities to La Causa during the interim, and it was graciously accepted.

The good news was that La Causa had insurance for the property damage. The bad news was that there was a $500 deductible which La Causa did not have. Lorenzo put on his teacher negotiating hat and made a deal with the insurance company. The volunteer labor would be the in-kind equivalent for meeting the deductible. La Causa could not claim the labor costs, but could expense all the materials. Additionally, Lorenzo, with the help of the school principal, negotiated bus transportation between the La Causa site and the Armadale Methodist Church. Since school was out, the private bus company that serviced the school district would make a little extra income.

The pastor's wife hosted a small coffee get-together for Corkie, Andrea Montez from La Causa, and Holly. She had made a deadly cinnamon coffee cake that was instantaneously devoured with cups of coffee and tea. The ladies needed the break and this was a golden opportunity to get to know each other better. But there was an underlying agenda.

As of today, the Armadale parish conference rooms were being used by Corkie's and Andrea's groups thanks to Reverend Starmont's generosity for the temporary relocation. They discussed the logistics and other issues of having La Causa staff and children on the church property. There was also one empty lodge that could be used for daycare. Corkie knew that it was difficult to project how long the church property would be needed by the displaced groups. La Causa projected that the transformation could maybe take at least two months to accomplish.  The fire department and the city inspector had to sign off on the clean-up before reconstruction and repairs could begin.

Corkie brought up questions about how the Armadale United Methodist Church could be helpful to the Oregon First campaign to defeat Proposition 105 without running afoul of any religious or political pushback. Corkie knew that Reverend Starmont and Sandra were aligned with their efforts, but she wondered if all the parishioners were of like mind. Sandra said she would email her a list of potential volunteers who were sympathetic to the cause.

More deliciously-smelling coffee and tea were served. The coffee cake was gone.

Finally, Corkie wanted to address the issue of vandalism. She had heard that several Mexican bars and restaurants had been spray painted with racist graffiti in the last few nights. Sandra reported that the tires of some of her parishioners had been punctured. Andrea mentioned that the same thing had happened at the Catholic Church. In most cases, the vandalism had been reported to the police. There were no witnesses.

## Chapter 42 – B.B.'s Deposition

***Wednesday, July 18, 2018***

The heat wave continued. The distorted air floated up from the hot streets. B.B. Barnes walked up the courthouse stairs with his attorney, Edward Church. Barnes carried a sports coat over his shoulder. He wore a white shirt with a frayed collar, but no tie. Mr. Church was on retainer with the Cook Brothers Gold Mine. From time to time, Church assisted Masters by providing legal representation for his employees. Normally, it was for driving under the influence (DUI) or for a domestic relations dispute. But today was different. B.B. Barnes was being deposed as a party for his alleged role in the May 18 incident involving Mrs. Margaret Fisher, and Marta Martinez and her daughter Samantha.

All of the parties to the litigation agreed to hold the deposition at the old courtroom. The room was old and stuffy, but very suitable for a deposition. The plaintiffs' attorney, Thaddeus Schiffman, had scheduled the deposition the previous week. Holly Acevedo sat next to Schiffman as co-counsel. Representing Twin Oaks in its official capacity was City Attorney Marsha Squires. Mayor Keough would not be in attendance, but his private attorney, Jeremiah Saxon, would represent him. Saxon was the retained legal counsel for Pastor McConnell's church and was doing this as a special favor to the pastor.

The deposition would be held in closed session, although all the parties stipulated that the information gathered could be made public. The public and the press loved transparency.

Barnes sat at the far end of the long rectangular wooden table with a microphone in front of him. A video camera was focused on him. The room was brightly lit. His attorney, Edward Church, was seated on his right. Barnes was already sweating. There was no air conditioning. Attorneys Squires and Saxon flanked Schiffman and Acevedo at the other end of the table.

The court reporter, Marjorie Reese, asked Barnes to raise his right hand. He was successfully sworn in. A bailiff guarded the back door. There were no members of the public or press allowed into the room.

"Mr. Barnes, thank you so much for being here today," smiled the old fox, Thaddeus Schiffman. By his grins and demeanor, one would think that B.B. and Thaddeus were buddies. However, everyone knew that Thaddeus really didn't give a rat's rear end about Barnes. He knew that B.B. was a bad guy who had injured his clients and he was going to nail him.

"For the record, I am going to introduce some documents and stipulations that have been previously agreed to by all the parties. You all have copies of them."

Since Schiffman had called for the deposition, he had almost free rein on how to run the session. The time on the antique wall clock read 10:07. If the deposition went past noon, they would take a forty-five-minute lunch recess. But no potty breaks! Schiffman was not about dragging his feet.

"Mr. Barnes, please feel free to consult your legal counsel at any time. We can repeat or clarify any question. Is everything understood?"

"Yes, sir."

"Okay, Mr. Barnes, please give us your name and current

address." Schiffman spent the next few minutes reviewing B.B.'s personal information and history. Then the plaintiff's attorney went into Barnes' employment with the Twin Oaks police department. Several documents were presented to him and he authenticated them e.g., payroll information, etc.

"Would it be fair to say that you received average to good performance evaluations during your tenure?"

"Yes, sir." Barnes had been prepped to answer only with one or two words, if he could. "Yes" and "No" were good responses.

"And these evaluations were made and signed by your immediate supervisor, Police Chief Marty Chiloquin?"

"Yes, sir."

"Directing your attention to March 16, 2018 of this year, did you assist ICE in the apprehension of Gloria Ocaso in your capacity as a police officer?"

"Yes, sir."

"And was this in violation of police department policy?"

"Yes, sir," Barnes hesitated, and then added. "but we work closely with the feds. We're all part of law enforcement."

"And you realize that this was in violation of the Oregon Sanctuary Law?'

"Yes, sir," Barnes took in a deep breath. "Police Chief Chiloquin informed me that it was."

"Did he give you a verbal reprimand?"

Barnes wanted to deny it. "You could call it that."

"Now, moving on to Friday, May 11, 2018, did you assist ICE in their interrogation of Sandra Starmont and Margaret Fisher and two others?"

"Yes, sir."

"And was this in violation of police department policy?"

"I didn't think so at the time."

"But this was in violation of Police Chief Chiloquin's specific instructions."

"I guess so. I was just issuing a traffic citation."

"As a police officer."

"Yes, sir."

"For a broken taillight?"

"Yes, sir."

"And ICE arrived coincidentally at the same time?"

"Yes, sir."

"Was there any kind of coordination between you and ICE on the stop?"

"I don't recall."

"And as result of this incident, Police Chief Chiloquin suspended you for three days as evidenced by the personnel action in your file?"

"Yes, sir."

"Did you contest this?"

"No, sir."

"Let's now go to the incident in question. The detention of Margaret Fisher and the Martinez family on May 18. Why did you pull over the Fisher vehicle?"

"She did not come to a full stop at the intersection."

"And again, coincidentally, an ICE van pulled up at the same time."

"I think so."

"During this stop, a passenger left the car and you pursued her?" Schiffman leaned in on the witness.

"Yes, sir."

"You tackled Samantha Martinez and she was injured. Is that correct?"

"Yes, sir."

"Did you call for medical assistance?"

"No, sir," Barnes regretted hurting the girl. "She was under ICE detention."

"ICE detention that you were cooperating with, is that correct?"

"Yes, sir."

"Again, this was in direct violation of the police chief's directive?"

"Yes, sir."

"And you knew this was in violation of the Oregon

Sanctuary Law?"

"Objection," Church blurted out. "He pleads the Fifth Amendment."

"Duly noted counsel," Schiffman didn't miss a beat. "This is a civil lawsuit. We will stipulate that this deposition can't be used for criminal prosecution. Now, Mr. Barnes, please answer the question." Schiffman knew that City Attorney Squires would not prosecute Barnes. It would be too messy.

Barnes looked at his lawyer. Church gave him a nod.

"Yes, sir."

"At what point on May 18 did you contact ICE regarding the Fisher vehicle?"

"I didn't."

"If you didn't, was there somebody else who did?" Schiffman was surprised at the answer. Ah, the value of discovery.

"Yes," Barnes blurted out. "Randy Miller."

"Do you know why Mr. Miller was working with ICE?"

"He was just trying to help with the campaign."

There was an awkward silence in the room.

## Chapter 43 – Show Me the Money

### *Thursday, July 19, 2018*

Police Chief Chiloquin was on his third cup of stale coffee in the office of City Attorney Squires that Thursday morning. Marsha wanted to debrief him on the B.B. Barnes' deposition the day before.

"Well, Marty," she was looking at her notes. "I think we did as well as could be expected."

The police chief nodded. His greatest skills were his abilities to listen and observe.

"I am relatively certain that the City and the police department are off the hook. Barnes admitted that he acted in violation of police department rules and against your direct orders. He was not acting within the scope of his official duties," Marsha paused. "I think his attorney, Church, has his hands full in representing his client. B.B. was a rogue agent. Too close to the feds."

Marty nodded again.

"But the elephant in the room is Keough," she frowned. "How is he involved? Was the 'campaign' that Barnes mentioned Keough's re-election or the pro-105 ballot measure? Barnes was a little squishy on that. He said that he really didn't know. I think there was a little CYA going on there."

"But, Marsha, correct me if I'm wrong," Marty's eyes were squinting deep in concentration. "What difference does it make? Using city resources for political purposes is against the law. We know that Thaddeus will probably depose Randy Miller now." The police chief had received reports of incidents of vandalism in the city. He believed that part of it was probably racially motivated, and suspected that there was a connection to both the mayor's and the Yes on 105 campaigns. He needed to make a phone call after this meeting.

"The question is what do with Randy? Bring him for questioning?" Marsha interrupted Marty's train of thought. "I'm not sure we have any grounds. He probably did nothing wrong."

"But he could point us in the right direction."

***

It was late in the afternoon. Mayor Keough wanted a cold drink. With alcohol. But he had an important task to perform. He went over to Masters' downtown office. Masters had agreed to meet with him in the late afternoon.

Fortunately, the place was air conditioned. The mayor gave a brief knock and walked into Willie's office. Masters was on the phone. He motioned with his right hand for the mayor to take a seat.

A moment later, greetings were exchanged. "How can I help you today, Mr. Mayor?" Masters was getting tired of Keough only coming over when he wanted something. He wondered why he had ever agreed to be the re-election campaign manager.

"I need some money," Keough smiled.

Masters tried not to roll his eyes. The honorable was always asking for money.

"Five thousand dollars," the mayor said matter-of-factly.

“For what?!” Masters asked in surprise.

“To pay for the volunteers.”

“You mean those Utah guys?” Willie was already providing the skinheads with lodging at the Cook Brothers Gold Mine. He made Andy and his half-brother daytime security guards there. He had no idea what the other guys did all day.

“Yeah,” Keough said smugly. “I promised that we would pay them.”

“With what money?”

“My campaign fund, of course.”

“First of all, you don’t have that much money in the bank,” Masters always had to backfill the funding shortages. “You need to make some phone calls . . .  drum up donations.”

“I will. I’m going to,” Keough replied. *When hell freezes over.*

“And we need to report this on your re-election finance report that is coming up. How should we report it?” Masters asserted with a slightly irritable tone.

“Under Miscellaneous Expenses.”

“Can’t do.”

“Why not?” the mayor demanded.

“Because the expenditure is for staffing, not miscellaneous,” Masters was trying to bite his tongue. “And I am not going to jail for false reporting.”

The conversation during the next few minutes got very

heated. In the end, Masters agreed to give the volunteers $500 each on the condition that they go back to Utah by the next day. Masters could not afford them to hang around, but Andy and his half-brother Elijah would be allowed to stay on. The two would be on the payroll for the remainder of the campaign.

After he left Masters' office, Keough was ready for his cold drink. Make that a double.

## Chapter 44 – Polling

### *Wednesday August 1, 2018*

The summer was flying by. The Oregon weather was beautiful with cloudless skies and sylvan smells. Tourism was up in Twin Oaks. The local politics had settled down, but Oregon First was still canvassing and phoning seven days a week. The operations at La Causa were back to normal. The vandalism had ceased. Life was good.

Corkie had almost totally abandoned the community center. She rarely saw Holly who was busy getting ready for the Fisher/Martinez trial. However, Corkie always stayed in touch with Gloria. Gloria told her that her caretaking job was going well. But the bad news was that her daughter, Yesenia, had still not been located. Gloria had lost weight and was distraught. There had supposedly been a Yesenia sighting in Texas, but that turned out to be a false lead. Corkie also heard a rumor that there were a couple of strangers who had been asking around for Gloria's whereabouts.

On the political front, Corkie was in touch with Monica Ruiz on a daily basis. Oregon First was preparing for No on Proposition 105 rally that was planned for Labor Day, September 3. The campaign's progress was on target.

"Corkie, I have some good news," Monica had called early that morning. "The statewide polls have Proposition 105 going down 60% to 40%."

"Wow!" there was a big smile on Corkie's face. She was exhausted and this was good news. But she knew that she could not take anything for granted and had to press on.

"In Twin Oaks, you guys are showing 42% No and 58% Yes," Monica added.

That was a deflator for Corkie. Their goal was to reach at least 50 percent against. *Need to keep on plugging.*

Corkie was never home anymore. Lorenzo cooked all the meals, usually for himself. She ate leftovers if she didn't go to bed first. He cleaned house and washed clothes. He had become Susie homemaker. He was teaching only two summer school math classes that left him with a lot of free time. Chispa really liked him being at home.

Reverend Starmont and Sandra were godsends for the local campaign. They procured dozens of volunteers for the weekly telephone bank that was being run out of a local labor union hall. They had upwards of a dozen phone lines. Sandra and her friend, Margaret Fisher, had even driven over to the phone bank a few times.

***

Police Chief Chiloquin was glad that things had calmed down in his city. But his law enforcement gut kept nagging at him. Something was amiss in town, and he didn't know what it was. He had a suspicion that the mayor was involved, but he couldn't figure out how. The city attorney, Marsha Squires, also knew something was wrong, but couldn't share information with the police chief because of attorney-client privilege.

However, Attorney Squires did share with Marty that Thaddeus Schiffman had deposed Randy Miller the week before. Randy denied working for any campaign when he made the call to ICE on May 18 that resulted in the detention of Margaret

Fisher and the Martinez mother and daughter. He said that he was simply doing Barnes a favor. When he was asked why Barnes asked him for the favor, he pleaded ignorance.

Marsha and Marty surmised that either B.B. or Randy was not telling the truth. And both had their money on Miller, who they knew had worked for Mayor Keough.

Marty had called his friend Ray Stone at the FBI for assistance. He wanted an outside agency to investigate. He thought it looked like voter suppression and civil rights violations. Marty had taken training classes at the FBI Academy, and Stone had been an instructor there. They got to be friends. The relatively young Stone had graduated from Georgetown Law School in 2002. Besides having a black belt in karate, Stone was a century (one hundred mile) bicyclist. He had participated in the Crater Lake Century race two years prior and had finished respectfully in the middle of the pack.

"Sorry, buddy," Stone replied. "We don't have the resources to come over there and help you. I really would, if I could. This administration is giving us b.s. assignments. They are not supportive of law enforcement. They have their own political agenda."

Marty understood.

***

Barnes was getting more and more frustrated every day. His night shift job was getting to him. He worked all night doing nothing. He kept seeing the black Humvee driving in and out of the gold mine at all hours of the day and night. They were supposed to be security guys like him, but he only saw Elijah Jackson making the rounds. Andy was never around. B.B. was always too tired to socialize much on his off hours. Occasionally, he got together with Randy, and they bitched about how they had been dumped by the mayor. Keough and Masters were letting the Utah boys run the show.

Tonight Willie Masters was on site. B.B. approached the monster Dodge Ram truck and waited for his boss to get out.

"Hey, B.B. How ya doing?" Masters was dressed in jeans and a cowboy shirt. He was wearing a Stetson cowboy hat.

"Okay, I guess," B.B. didn't know how to begin.

"Something on your mind?" the boss stopped and stared at B.B.

"Yeah, those Jackson boys work the day shift," B.B. began. "And I have to work nights. And one of them is never here! It's not fair!"

"I know how you feel," Masters was fed up with the setup also. He was losing money carrying the mayor's load. "B.B. I can tell you this. After the election, things will be better. I promise you." The boss extended his hand and they shook.

B.B. was surprised. There was no pushback from his boss. Things would get better. He just had to wait a little longer. On the other hand, the Jacksons were getting away with murder.

## Chapter 45 – The Candidates' Forum

### *Wednesday August 15, 2018*

Willie Masters was waiting in his downtown office for the mayor to arrive. The Twin Oaks League of Women Voters was having a candidate and ballot measure forum that evening at the city hall auditorium. The mayoral race and the two open city councilmember positions would start the program. Then the pros and cons of Proposition 105 to repeal the State Sanctuary Law would be debated.

Masters was anxious to go over talking points with Keough. He kept it down to three main topics that the mayor had to emphasize: the crime rate was down, taxes had not been raised, and the city was trying to resolve the illegal alien problem. Willie knew the mayor well and knew that most of this preparation was for naught.

There was a tap on the office door. Mayor Keough walked in confidently. He was ready to rumble. Accompanying him was Andy Jackson. The Utah state militia guy was now a constant companion to the mayor, almost like a body guard. Masters had noticed recently that Andy was directly imposing himself upon the mayor. He now had the mayor's ear.

Keough and Masters shook hands. "Mitch, how are you feeling about the forum tonight?" He did not want to characterizes the town hall as a debate. He just wanted the mayor to recite the talking points and move on. He also did not want the mayor to go on the offensive and attack the opposition.

"Fine! Fine! Just want it to be over," Keough huffed. "What

a waste of time! I'm winning in the polls, ain't I!"

"Yes, you are," Masters scrambled some papers on this desk. "You are in the mid-forty percent range."

"So what's the problem?!"

"The trend line has been flat for the last month," Willie looked at the charts. "And your unfavorables have gone up."

"What do you mean? The folks should love me. I'm trying to get rid of the illegal alien problem here in town."

There was another knock at the door. Pastor McConnell entered. "Sorry, I'm late. Helping out a parishioner." He took a seat.

"No problem, Pastor," Masters segued out of the forum preparation. He knew that Mitch Keough was going to do what he was going to do anyway. The mayor never followed a script. He was the proverbial bull in a china shop. "We were just going to talk more about the campaign plan for the next eleven weeks," Masters continued.

They spent a great amount of time focusing on the three-day Labor Day weekend festival at the park. They had procured a booth and there were enough volunteers. They would have brochures, buttons, and posters. The mayor would be there in person.

"What about tee shirts?" Keough blurted out.

"It's a question of funding, Mitch," Masters was perusing other papers. "Our working capital is low. You need to step up the fundraising. How are you doing on the phone calling? We haven't seen much money come in lately."

"Been busy. We should be able to buy tee shirts on credit," Keough retorted. "If not, Willie, you should be good for it."

"Like I've said in the past, the campaign finance reports are due in two weeks," Willie was nervously trying to make his point. "I can't have my name or Cook Brothers stand out on the reporting."

"Who cares?"

"Well, Mitch, I don't want to go to jail. Or worse."

"Oh, Willie, you're such an old lady," Keough laughed.

"While we're talking money," Pastor McConnell piped up. "I was talking to Andy. We think that this campaign needs a shot in the arm. Something to arouse the electorate. Andy has some ideas. This means bringing back the Utah boys."

"What?" This was the first Masters had heard of this. He knew that these other three were scheming behind his back. "What are you planning?"

"Don't know yet," Jackson said with a devilish smile.

"But will it cost money?" Masters asked.

The other three nodded yes.

"Also, we need a little reward money," Keough grinned at Masters.

"Reward for what?" Masters squinted and shook his head.

"We're running the campaign against the illegals."

"So?"

"We're been revving up people against that woman who was

cut loose by the Commie court. That illegal alien woman! She's going to be our poster child!" Keough laughed.

***

The president of the local Women's Voter League, Katherine Halley, welcomed the community to the candidates' forum. She explained that the candidates would be given three minutes for opening statements, and then there would be a fifteen-minute question and answer session with the three moderators. Responses could not go over ninety-seconds. Then each candidate would have one minute to close. The same rules applied to the pros and cons discussion on Proposition 105. The moderators were Pete Adams of the local newspaper, Sally Huntley from the local Chamber of Commerce, and Marisa Haggerty from the Farm Bureau.

In the audience, Lorenzo sat with Corkie and her Oregon First and La Causa colleagues. Sandra and Dell Starmont sat right behind them. The temperature in the room was stifling. Someone was wearing a sweet, nauseous, floral perfume. The air conditioning seemed to be on low.

"Our first speaker will be the incumbent mayor, Mitch Keough, followed by the challenger, Gordon Saunders," Ms. Halley began. Keough adhered fairly closely to the talking points in his opening remarks. Masters had a shocked look on his face when he listened to the mayor. On the other hand, Saunders was a chronic candidate. He had run for every political office from dog catcher to Congress. He rambled on and on about the good old days of the Truman Administration.

The questioning by the panelists went smoothly as Masters had predicted. Keough was on fire. He was hitting all the high points. Saunders kept saying that he would look into the matters once elected.

But in his closing, Keough railed on and on about the illegal aliens and the danger that they posed to the community. Equally bad, Saunders talked about the threat of socialism in the country.

More people came in, as some people left. Most of the audience was composed of seniors. Corkie was getting nervous. She was going to be the spokesperson for the No on Proposition 105 side of the debate later on. The city council candidates nearly put everyone to sleep. This portion of the program was uneventful.

After a ten-minute break in the program, Corkie made her way to the front. The Yes on Proposition 105 would be represented by Betty Wilson from the Lake County Sheriffs Association. A copy of the ballot measure was projected on both sides of the stage.

Wilson was wearing an aqua blue polyester pants suit that covered a paunch. She began first, "We are a nation of laws. These laws have to be obeyed. Law enforcement and police are all on the same time. Why can't we work together?" She did an excellent job in her three minutes.

Then it was Corkie's turn. Her hands were sweaty. She and Lorenzo has prepped for hours. She was good to go. "In 1987, the Oregon Legislature in a bipartisan effort told cities and law enforcement, that they no longer had to be minions of the federal government. Cities and counties could control their own law enforcement priorities. Crimes against persons. Crimes against property. Cities and counties could control their own civic priorities. Resources. Staffing. Jails. In Oregon we have a tradition of welcoming all people. And we want all people to be treated equally and justly. We need to keep our own Oregon values."

Then the questions came. Pete Adams asked which groups

supported or opposed the measure.

"Let's start with you, Ms. Wilson."

"Law enforcement, the Federation for American Immigration Reform, Oregonians for Immigration Reform, and the Republican Party. All these groups favor the measure."

"Ms. Becerra, same question."

"We have over a hundred groups opposing 105, including most law enforcement agencies (Corkie made a pregnant pause here). Doctors, labor, religious groups. I only have 90 seconds to answer, so I would urge you to pick up a brochure at the Oregon First table to see the complete list," Corkie smiled. Score one for the good guys.

The next question was from Marisa Haggerty from the Farm Bureau. "What would the Bible say about Proposition 105?"

"Well, according to my pastor, Pastor McConnell, the Bible says under Matthew 22:21 that Jesus said 'Render to Caesar the things that are Caesar's; and to God the things that are God's.' The Bible wants us to obey the law of the land."

"Ms. Becerra, your response."

Corkie responded, "I also like Matthew who stated under 22:37-40, that Jesus said 'Thou shalt love the Lord thy God with all thy heart, and with all thy soul, and with all thy mind. This is the first and greatest commandment. And the second is like unto it, thou shalt love thy neighbor as thyself. On these two commandments hang all the law and the prophets.' I believe that the Bible tells us that Love is the ultimate requirement. I also believe that we should adhere to the Oregon Sanctuary Law which is the law of the land."

A few more questions were asked and then Wilson and Becerra were asked to close.

Wilson talked about how illegal aliens were taking over. They got free governmental services. They didn't speak English. She received moderate applause when she finished.

It was then Corkie's turn. She made a strategic, but risky closing. "For my closing, I want to read you a statement about who we are as Oregonians:

> ***Oregon is home to thousands of immigrants and refugees, as well as to the families who've been here for generations because a family member courageously immigrated to the state. Today, immigrants are critical to the state's cultural and economic vitality. We are your neighbors, your friends and your colleagues. Oregon is our home.***
>
> ***Dignity and Respect are Core Oregon Values. We chose Oregon because it is a special place where its people believe in constitutional and human rights. We must protect those rights for everyone who calls Oregon home. All Oregonians should be treated with dignity and respect regardless of where they were born.***
>
> ***Tragically, Oregon's values are being threatened by local and national white supremacy groups that continue to push racist, anti-immigrant and anti-Muslim policies which are tearing apart our families and Oregon communities. We are fighting for our way of life. This is a watershed moment in defining who we are as a state; it's time to stand up for the compassion and values that make Oregon a place we are proud to live in.***

> ***Oregon First is a statewide coalition that defends against anti-immigrant and anti-Muslim policies and ballot measures and works to ensure that all Oregonians, regardless of country of birth, are treated with dignity and respect.***
>
> This quote is from our own Governor Kate Brown."

There was mostly applause with a few boos.

It was almost nine o'clock when the forum ended. Lorenzo and Corkie helped clean up. Corkie was carrying a box of campaign materials down a small landing. She heard someone yell out, "Watch your back!" She felt someone shove her. She fell forward with the box breaking her fall. By the time she got up, there was no one around.

She was still noticeably shaking as Lorenzo drove them home. *Was that an accident?*

## Chapter 46 – Explosions

***Thursday, August 16, 2018***

The room was a sterile green and there were a dozen medical contraptions within. An empty breakfast tray was stationed next to the bed.

"How are you feeling, Lorenzo?" the police chief leaned over toward the patient.

"Put me in, coach," the injured man smiled and then started to choke, his body twitching in pain.

"Just relax," Chiloquin spoke calmly. "Just have to ask you a few questions. You were really out of it last night." He handed Lorenzo a plastic cup filled with water.

"How's my wife?" Lorenzo said in a panic as he was starting to become more alert. He sipped some water through the straw. He had probably been given some potent pain medication the night before when the ambulance brought him to the Emergency Room of the hospital.

"Oh, Corkie's fine. She is one tough lady," the chief said dismissively. "But she is going to have to explain her black eye to folks." He laughed.

"Does she have any injuries?" Lorenzo persisted. "Any broken bones?"

Chiloquin nodded no. "You guys were lucky. You had your seat belts on." The chief knew that half the people never wore theirs, even if they had kids. "But most of all, the airbags deployed properly."

"My truck?"

"Fixable. Your windshield and all the windows are smashed. Do you go to Joaquin's? He'll do you a good job. I think the problem will be getting the airbags replaced. The warehouse is probably on the other side of the world."

Lorenzo's mind raced. He would try to call his insurance agent this morning. He didn't know what was covered. Crap! He might have a deductible. In any event he would need a rental car. *Got to wake up and get it together!*

Chiloquin opened up his notepad and looked at Lorenzo. "Are you able to tell me what happened to you and Corkie last night?"

Lorenzo slowly nodded yes. "We were driving back from the League of Women Voters political forum down at the city hall. We had packed up all the boxes in my pickup and were driving home. It was already dark. I'm sure I had my lights on. The sky was overcast and dark. I think it was sprinkling a little. We came straight home. We had not been drinking. We were hungry. At least, I was. Corkie was probably still wound up from her presentation."

The police chief was aware of the prior night's forum. One of his officers had been assigned as security. He knew that there was a contentious climate anytime Proposition 105 was in the picture.

Suddenly a nurse came in and asked Lorenzo if he needed to go to the bathroom. He had opted out of the catheter. He nodded no and continued his conversation with the chief.

"We turned onto our private road. I'm not sure, but I thought

I heard a snap. Across the windshield. Then another. An explosion went off somewhere on my side of the truck. There was all this smoke and debris. Then I think there was another snap as I tried to brake and turn to the right. Then two more explosions. One on the right side and one to the back. My airbag deployed and it smashed me in the chest. That's why I have two cracked ribs. My ears were ringing. I couldn't get to my phone. It was totally f*cked up."

Chiloquin pressed him a little more, but decided enough was enough.

"Any idea who did this?"

"No," Lorenzo replied. "But Corkie told me someone shoved her at the forum. She didn't know if it was by accident or on purpose, but they said something that sounded like a threat or warning."

"Thanks, Lorenzo, you've been very helpful," the chief closed his notepad. "Anything I can get you?"

"No, thanks, Marty. They're supposed to release me this afternoon," Lorenzo was starting to fade. "I have to deal with the insurance people now."

"Get some rest, my friend," Chiloquin patted Lorenzo carefully.

Corkie was in the hospital lobby wearing sun glasses. She was with Sandra. Chiloquin questioned her and she gave her story. When asked about the shove, she said that she thought someone had yelled, "Watch your back!" She thought it was someone from the pro-105 campaign, but didn't know for sure.

After Chiloquin drove back to the police station, he made a call.

“Hey, Ray, I think things are heating up in town. We need your help.” The police chief had again called his friend at the FBI.

“We’re still busy, Marty,” FBI agent Stone said. “But let me see what I can do. I’ll get back to you.”

***

By noon, half the town was aware of the “bombing” of the Becerras. There were rumblings and conspiracy theories being promulgated. Mayor Keough decided to exploit the situation and called for a special city council meeting that afternoon. Nobody was happy about the mayor’s decision to bring the state militia to fight the “invasion of illegal aliens” in their town. Besides one press person, there were hardly any members of the public present because of the short notice for the special meeting. But there were flyers lying around on empty seats with a U.S. flag logo listing all the “evils” that the illegal aliens were perpetrating, especially mentioning Gloria Ocaso’s name. Keough had told Masters that he had nothing to lose since he was ahead in the polls. His mayoral opponent Gordy Saunders was the village idiot. Pastor McConnell had firmly proclaimed that Keough had to mobilize his political base.

“I want to move Resolution . . .” the mayor started the meeting. It was a similar resolution to his previous attempt, calling for the state militia to come to Twin Oaks and round up all the illegals in town. “These illegals are threatening the town people with vandalism and physical force.”

Normally, there would have been a lot of debate, but City Councilmember Alice Williams called for the vote. And again, the vote was 3-3 resulting in the motion failing.

Before Keough could gavel the close of the meeting,

Councilmember Kirby moved that the City offer a reward of $500 for information regarding the bombing of the Becerras. The motion was seconded by Foster Grey. The mayor tried to protest that the motion was out of order, but Williams again called for the vote, stopping all debate. The motion passed 5-1 with Keough voting no.

***

Police Chief Chiloquin was walking past Susan Sommers, the police station receptionist. She yelled out. "Hey, Marty, what's up? A zillion people are calling in about the Becerra bombing. And emails too. They want to know about the reward money. And something about Gloria Ocaso."

## Chapter 47 – Red

***Monday, August 20, 2018***

The week of August 20 began with a pall over Twin Oaks. What was once a happy, neighborly town seemed to turn into an occupied territory almost overnight. Two black Humvee vehicles had been driving around town with U.S. flags whipping from their backsides. They were occupied by paramilitary types with shaved heads who wore fatigues and dark sunglasses. Each morning one of the vehicles would drive in and park in front of the Yes on Proposition 105 storefront headquarters downtown.

A city police officer, Oscar Perkins, who was on parking enforcement duty asked the men who were pacing in front of the building what was going on. He had noticed the Utah license plates.

"Oh, we're just here to give support to the campaign against the illegal aliens," the paunchy leader of the four skinheads said.

"Are you working on the Proposition 105 campaign?" the officer probed.

"Not really. We're working for the mayor."

The officer's brow furrowed. *Why would the mayor be involved with out-of-staters?* "Are you volunteers?"

"Naw, we get paid," the guy grinned. "But not enough."

Officer Perkins left, and an hour later when he returned to the police station he filled out an incident report on the Humvee. The yellow copy would be sent to the police chief later on. When

Perkins finished, he went to the coffee room and snagged a chocolate-frosted crueller. He said hi to the police cadet, Dana Brando, who was confined to the cubicle in the corner of the workroom.

"How you doing?" Officer Oscar asked him. Dana was a volunteer who had recently graduated from the Police Academy in Salem, Oregon. He was looking for a job, but needed some experience. Marty Chiloquin had liked the guy's résumé and brought him on board.

"Since they offered that reward, the whole town has gone plum crazy," Dana was glad to talk to a real police officer. His only other contact was Susan Sommers who forwarded telephone calls or emails to him that had to do with the vandalism in town or the bombing of the Becerras' car. At the moment he was creating an Excel spreadsheet trying to categorize the various call-ins.

"Really! Like how?" the police officer's curiosity was piqued.

"Well, lots of campaign posters have been spray painted over," Dana responded. "Customers being harassed at Felipe's Mexican Restaurant by skinheads."

"Any description of these guys?"

"Just a bunch of soldier types dressed in camouflage."

A minute later, Oscar went back to his cubicle and revised his incident report. He walked a copy of the IR over to the police chief's office. Twenty minutes later he was back on parking patrol, but not before snagging another donut.

***

Across town, Corkie was holding her daily staff meeting with her key political coordinators. The damaged building had finally been repaired, and La Causa, the child care center, and the No on Proposition 105 headquarters had been able to move back from the Armadale church property.

"Mando, you're up," Corkie was going through her daily checklist. Armando Nuñez was the lawn sign coordinator, among his other duties. "What do you have to report?"

"We have had over a dozen lawn signs spray painted or destroyed. I made a list of the locations and emailed them to the police station," the young Latino idealist said. "Some guy named Dana responded and said they're working on it."

"Can we replace them?"

"Yes, probably today even," he answered. "The good one at the vacant lot on Fifth and Grand was entirely gone. Lots of traffic there."

"Thanks, Mando."

Corkie knew that the local campaign was being successful. They were running at full capacity. The recent events had been setbacks, but these could be overcome. She was still wearing sunglasses and lots of makeup. Lorenzo had gotten his pickup back. He was still fighting with the insurance company over his comprehensive coverage and the $500 deductible. He was resting at home and Chispa was very happy to have a companion.

"Mercedes, you're next," Corkie continued.

They were over half way through the meeting when a young olive-skinned Latina girl with long black hair wearing black jeans and a blue No on Proposition 105 tee shirt entered the room. Her body language showed that she was flustered.

"They're outside!" she cried out.

"Who?" several people yelled out.

"Those soldier guys who are stopping everyone."

Corkie got up and walked to the front door. She looked out. There was a black Humvee parked about 75 feet from La Causa. Several paramilitary skinheads were just standing around. Her first instinct was to confront them, but they weren't on private property. There was nothing she could do. She knew that Lorenzo would be pissed if she didn't call him. He would rush right over, probably with a rifle. That was no good. She decided to call police chief Chiloquin.

Within a half hour a police car pulled up behind the Humvee with its lights blinking. The police officer, Gale Devine, got out of the car and walked toward the five guys. Her partner stayed behind the passenger side door of the police car

"Names and identification!" she barked at them.

The men all reached into their back pockets. The pale-skinned one with red-hair stubble protested, "We have a right to be here. It's a free country."

"We have reports that you are harassing staff at La Causa."

"They're just illegals. They have no rights," one of the militia's lieutenants defiantly blurted out.

Devine said nothing. She had been hired as the replacement for Barnes. She had done a tour of duty in Afghanistan and had worked for the Portland Police Department for five years. After enduring a messy divorce from her African-American husband who was a detective for the Portland Police force, she decided to move. She had no children and she took no prisoners.

She took out her cell phone and took photos of all five IDs. Then she looked each of the goons straight in the eye and took their photos.

"You can't do that," objected the one called "Red."

Devine ignored him and took several photos of the Humvee.

"Now you all get back into our vehicle and get out of here," she ordered. "Don't let me see you around here again."

## Chapter 48 – Tail

***Wednesday, August 22, 2018***

The furry creature was at her feet as Corkie convened her Oregon First staff meeting that Wednesday. The meeting scheduled for Tuesday was cancelled because Corkie had had a conference call with the state campaign headquarters in the morning. She reported that things seemed to be going well. The polls were showing an increased opposition to Proposition 105. Several state and federal legislators (mostly Democrats) from her area were also opposing the measure. Corkie reported on the campaign-related vandalism and requested more lawn signs from the state campaign headquarters. Chispa rearranged his body, quietly laying across Corkie's white running shoes.

Lorenzo was insistent that his wife have their dog with her in light of the potential threats lurking about. Chispa was only too happy to be petted, pampered, and given an occasional treat. Lorenzo was getting better. He had only a few more days of recuperation before he returned to his doctor for a follow-up visit. He was already preparing for teaching his high school classes in the Fall.

"Okay, Mando, it's your turn," Corkie said. It would have been more fair if she rotated the reporting, but she already had a template for the agenda. She didn't want to get confused. Chispa looked up as Armando began.

"Well, we replaced the lawn signs that were all messed up. On Monday night. I think it was seventeen." Armando was wearing a Che Guevara tee shirt and blue jeans. Some of the younger girls had a crush on him. "And the next day, they were all gone. Couldn't find any of them. Wrote down the locations and emailed the info to Dana at the police station."

"Have they ever found any of the signs?" Corkie asked.

"No."

"Do we have enough replacement signs?" Corkie asked. "I did ask the state for more. When we'll get them is anyone's guess."

"I'm not finished!" Mando interjected. "Rafa and I staked out the Fifth and Grand location. Rafa has a silver Honda Civic. Around midnight a big Humvee comes racing by and stops. A guy jumps out. He looks like a paratrooper dude. He yanks up the sign and throws it in the back of the Humvee."

Corkie knew that the town closed down at 11 p.m. and that no one was around after that. "Well, at least we know it was a Humvee. It was probably the same one that was around La Causa on Monday."

"But, dudes, it gets better. Rafa took a video of it with his cell phone. We sent it to Dana. It was kinda dark, but he thinks they are going to send it to some lab at the FBI or something like that."

***

Dana had forwarded the video to Chiloquin. The police chief found the photos too grainy, but could discern that the perpetrator had been in a Humvee. Not many in Twin Oaks. Just the ones the Utah boys were driving. He called Stone, and sent him the video. The FBI agent said that his SID (Scientific Investigative Department) would check out the video. In less than an hour, Stone came back with an enhanced version of the photo that clearly showed the Humvee license plate.

"Thanks, Ray, I owe you," Marty said.

"Yeah, you owe me two," Stone said. "I'm flying down to Medford tonight. I'll rent a car. But I'll take a steak dinner."

"Done," Marty smiled. "And Ray, can you bring some night surveillance equipment with you?"

"Now we're up to surf and turf."

***

Officer Gale Devine and her partner Mike Suarez were parked a block down the street from the Yes on Proposition 105 headquarters in an unmarked white Chevy van. One of the Humvees was parked out in front of the building. The two police officers were age mates. She was 33, 5'8" and full-bodied. He was 32, 5'11" and weighed about 175. His features were non-descript. Most of his work was as a detective, but he also worked undercover. He couldn't have any distinguishing marks.

Gale could have had a romantic interest in Mike, even though he really wasn't her type. But she knew that he lived with his girlfriend and her daughter. She believed in monogamy, even though her former husband hadn't.

Mike was coming back from a bathroom stop, when Gale motioned him to jump in. She had moved over to the driver's side. "They just left."

Their van maintained a two block distance behind the Humvee. It was early evening and that helped them conceal their pursuit. They would keep their headlights off for as long as possible.

Mike radioed the dispatcher and gave their coordinates. They were patched into the chief's office. "Subject One proceeding east on Grand. Going at the limit."

Traffic was light and Gale let a SUV pull in front of her. The police chief had called for backup to run parallel to the Humvee two blocks over. The Humvee proceeded in a southeasterly direction, obviously unaware that anyone was following them. It continued out of town toward the foothills.

"It doesn't look like they are going to the California part of town," Suarez reported. In his office, the police chief was using old technology to track the Humvee: colored chart pins on a map of the metropolitan area of Twin Oaks. The backup car had now fallen behind Gale and Mike.

Suddenly, the brake lights of the Humvee went on. It was stopping at a gas station that housed a small market. Gale and Mike pulled off to the side of the road. Their backup went past the gas station. They would try to find a turnoff down the road.

Mike called in to apprise the chief. Chiloquin told them to be patient. Things would either work out or they wouldn't. Gale took out her binoculars. She observed two subjects coming out of the grocery store with a couple bags of provisions. They were laughing. That was a good sign. They didn't have a clue that they were being followed.

Two minutes later the Humvee sped out of the gas station. Mike and Gale waited a few seconds before continuing their pursuit. Two miles up the road, their backup appeared behind them. Mike and Gale decided to give the Humvee more distance. It was now dark and they had to turn on their headlights.

The highway was desolate with only power line poles visible on the right. It was getting darker and darker. Three miles later there was a sign pointing to the right. It was the entrance to the Cook Brothers Gold Mine. The Humvee turned right.

Mike was instructed to continue for another mile and then pull over and wait. Their trailing car stopped short of the gold mine turnoff.

Fifteen minutes later the two police cars were driving back to town.

## Chapter 49 – Redemption

***Thursday, August 23, 2018***

"Morning, Willie," the police chief was just eating a quick lunch consisting of a ham and cheese sandwich and a bag of corn chips at his desk. He was now calling Masters at his office.

"Morning to you, Marty," he rarely talked to the chief of police. "What can I do for you today?"

"We need to meet and talk over a few things."

"We can do it here in my office or at yours. Whatever works for you," Masters was trying to be amenable. He didn't know what was going on, but it didn't feel right.

"Someplace that isn't public or where there aren't a lot of people around."

*Uh-oh! This sounds really serious now!* Masters was trying to think quickly. "How about my house? My wife is working today." Sue Ellen was a librarian at the public library.

By two o'clock Marty was walking up to the Masters' palatial country mansion. The gardens were beautiful manicured on both sides of the walkway. There was an avenue of maples that surrounded the home. Willie was sitting on one of the white rattan rocking chairs on the front porch. He motioned to the rocker next to him, as Marty approached.

"How you doing, Marty?"

"Fine," said the police chief with a poker face. "Beautiful spread you have here. Hate to see you lose it." Marty had only been here twice before on social occasions. He saw Willie as a practical businessman who played the odds. He needed to fire a warning shot across Willie's bow to show that he meant business.

Willie was taken aback, but tried hard not to show it. He calmly replied "Well, what's on your mind?"

"We have reason to believe that a group of Utah militia guys are up here in our town causing trouble," Marty was looking straight ahead at the trees. In a few weeks, summer would be ending and the foliage would begin changing colors. He turned and then looked at Willie. "And that they are staying at your gold mine."

*Aw, sh*t! Can't believe we got busted. Should have known it was only a matter of time with those toy soldiers.* Masters was angry, especially because he had allowed himself to get sucked into the mayor's spider web. *Need to cut my losses.*

"Tell me what you need to know, Marty," Masters was capitulating. "I won't bull sh•t you."

"How did this all start?"

Masters told him how Pastor McConnell had summoned some of his political sympathizer contacts from Utah. They were part of the Three Percent movement. Pro-guns. Pro-White Supremacy. Anti-People of Color. He shared that Andy Jackson was their group leader, and how he and his brother Elijah were on the gold mine payroll. Initially, they worked the day shift, and afterwards, it was Elijah working alone while Andy spent his time in town hanging out with the mayor or Pastor McConnell. Now, neither Andy or Elijah were doing anything for the mine. Barnes had to pick up a little of the slack. He complained, but enjoyed the overtime. Barnes and Masters were counting the days until the Utah boys were gone. H

Chiloquin had his poker face on as he heard all of this. *I think it's obvious that Masters is being used, or maybe letting himself be used.*

"What are these Utah boys up to?" Marty pressed.

"Don't know for sure," Willie's mouth moved to the side. "But I know it's no good. B.B. says he saw those guys taking dynamite from our special storage unit. We keep explosives there behind a cement barrier. Very limited access."

"Did B.B. confront them?"

"No, he says that the Utah guys go out of their way to avoid him. B.B. is fed up with them. He wants them out. And so do I."

"How does the mayor figure into all of this?"

"Well, he let Andy bring his militia unit here from Utah," Masters was on a roll. "And he pays them with campaign funds. That's illegal. I'm not going to pay them! I won't go to jail for him!"

***

Early that evening Officers Gale Devine and Mike Suarez had parked their patrol car just outside the Cook Brothers Gold Mine Company facing east. FBI agent Stone accompanied them, loaded down with all sorts of surveillance equipment aimed at the inside of the gold mine grounds. They walked about a hundred yards on the dusty, gravel road to the front gate, stopping every 25 yards to check for heat signatures on the camera. There was only one body registering. It should be Barnes working the night shift. The miners had already gone home for the day.

Barnes, dressed in his Cook Brothers tan security uniform, greeted the trio with a head nod. He didn't say a word. It was a good thing because the cameras were rolling and sound was recording.

He led them to the building where the Utah boys were lodged. He unlocked the front entrance and walked in first to make sure no one was there. He gave a thumbs up for the all clear. The two police officers and the FBI agent were all wearing blue latex gloves. They went through each room systematically taking dozens of photos and making explanatory narratives with recorders. They found a whole cache of automatic weapons. *This is good stuff,* thought Stone. *Old Marty had been on to something.*

Barnes then led the three law enforcement officers to a warehouse. It was padlocked, but Barnes had a key. It looked more like a refurbished barn and smelled just as bad. In one corner were two boxes of dynamite, some flash-bangs, hand grenades, and more automatic weapons. Stone took his time filming the scene. He figured that they didn't need to take fingerprints because Barnes would be a witness to having seen the Utah boys in the warehouse. Officers Devine and Suarez were ready to go, but Stone moved closer to the TNT boxes. He lifted the lids. The boxes looked fairly new, but they were filled only half way. There were dynamite sticks unaccounted for.

Stone filmed the scores of Humvee tire tracks. They would be a challenge to decipher.

It was starting to get dark. Stone wanted to see the special storage unit where additional and more powerful dynamite was stored. Again Barnes had the keys to grant them access. Stone looked at all of the TNT boxes. None had been opened, but Stone noticed some crystallization on the outside of a few boxes.

That was not a good sign. It meant that these were old and perhaps, more volatile.

Gale's phone suddenly buzzed. "Big Bertha, this is Oppenheimer. Over," Oscar spoke into his car radio. He was stationed three miles down the road, just past the gas station. He had been watching for any of the Utah vehicles to return to the mine. "Do you read me? Over."

"Read you, Oppenheimer," Gale spoke into her police radio.

"Two bogies just passed me, doing the limit! Over."

## Chapter 50 – Fried Eggs and Bacon

### *Tuesday, September 4, 2018*

Tuesday morning after the Labor Day weekend came early and the sounds of the Dixie Chicks country western music along with the smell of bacon permeated the downtown diner. It seemed as though the whole town was relieved that the Labor Day weekend had been quiet and peaceful. Maybe things were getting back to normal.

Holly was at least 30 minutes early as she sipped her coffee. She was feeling jittery. Lorenzo had made her a double Bustelo espresso when she begged off having breakfast with him and Corkie. Holly had driven to Twin Oaks a day early, to be ready for the mandatory pre-trial mediation session that was scheduled for today. The plaintiffs and her co-counsel Thaddeus Schiffman were having a breakfast meeting to discuss strategy in the case of Fisher/Martinez against Keough and Barnes as a result of the May 18 incident. Following Holly's trial strategy, the other defendants, the Twin Oaks Police Department and ICE, had been dropped from the initial legal pleadings per mutual agreement. This maneuver would increase the plaintiffs' chances of prevailing and preserve their scarce resources.

When she arrived into town, Holly had met Corkie at the park where the No on Proposition 105 campaign had a booth for the Labor Day weekend to help persuade people to their side, and hand out buttons and stickers. She had shared with Corkie that the Presidential administration was more screwed up than anyone could even imagine. All immigration applications were taking forever. That meant Gloria was still in limbo. Corkie shared that Gloria was doing well as a caretaker. Both of them were saddened that there were still no leads as to Yesenia's whereabouts or condition.

Lorenzo stopped by and offered to accompany Holly around the park. The local high school band was playing. Minutes later they were enjoying boysenberries with vanilla ice cream. Holly knew that Lorenzo had used the escort ruse to score the deadly dessert.

Holly spent the night with Corkie and Lorenzo that Monday night. They hadn't seen each other much that summer with Corkie working on the Oregon First campaign. Holly told them that Monica Rizal, the summer intern, had wanted to come along, but the law school was back in session. They caught up on all the events over dinner and the wine that Holly had brought them. Corkie told her about the leaflets that targeted Gloria Ocaso as an illegal immigrant. Holly was pissed. She would have to call Manny the next day. Holly called it quits before they opened a second bottle of wine. She had to be fully alert for the next day's mediation.

Thaddeus Schiffman was the last one to join the group in the large booth in the back of the diner. Holly was there with their clients Margaret Fisher and Marta Martinez. Sitting next to Margaret was Sandra Starmont.

Only Holly ordered a real breakfast. Nothing like fried eggs and bacon before a court proceeding. The others had coffee or tea and nibbled on some freshly made banana almond muffins. The veteran waitress, Sally, filled up their coffee cups and asked what Thaddeus wanted. He ordered oatmeal.

"Like we told you before, this is not the trial. That's scheduled for next week," he put milk and sugar into his coffee as he spoke to the plaintiffs. "By law, we are required to sit down with the defendants to try to work this out. The judges really don't like trials that much."

Holly was amazed on how smooth Thaddeus was. He would be really good in front of a jury. She was glad to be here to learn from him.

"You won't have to testify today," Schiffman continued. "We just have to listen. Most of the time you won't even be in the room." The three other women looked bewildered. "Holly and I will do most of the talking."

By ten o'clock all the parties were seated in the adjunct courtroom around a large conference table. All the parties agreed that this session would not be recorded. A small, wizened man with frizzy grey-blonde hair sat at the end.

"Good morning, I'm Barry Greene," the retired judge from Chicago began. "I'm your mediator today. This is a very simple process. First, I will ask you to only address me, not the other parties. This is intended to be a non-confrontational meeting. We're going to try to resolve this in a friendly manner. No kicking or biting," he smiled wryly.

The people around the table also gave nervous grins. He went over the ground rules about breaks, the order in which the parties would meet with him individually, and his own recommendations. The parties stipulated that the mediator's recommendation would be confidential and non-binding.

For the defendants, Alvin Beckham was representing Mitch Keough in his personal capacity; Marsha Squires represented the City of Twin Oaks; and Otis Tyler represented B.B. Barnes in his personal capacity. Mayor Keough was not present; B.B. Barnes was.

Barry Greene explained the mediation procedure again. He

knew that mediation was foreign to most people and he wanted everyone to feel comfortable. First, he would meet separately with the plaintiffs. Then he would meet with Mr. Beckham and Ms. Squires and finally, with Mr. Tyler and B.B. Barnes.

Upon Greene's request, the defendants left the room. Greene gave a big smile to the plaintiffs that showed his beige-tainted dentures. "Okay, ladies and gentleman, want do you want?"

Thaddeus knew Greene fairly well. He was fair, but was always determined to squeeze out a deal. Greene's success rate at settlement was at 90%. Judge Lyndon Cummings loved him. "Money, admission of wrong doing, and assurances that it won't happen again," he replied.

The mediator nodded. Thaddeus was talking his language. No platitudes about Justice or the American Way.

The original lawsuit asked for $10,000 in general damages for Margaret Fisher and the same amount for Marta Martinez. For Samantha Martinez, the amount was $50,000 for general and specific damages. The plaintiffs were also asking $200,000 in punitive damages, plus costs and attorneys' fees. Thaddeus took a serious tone when he explained that his clients had been berated and incarcerated unjustly by the defendants. It was ethnic profiling gone wrong. Plus, Samantha Martinez was physically injured by the police officer and is still recovering. Everybody had been traumatized by the tragic incident.

"Okay, Thad, what's your bottom line?" Barry Greene cut to the chase.

"We probably could drop the punitives if they would admit to wrongdoing and stop working with ICE," Schiffman was following the legal strategy that Holly and he had come up with. They knew that getting punitive damages was going to be an uphill battle anyway. "Costs and attorneys' fees are a maybe."

Fifteen minutes later the plaintiffs' team exited the room and went to the cafeteria to wait. Alvin Beckham representing the mayor in his personal capacity and Marsha Squires for the city then entered the room.

Greene went through the same spiel.

Beckham shrugged and said plainly, "Keough doesn't want to settle."

The mediator looked at him sternly. "And he knows what that means?"

The attorney nodded yes.

"Okay," Greene pondered for a moment and then asked. "Okay, Ms. Squires, what about the City?"

"Well, we're in the same boat," Marsha said. "Based on Mr. Barnes deposition and all the documentation, Barnes and Keough were acting outside the scope of their official capacities as governmental employees. I have talked this over with the city's insurance carrier and they agree. We are offering nothing."

"Okay," Greene nodded. He was not going to take these positions as final. He had a few tricks up his sleeve.

Fifteen minutes later, Barnes's attorney, Otis Tyler, was sitting in front of Barry Greene. Marsha Squires was also at the table. The mediator went through the same speech.

Tyler tapped his pen on the table. "Mr. Barnes wants to make a deal," the attorney turned to look at Squires. "He is willing to testify against the mayor. But he wants to be dropped as a defendant."

Greene was a little surprised, but not really. Nothing was ever predictable during these mediations.

"But they already have his deposition," Marsha Squires interrupted, which technically violated the mediator's ground rules. She looked at B.B. incredulously. *How far from grace had he fallen?*

"You really need to hear what he has to say," Tyler persisted. "It's dynamite."

## Chapter 51 – Country Justice

***Monday, September 10, 2018***

Thaddeus Schiffman was a Jimmy Stewart type country lawyer. And, when he saw an opening, he took it. The trial for Fisher and the Martinez family versus Keough et al. was set for the next day. But after the dynamite testimony that Barnes was offering in exchange for being dropped from the lawsuit, it was a slam dunk. He knew in reality that B.B. was judgment proof. Not even a pot to piss in. Thaddeus knew that one couldn't get blood from this turnip. But now the big dog was cornered and was about to be spayed.

Superior Court Judge Lyndon Cummings had called a special meeting of all the attorneys in the case that Monday morning in his chambers. Mayor Keough was there with his attorney Alvin Beckham. Marsha Squires represented the City and Otis Tyler was defending B.B. Barnes. Thaddeus Schiffman was present for the plaintiffs. Stiff-backed wooden chairs were squeezed around the judge's desk.

"I read Mediator Barry Greene's recommendation on this case. He strongly recommends a settlement," the judge was in a cranky mood. "Why isn't this case being settled?"

"The mediator's report is only advisory, your honor," Beckham spoke up.

"I want my day in court!" Keough interrupted.

"Counsel, please remind your client that he is not to speak. You are his spokesperson," the judge admonished Beckham.

“Yes, your honor,” Beckham gave Keough a dirty look.

“Mr. Schiffman has filed a motion for summary judgment against the defendant Mayor Keough,” the judge went on. The other attorneys were surprised. That meant that the court could enter a judgment against Keough without a full trial.

“This motion will be heard on Monday, September 17, before the trial begins. You are all on notice as of now.” The judge had pushed the trial date back another week, trying to force a settlement.

The mayor’s attorney, Alvin Beckham, looked perplexed.

“I want to speak to the jury,” Keough blurted out. “They love me. They understand me.”

“Mr. Beckham, please advise your client that he is excused,” the judge would not tolerate insolence from anyone, including the mayor.

Beckham leaned and whispered to his client that he had to leave the chambers. “That’s bull shit,” could be heard from the mayor when the door closed after him.

A minute later the judge continued, “And just for the record, Mr. Schiffman has decided to waive his clients’ right to a jury trial. This will be a trial from the bench. That should shave at least a few days off the proceedings.”

The judge paused. He was frustrated. He directed his gun sight to Beckham. “Alvin, everybody seems to have made movement from their original positions. Everybody has compromised except you. As I read the evidence, I am leaning toward granting the motion for summary judgment. I don’t really see any issues of fact. The mayor screwed up big time. There really is no need for a trial. It would be a waste of the taxpayers’ money. I'm going to give you one more chance. You need to have a "come to Jesus" talk with Mitch. Get it done, Alvin!"

***

The following Friday had been slow and Police Officer Oscar Perkins was on special traffic enforcement duty in downtown Twin Oaks late in the afternoon. It was almost five o'clock and everybody wanted to get home. Traffic was getting a bit heavy.

The three lady campaign volunteers for the Yes on Proposition 105 were just leaving their headquarters. The young brunette took out a key and locked the front door of their office. The three coworkers walked out together to the municipal parking lot where each had a car. The four Utah boys were milling around in front of their black Humvee that was parked in front of the building. Going back to the gold mine was a drag. So boring. Nothing to do. They were not allowed to drink or smoke there. They had to maintain strict military discipline.

The city hall tower clock struck with five tolls. Suddenly, a white police cruiser came racing on the wrong side of the road toward the Humvee and screeched to a stop in front of it. Simultaneously, other police cars pulled up beside and behind the Humvee. The multipurpose Humvee vehicle was pinned in.

Officer Gale Devine walked up to four Utah militia with her right hand on her gun. Two other officers provided backup. Officer Perkins was one of the cars that responded. He was already in radio contact with the police chief. "Hands up!" she shouted in an authoritarian tone.

Two of the guys obeyed and the other two didn't. "I said raise them!" she repeated.

"What's this about?" shouted out one of the guys who seemed to be their team leader. "We're here legally! We didn't do anything!"

"All of you, hands against the car!"

"And what if we don't want to!"

Gale knew they were testing her. "Probably get shot for resisting arrest."

"Are we under arrest?" one of them blurted out in surprise.

"Now, down on your knees," Gale shouted out. "Keep your hands up!"

"You're going to be in deep shit, when the mayor finds out," threatened the team leader.

"Who is the owner of this vehicle?" she roared.

The four guys looked at each other. Nobody knew. Nobody stepped forward.

"Do any of you know where this vehicle's registration is?"

"Okay, you," Gale pointed to the wimpiest of the guys. "Read this. It is a duly-authorized search warrant allowing us to search this vehicle. Is that what this paper says?" She shoved the document in front of his face.

The guy was nervous. His lips moved as he read. He then nodded his head.

A police van pulled up close to the Humvee and stopped. An officer with a k-9 dog jumped out. He was followed by a technician.

"We are now going to search the vehicle. Is there anything you want to say before we do?" Gale knew that at least two of them wanted to say something, but didn't.

The vehicle was registered to the Utah State Minutemen in Salt Lake City. The search yielded four assault weapons, four Glock handguns, twelve sticks of dynamite plus other explosives, and the mangled remains of two No on Proposition 105 lawn signs.

An hour or so later, the four Utah militia men were occupying a cell in the city jail. They had been read their Miranda rights. They called their leader, Andy Jackson. Andy had a difficult time finding an attorney to represent the four thugs. It was the weekend and no one was around. Their arraignment was not until Monday. Their Humvee was towed away to the police impound. They were charged with several state law violations. FBI agent Stone was working on drafting federal charges.

After the arrest, the police chief sat in his office reviewing the state and federal paperwork that Stone had given him. *I think Stone and I can flip one or two of these guys,* he thought.

# Chapter 52 – Contempt

## *Monday, September 17, 2018*

Corkie was on her second piece of avocado with salsa toast at the breakfast table. She was relaxed. She had taken the prior day off (a Sunday!) and had spent quality time with her husband. They both needed to reconnect after all the stressful events of late.

During his rest and rehabilitation period, Lorenzo had restained the back deck and had gotten his old Dodge pickup to run. His radio antenna was missing and he couldn't find another one. Even the junk yard didn't have one. *Oh, well.* Today he planned to drive it to his high school to drop off some materials, since school had already started.

"Mi amor, could you please pick up some celery and blueberries on your way home from school today?" Corkie requested. Lorenzo had been the chief cook and bottle washer for the past week. The barbequed tri-tip and Holly's pinot noir had been a winning combination the night before.

"No worries," Lorenzo was sipping his coffee with soy milk. "What are you up to today? Same ol', same ol'?"

"Yeah," she sighed just thinking of her week ahead. "Going to meet Sandra at the courthouse this morning. The trial against the mayor is supposed to start today. But they may settle."

***

The bailiff had called the case of Fisher and the Martinez family versus Keough et al. Superior Court Judge Lyndon

Cummings pounded the gavel with emphasis.

"This court is now in session. Are all parties present and accounted for?"

The attorneys at both tables in front of him answered in the affirmative.

"Mr. Schiffman, are you ready to proceed?"

"Yes, your honor," Margaret Fisher and Marta Martinez were seated next to him. Holly was not present.

"Before we proceed, Mr. Schiffman," the judge said sternly, "I believe you have a motion to present to the court."

"Yes, your honor, we are moving for summary judgment. All parties have been duly noticed," Thaddeus asserted. "There are no real issues of fact. We feel that the court can rule on the pleadings and the attached affidavits."

"Mr. Beckham."

"We object, your honor," the mayor's attorney countered. "We have not determined the mayor's state of mind. This is a question of fact."

"Nice try, Mr. Beckham, but this is not a criminal case. What the mayor thought or didn't think is irrelevant," the judge said in an irritated tone. *Ol' Mitch wasn't thinking at all when he decided to stick it out and not settle.* The judge had known the mayor for many years and thought he was a pompous ass. He had always voted for him, but not this year.

"I am granting the plaintiffs' motion for summary judgment," the gavel cracked. "I am awarding the plaintiff, Fisher $20,000 in specific damages and $10,000 for punitive damages.

"For the Martinez', $50,000 in specific damages plus $20,000 in punitive damages. In addition, I am awarding the plaintiffs all costs and attorney fees.

The mayor was sitting in the back of the courtroom. Beckham didn't want him upsetting the judge again. Corkie and Sandra, were also in the back, wanted to stand up and applaud. They had the biggest smiles on their faces.

"Your honor," Marsha Squires stood up. "Based on summary judgment just granted, we are moving for a dismissal on behalf of the Twin Oaks Police Department.

"Motion granted!" Judge Cummings slammed the gavel.

"Your honor!" Otis Tyler jumped up. "Otis Tyler, representing the defendant B.B. Barnes. We also move for a dismissal on his behalf per the stipulation."

"Granted," the judge smacked the gavel again. He would have limited the damages against the mayor to $50,000, but that fool had pissed him off by wasting his time and not settling. *What an idiot!*

Within thirty minutes after the case ended, Schiffman was walking into the Clerk's office to file a $125,000 lien against Mitch Keough's house and property.

***

Later that day, in the same courtroom, the bailiff had called the case of the People of Oregon versus Brady, Gunderson, Melville, and Heller for illegal possession of fire arms, and sixteen other criminal counts. These Utah state militia men were represented by Tors Lindstrom, a real estate attorney. He was called by the Pastor McConnell when the defendants couldn't find any lawyer who would take the case. No self-respecting attorney was going to defend some out-of-state rednecks.

Marsha Squires was representing the prosecution. She presented the charges. Lindstrom was not a criminal defense attorney and didn't know that he could waive the reading. Judge Cummings rolled his eyes and wiggled his butt in the high-backed leather chair. His hemorrhoids were killing him and the pillow didn't help.

"Mr. Lindstrom, how do your clients plead?" the judge asked.

"Not guilty on all counts, your honor," Lindstrom said professionally

Judge Cummings muttered a few words to his clerk and then yelled, "Trial set for Monday, September 24." The gavel sounded.

"Your honor, at this time we would request bail," Lindstrom moved.

"Your honor, the People oppose any type of bail," Marsha Squires jumped up, loaded for bear. "The defendants are a flight risk, they have no visible means of support, and the violations involve military grade weaponry."

"Your honor, they were simply exercising their First and Second Amendment rights," lamented the defense attorney.

"And your honor may recall that you had a similar case recently and you sent the offender back to Utah after a civil compromise," Marsha was angry as she spoke. "Why are these guys from Utah still interfering in our elections and threatening our town folk?"

"Cash bond, $50,000 each," Cummings cracked his gavel.

"But your honor," Lindstrom complained. "They can't raise that kind of money. They'll be in custody until the trial."

Just then, the back doors of the courtroom swung open. Two men in suits rushed in.

"Your honor, if I may be heard," said a man in a navy pin-striped suit and wearing wire rimmed glasses. "Dennis Milbanks, Assistant U.S. Attorney."

Judge Cummings nodded yes. "State your business."

"We're here to take custody of these four defendants. They have been named as defendants pursuant to a federal indictment involving interstate voter intimidation . . ." Milbanks' face had beads of sweat as he quickly recited a litany of charges. He and Stone had sped over the mountain after they got the federal indictment against the Utah boys.

"Without objection," Cummings slammed down his gavel. The local government wouldn't have to foot the bill holding these four skinheads in custody. The feds would. He smiled.

"Your honor, the People would like to postpone the State's case pending the outcome of the federal case," Squires quickly blurted out.

"Without objection." Slam! The defense attorney should have objected that this violated the Sixth Amendment right to a speedy trial, but he really wasn't a criminal defense attorney.

In the back of the room, there was an "Oh, f*ck!" from an ex-Marine. He picked up his cell and spoke, "Elijah, call base and tell the rest of the guys to get the hell out of Dodge. Pronto!"

## Chapter 53 – Resignation

***Tuesday, September 18, 2018***

The day after the arraignment hearing, Andy Jackson was fuming. He had just lost his men. *We got played! We may have lost a skirmish, but we still have more bullets!* He called Pastor McConnell to get some guidance. Andy didn't know the terrain. He needed insider intelligence.

Pastor McConnell called Masters. They needed to talk. The reverend told him to make sure that the mayor came, too.

"Where should we meet?" Masters asked. He was busy and didn't want to lose an hour or two in a political bull shit session.

"Your office," it wasn't a request.

"Okay," Masters said. This would work out okay. He didn't have to drive and the mayor only had a three block walk. *That should take him a good half hour*, grinned Willie to himself.

Forty minutes later, the mayor, red-faced, huffing and puffing stumbled into Masters' office. He saw Andy Jackson with his half-brother Elijah, Pastor McConnell, and Willie.

The reverend began, "Andy, here, says we have a problem. Half of his guys are in jail. The other half had to leave town."

"Why? What's happened?" bumbled the mayor.

"Your police chief set us up with the feds!" Andy said angrily. "My guys are facing federal charges. And we're going to need some big bucks to get them out of jail!"

Nobody said a word. Masters thought, *not another friggin' dime from me. Time for the mayor to pony up.*

The mayor started to speak, but Pastor McConnell cut him off. "Andy, we each have our own responsibilities here. The mayor is running for re-election. Masters is his treasurer and campaign manager. I'm working for the Proposition 105 campaign. And you are the commander in charge of supporting all these efforts. Son, you are responsible for your men. And only you. Do you understand what I'm saying?"

Andy nodded his head. "Yes, sir." *They were throwing him and his men under the bus. It was that liberal police chief's fault. Why couldn't he be working in an Indian casino, instead of defending illegal aliens. He wasn't an American!*

"Well, now that we are all here. Let's talk about the mayor's race," Masters wanted to take control of the meeting. He didn't like Jackson taking over. He was a dangerous man.

"I can assure you my congregation is one hundred percent behind you, mayor," the reverend gave an unctuous smile.

"Well, the polls are looking good, Mitch," Willie reported.

"What about that trend line thing you talked about?" Keough asked.

"It's dropped a little, but you're still ahead."

"I'm going to be making a speech at the Chamber of Commerce this weekend," the mayor boasted. "That should pump them up!"

"How are we doing on fundraising, Mitch?" Masters broached the subject knowing the probable answer.

“A little slow,” the mayor’s eyes scanned the others. “You can backfill us. You’ll get paid after I get re-elected.”

Masters was about to argue.

“We need to get paid right now!” Andy Jackson stared straight at Masters. “We were promised we’d be paid.”

“I never made any such promise,” Masters was defending himself. Jackson was physically intimidating, but Willie believed in keeping pristine financial records.

“It was probably your boy B.B. who tipped off the police chief,” Jackson made the accusation. “Once a cop, always a cop.”

Masters didn’t respond. B.B. had quit his security job with Cook Brothers Gold Mine Company that morning, after the lawsuit was dismissed against him. He had dodged a bullet. He had no real future in Twin Oaks. He could never get back on the police force. B.B. had told Willie that he was moving to Coeur d’Alene, Idaho. He had a state forestry job lined up at Hayden Lake. His cousin who lived near Lake Pend Oreille had gotten him the position.

“Well, he definitely sold me out,” the mayor exclaimed. “He was bad news. Speaking of B.B., I haven’t seen Randy in a while.”

“I think he has a real job now,” the reverend said, not really caring if he was offending the mayor.

“We need to get paid, Goddammit!” Andy said.

“Son, please do not take the name of the Lord in vain!” admonished Pastor McConnell. “You know better.”

“I don’t really care!” Andy shot back.

The mayor tried to smooth the waters. “Willie, just pay these guys. We’ll make it right down the line.”

“Sorry, mayor, no can do,” Willie was frustrated. He had painted himself into a corner. The campaign financial reports were due the following week.

“But I’m telling you, you have to,” the mayor was trying to order him to do it.

“Sorry, gentlemen, I resigning as campaign manager and treasurer,” Masters spoke with conviction. *Good luck finding someone to do the campaign finance report. They’ll probably all land in jail.*

“You can’t do that!” protested the mayor.

“I just did.”

## Chapter 54 – High School Scene

***Friday, September 21, 2018***

This was Oktoberfest weekend in Twin Oaks and the town was ready to celebrate. There had been no school. It was late afternoon and the sun was unseasonably hot. Lorenzo had spent the whole day running errands that he had neglected while he had been sidelined with his cracked ribs. Lorenzo's old pickup truck didn't have air conditioning, so Chispa just stuck his head out of the passenger side window. Life was good for him.

His last task of the day was to pick up some school materials that he needed for the following week. Since it was a day off for the students, Lorenzo didn't expect anyone to be at the high school. He was really surprised when he saw a black Humvee pull out of the school parking lot. It had tinted windows, so he couldn't tell how many occupants the vehicle contained. He knew that the Humvees were associated with the Utah skinhead militia guys who were harassing people in town. He had also heard about them carrying an arsenal of weapons. Had he heard that they even had dynamite?

He kept driving past the high school and looked in the tiny rear view mirror to see if the Humvee occupants had recognized him. He saw no brake lights. He made a U-turn and drove back into the high school parking lot. He and Chispa got out of the truck. He was walking to his office at the school, but then stopped. He systematically started inspecting the buildings, going from left to right. He didn't know what to look for. Any signs of breaking and entering? Strange objects out of place? He took out his cell phone and called the police station. *Better to be safe, than sorry*, he was thinking. Chiloquin was not in, but

Lorenzo talked to Dana who said he would forward the message immediately to the police chief. Lorenzo finally ended up retrieving his materials from his classroom and driving home. Chispa was panting with his tongue out. Lorenzo let him drink from the portable doggie water bowl. He was happy for the outing.

***

Within the hour Police Chief Chiloquin had ordered a police technician who had bomb squad training to the high school to check it out. FBI agent Stone was still in town. Chiloquin contacted him. Stone advised Chiloquin to set up some a camera surveillance system at the school. Marty wasn't quite sure how to do it, but with Dana's assistance he would make it work.

"Did Lorenzo get the license plate number?" the chief asked Dana.

"Negative. He just said it was a black Humvee."

A minute later Marty called Masters at home. "Hey, Willie, I have a few questions."

"Go right ahead," Willie had felt a catharsis when he quit the mayor's campaign. He wasn't even sure he was going to vote for him. *But better the devil you know than the devil you don't know,* he figured.

"Did a Humvee leave the gold mine this afternoon?" Marty knew that the other Humvee was in police impound.

"That's what one of my men reported to me."

"Do you know how many guys left town?"

"No, why are you asking?" Masters was getting concerned

about the questions.

"Got a report of a Humvee hanging around the high school late this afternoon."

"Maybe that was Andy Jackson or his brother."

"I don't understand, Willie. I thought the Humvee was on its way back to Utah."

"No, Andy and his brother, Elijah, are still around. They left my property with the others, but are staying at Pastor McConnell's retreat house about five miles out of town."

"And they have a Humvee too?"

"Yeah, didn't you know that?"

*Sh*t, how did I miss that?*

***

Marty Chiloquin called Principal Kokoro. He advised the principal to shut down the school until further notice. He gave the principal a vague excuse that there might be threats of vandalism over the weekend. In reality, his team had found smoke bombs in the high school ventilation vents, flash-bangs in the school labs, and some light explosives next to some fire alarms. They were set to be triggered by remote control or a cell phone. *Why target a school?* Chiloquin wondered. It didn't make sense.

The high school students would be elated. Their parents not so much. They would be told it was a natural gas leak. The detonation was probably scheduled to occur during the weekend when no one was around. S*omeone would probably spray paint something. Some kind of illegal alien message. Good strategy for* *the bad guys: low cost, big bang, big reward.*

The police quickly came up with a game plan. Dana would monitor the cameras that had been secretly installed at the high school. If he saw a Humvee or anything fishy, he would immediately sound the alarm.

Everybody at the police department, including reserves, were on duty or on call. They would miss Oktoberfest, but they loved the overtime. Nobody had seen the Jackson Humvee in town, but an FBI team was monitoring the McConnell retreat house. Stone had called in reinforcements. Chiloquin had offered the police station as the staging area, but Stone respectfully declined. They had their own standard operating procedures.

# Chapter 55 – The Buddhist Motorcycle Club

## *Saturday, September 22, 2018*

On Saturday morning, Marty was eating breakfast with his old Air Force buddy, Trevor Keyes. Trevor was the same age as Chiloquin, but was 6'2", 220 pounds, and sported a long braided greyish brown pony tail and bushy beard. Trevor had grown up in Oakland, California, and had attended Peralta C.C. In 2015, he had moved to Twin Oaks after his son, who was a police officer in Los Angeles, was killed. Trevor managed the local auto/motorcycle parts store in town. But what made Trevor interesting was that he was the leader of the B42 Society. The B42 was a Buddhist motorcycle club composed of old military veterans who had strong beliefs in the Second Amendment. He hated the National Rifles Association because of the misinformation it put out regarding the origins of this Constitutional right. He believed in the security of a free State and was a strong supporter of the State of Jefferson movement. This movement was an effort to encourage parts of Northern California and Southern Oregon to break away and form their own state.

"We're tired of being second class citizens," Trevor would rant.

"Well, at least your people weren't murdered in the name of Manifest Destiny," Chiloquin would counter.

Chiloquin dipped his wheat toast into the egg yolk and scooped up a piece of bacon. Trevor was making great progress on his stack of pancakes drenched in butter and syrup. They were both on their second cups of coffee.

"What happened to those state militia guys from Utah?" Trevor asked. "They looked like stand-up guys."

For Marty, that was like throwing a grenade into a church. Marty started to tell him about the vandalism, threats, and the bombing of the Becerras' car.

"Yeah, I heard about that," Trevor said. "The mayor blamed it on the illegals."

"That's what this is all about," Marty continued in an agitated tone. "The undocumented here and the people of color are being set up. They're being blamed for everything."

"Well, that sounds like America."

Marty explained the recent encounters with the Utah paramilitary group.

"They're all gone now, aren't they?" Trevor asked.

Marty trusted Trevor implicitly. Trevor had helped him solve many a case off the books. So he told Trevor about the impending threat at the high school.

"I don't get it," Trevor scrunched up his face. "Nobody's around. Nobody is going to see it. It would look like a prank."

"But the mayor would probably blame the aliens."

***

Normally, Dana got off work at five on Saturdays, but tonight he was working late. In addition to his normal duties, he was monitoring the hidden cameras at the high school. It was five minutes after five when he got a call on the emergency communications channel.

"Black Humvee just passed by me, over," Officer Oscar Perkins was parked about a mile down from the high school in an unmarked police car.

"Prom Queen, we are in play, over," Dana sent the "good to go" call to the fed SWAT team stationed around the high school.

A few minutes later a Humvee drove slowly past the high school. It went down the road a bit and made a U-turn. It drove back to the entrance of the high school parking lot. As soon as its tires went over the yellow lines onto school property, a dozen flood lights came on all around it. The Humvee stopped. A bull horn yelled out.

"Turn off your engine and get out of the vehicle, now!" screamed Stone.

No response. The windows were tinted and no one could see in.

"You have until the count of three! One! . . ." Stone yelled.

The Humvee started to back up. Shots were fired from the SWAT team. All four tires were shot at, but the tires seemed impenetrable. The vehicle kept moving back slowly. Then a dozen shots of paint bullets hit the windows and splashed big time. It was now impossible for the Humvee to see.

"This is your last chance! Two! . . ." Stone yelled louder.

The driver side door opened slowly. The skinhead had his hands over his head.

"On your knees. Keep your hands up!" Two SWAT team members secured him with plastic ties and searched him for weapons. Two others started going through the vehicle from front to back.

“Find anything?” Stone asked his men.

“Automatic weapons. A Glock. Some Donnie and Marie cassettes. And a cell phone.”

“Who is this vehicle registered to?”

“Utah State Militia.”

Stone told one of his men to read the detained man his Miranda rights. He did, and the prisoner acknowledged that he understood them.

“I want to make my phone call,” the prisoner said. “I know my Constitutional rights.”

“What’s your name?” Stone asked.

Silence.

“I’m going to ask you one more time, what is your name?” Stone said in an angry tone.

Silence.

Stone had a black belt in karate. In a nanosecond, his right fist connected with the prisoner’s left elbow.

There was a look of shock, and then of pain, as the prisoner’s eyes opened wide. He screamed. “You can’t do this to me!” His grabbed his left elbow with his right arm.

“Your name!”

Stone started to step forward again.

The prisoner flinched. “Elijah Jackson.”

Stone had been briefed about him.

"You are Andy Jackson's brother, is that correct?"

Elijah's eyes were watering from pain. He couldn't move his left elbow. He nodded affirmatively.

"Where is your brother?"

Elijah was shaking his head no. He wasn't going to give up his brother.

"We're here to save hundreds of lives," Stone said sternly. "We'll do whatever it takes to save lives."

"Nobody is supposed to get hurt," Elijah babbled. "Just mess up a few buildings."

"Where's Andy?" Stone had turned off his recording device before the interrogation in case things got messy.

"I was working alone."

As if on cue, Elijah's cell phone buzzed. A text message appeared on the screen that said:

**Did you trigger the devices yet? Don't see nothin'!**

## Chapter 56 – Was Ist Los?

### *Saturday, September 22, 2018*

For Oktoberfest weekend, everyone in Twin Oaks was German. Some folks dressed in lederhosen or wore dirndls. The oom-pah-pah music rumbled. Beer gardens were set up at the four corners of the city park. Everybody was eating bratwurst and sauerkraut. Hundreds of people were enjoying the festivities.

At around seven o'clock, Stone called Chiloquin, who was the only person left at the police station besides Dana and the night shift. They updated the status of the information they had gotten from Elijah and reviewed their plan of action.

"You don't have to thank me for doing your job," Stone goaded.

"Hey, this guy is a federal prisoner," Marty shot back.

"Marty, your memory must be going," Stone kept taunting. "Remember, you called me first."

"Just keep those guys out of my town, partner," Marty was appreciative. "Thanks." Under the right circumstances, he had no problems working with the feds.

The police chief decided to let Dana go home. The young man had endured a long day. Welcome to law enforcement. Chiloquin decided to go over to the park and check out the situation. He was greeted with hellos and handshakes. He was starving. He was tempted to have a bratwurst. Maybe with a little mustard and sauerkraut. The police chief gave wide berth to the mayor who was smiling and shaking hands at the Yes on Prop.

105 booth. He walked on toward the crafts stands. He liked the colorfully beaded and plant fiber baskets that looked similar to the ones that his Klamath grandmother used to make. He wanted to buy one for an upcoming birthday present, but he couldn't tonight because he was on duty. He found his friend Trevor Keyes at the bratwurst concession. Marty bought two which he doused freely with mustard and grabbed a soft drink.

As Marty and Trevor chatted for a while, Marty's eyes were constantly surveilling the surroundings.

"Sounds like your team did a great job catching the bad guys," Trevor was finishing off his wurst.

"That's just it, Trevor, we only caught one guy," Marty's mind was in overdrive. "And it was really just a bunch of smoke bombs and flash bangs."

"Dude, that's why I was in Tactical, and you were in Communications," Trevor said. "That's a classical diversionary move. The halfback goes up the middle, but the quarterback still has the ball."

*Crap! We were played. We would have sent our police and fire personnel to the school, leaving the park unprotected. It was a divide and conquer move!*

He placed a call to Stone and quickly explained his thinking. "I think we need to pull all our officers from the high school and deploy them to the park."

"No problem. Can do," Stone had almost arrived at the jail. "Meet you at the park." He would call his team in.

"Any more from the brother?" Marty asked.

"No, he keeps saying that no one was supposed to get hurt."

That struck a chord with Marty. "Ray, didn't he say that all they wanted to do was mess with a few buildings?"

"Yeah, the school."

"No, Ray, I think the target is the police station! Change of plans, meet me there!" Marty rushed to get off the phone.

Trevor had heard the entire conversation. "Want me to come with you, Marty?"

Marty shook his head with a dismissive "no." Chiloquin had to get back to the station. *Who was still there?* he wondered. Hopefully, Dana had gone home. Marty hurried over to the police station. The civic center was sparsely lit. Oregonians liked to conserve energy. It helped the environment, but it also aided the burglars. On the way over he called the station and put them on high alert. He also called officers Gale Devine and Mike Suarez who were teamed together tonight and ordered them to secure the police station.

It was deathly quiet as he approached the police station. The night was dark. He pulled out his Maglite as he got out of the car. He called the watch commander again.

"I'm in front of the building," Marty said. "I'm going to do a circumference inspection." He wanted to add "so don't shoot me" but didn't.

He carefully walked around the station, slowly, step by step. His head turned from side to side, studying every dark corner. After five minutes, he called the watch commander a third time. "Clear," he reported. "Going to look around the other buildings."

Stone still hadn't arrived and neither had Gale and Mike. Marty knew that he should wait for backup before walking over to the city hall across the plaza, but his mind was sending him mixed signals. *Maybe the park is the real target. It would make sense. Did I personalize this? Did I want the police station to be the target? Things here are too snug and cozy. The park will be closing down soon. Maybe I need to get back there.*

The answer to his questions came suddenly. “Hands up where I can see them. No sudden moves, Chief,” the military voice barked. “Turn around.”

In front of Marty stood an athletic figure in military fatigues and black camo face paint standing next to a bronze statue. He was pointing an AK-47 at Marty. “You should have stayed on the res, Chief,” Marty knew it was Andy Jackson. “We stole your land fair and square.”

Marty was thinking whether he should be quiet or engage. He decided to buy time.

“Andy, what do you hope to accomplish?”

“We need to get rid of all the illegals, niggers, redskins, just to name a few,” Jackson laughed. “We need to make America great again.”

“And how do you plan to do that?”

“Blow up a few buildings. People will blame the illegals and get rid of them. The mayor will get credit for repairing the city hall. Everything will be good.”

“But you’re going to get caught,” Marty was getting desperate. He didn’t know what else to say.

“But not by you,” and with a lightning quick motion, Jackson swung the butt of the AK-47 into Chiloquin’s mid-section. Marty exhaled a painful puff of air and collapsed. “You should have stayed out of this.”

A shadow fell over Chiloquin as Jackson stepped over his fallen body. He laid down his automatic weapon and drew the Glock out of his holster. Then he unsheathed a Bowie-sized knife.

Jackson paused. “Gonna shoot you first. And then scalp ya. With a little luck you may die from the bullet.” The handgun was pointed to the police chief’s head. “Adios, amigo.”

There was a powerful gunshot. Followed instantaneously by another. Blood was splattered everywhere. There was a cry of pain. A body flew sideways.

“Marty, are you all right?” a third person carrying a shotgun, ran up to Marty’s still body.

Chiloquin didn’t move at first. Then, he turned over and faced his rescuer. “Trevor, what took you so long?” he hissed, his ears still ringing from the gunshot sounds.

Holding his left hand over his stomach, Andy Jackson was rocking back and forth in pain. With his shotgun in hand, Trevor took a few steps and kicked the knife, the Glock, and the AK-47 out of reach. Andy’s hand was mangled and his chest was polka-dotted with blood. Marty got up and looked down at Andy.

“Marty, should we call an ambulance?”

“Not for me,” Marty was staring down at the shot man.

“How about for him?”

“He can call one himself.”

“He might bleed out.”

“He might,” replied Marty acidly.

“Are you going to read him his Miranda rights?” Trevor’s late son had been a police officer and he knew that Marty had to follow protocol.

“No. He’s not in custody,” Marty then kicked Andy in the groin with all his might. Andy looked like he was going to throw up. “Self-defense,” Marty looked at him scornfully.

After what seemed like an eternity, Andy looked up and said in a hateful tone, “F*ck you, injun!” The insult was met with another kick in the groin. This time Andy vomited dinner and blood.

“We can play all night. Where are the explosives?” Marty asked sternly.

“F*ck you, you dumb injun,” Andy mumbled through his bloody mouth. “I told you already.” His head motioned to the city hall. *Crap! That’s what he had said before.*

“How are you going to trigger it?” Marty pursued.

Andy remained silent. He stirred making serpentine motions.

“We’ve got your brother,” Marty said. “He’s looking at 20 years minimum.”

Andy looked like he was grabbing his stomach.

“Maybe even life, for all the conspiracies you guys are involved in,” Marty was playing him. “Attempted murder of a police officer will add 20 more. You just screwed him double. Where is the detonator?”

Andy rolled over. He lifted up his head and smiled. In his right hand he held out his cell phone with his thumb over the phone keypad. He started to move his thumb downward.

There was a loud gunshot. Marty looked at Andy whose eyes seemed to have popped out of his head. The paramilitary criminal was missing his entire right hand.

Seconds later Marty was searching Andy, who was rocking back and forth, and crying out in pain. Marty found a combat knife sheathed behind Andy's back. He called for the bomb squad. Officers Devine and Suarez radioed that they were parking and were on their way over.

"And send for an ambulance," Marty said to the night watch commander.

As he was hanging up, Ray Stone ran up to him. "Are you all right?"

"Yeah, got another one for you."

***

After the Oktoberfest shooting, Andy Jackson had been taken into federal custody while in a Portland hospital. He was still in ICU. The doctors were trying hard to save one hand. He had been unconscious since he arrived at the hospital. When he awoke and was stabilized, he refused to talk.

At the same time, the U.S. Attorney had taken Andy's brother, Elijah, apart like skinning a rabbit. Elijah was told that his brother might not make it, and if that happened, all the criminal charges would fall on him. If Elijah cooperated, maybe Andy could be moved to a better facility, maybe Letterman Hospital in San Francisco. In the end, Elijah spilled his guts implicating the mayor and Pastor McConnell. When asked about Willie Masters, B.B. Barnes, and Randy Miller, he bragged that they weren't even players. By the following Thursday, a federal indictment against Keough and the Jackson Brothers was issued.

Elijah was offered a deal if he testified against Keough and his brother. He balked. But even without his testimony, the U.S. Attorney had enough evidence to put the three away for a long, long time. Police Chief Chiloquin had told the U.S. Attorney that Masters had cooperated with the legal authorities and recommended that no action be brought the gold mine owner. The federal prosecutor agreed and said that being played by the mayor was embarrassment and punishment enough. Although the Jackson brothers were already in police custody, the U.S. Attorney was contemplating holding off arresting Mayor Keough until after the election.

## Chapter 57 – Election Night

***Tuesday, November 6, 2018***

The last six weeks before the election zoomed by. The hot summer days were gone. They were replaced by daily autumnal showers. The temperatures were colder and the deciduous trees were displaying a rainbow of colors. The campaign season had dominated the Fall with volunteers for all the candidates going door-to-door in the inclement weather. The Yes on Proposition 105 effort was reinforcing its base with daily diatribes by the mayor. Keough followed strict message discipline. Higher crime rates were due to the illegal aliens. Taxes were the fault of the illegal aliens. The shortage of jobs was caused by the illegal aliens. And the lack of governmental services to residents was also the fault of the illegals. Everything that was bad was their fault. The mayor wanted to make America great again.

Lorenzo was busy at school. He seemed to have a good crop of students in his classes this year. At school, he was officially apolitical. None of the students were of voting age anyway. The local teachers' union had taken a No position on Proposition 105. Luke Esquivel was angry at the union for doing so and complained about having to pay union dues. On the other hand, he never turned down a pay raise.

Corkie looked like she hadn't slept in weeks. Theoretically, today was the last day of the campaign, but things were never that simple. The Oregon First campaign would have a party at La Causa starting at 7 p.m. Mando and Rafa were in charge. That meant more pizza. TV monitors would be on all evening updating the election results. Corkie had bought fifty ten-dollar Subway Sandwich gift cards for all the volunteers out of her own pocket.

The Oregon electoral process was completely vote by mail. Most people voted early so they could get their civic duty out of the way. The city and county clerks had already begun counting the ballots. Voter turnout was expected to be high, especially among the millennials. The Democrats nationwide were expected to make a statement. At the Congressional level, the goal was to take back the House. As for the U.S. president, he was against everyone and everything. The Yes on Prop. 105 campaign had even sent out a copy of the president's endorsement of the measure.

The pro-105 campaign headquarters had an advantage. They were only two blocks from the city clerk's office. They had volunteers who would shuttle there every thirty minutes to get the latest voting results. The online site was always at least twenty minutes behind. Their building was decorated with dozens of American flags, both big and small. The campaign party was scheduled to start at 4 p.m. The mayor would be there, praising the troops. City Council candidates, Baumgartner and Warden, would be hanging out there also. Select supporters would be served alcoholic libations and hors oeuvres in the back room.

The press and TV cameras were stationed at both headquarters. Sheets of rain came down in hourly segments the entire afternoon. Groups of seniors started arriving at the Yes on 105 campaign headquarters. They wore red MAGA (make America great again) baseball caps.

A black SUV pulled up and stopped on the street in the yellow-painted loading zone. Three seconds later a second SUV drove past the first one for 100 yards and then made a U-turn. It parked across the street from the first SUV. Four men wearing black FBI vests, helmets, uniforms, and vests jumped out of the first vehicle. They were all caring automatic weapons. Two of them went to the back of the Yes on 105 building. The other two stationed themselves in front of the building.

Two middle-aged gentlemen nicely attired in suits exited the first vehicle and carefully crossed the street, looking both ways for approaching traffic. FBI agent Stone and his colleague U.S. Marshall C.J. Tipton gave a nod to the two FBI agents securing the front door. Tipton entered the establishment first. All of a sudden the front office area went silent. What was a 6'5" 260 pound African-American doing in their establishment? He was followed by Ray Stone who was only 5'10" and 180 pounds. Nobody said a word until the person who ran the office, Agnes Warhol, approached the two feds.

"May I help you, gentlemen?" she asked politely, her voice trembling.

"Yes, ma'am," Tipton said in his bass voice. "We are looking for Mayor Mitch Keough."

"I'll get him for you," Agnes offered.

"No, thanks, just point him out," Tipton countered. They didn't want to give Keough advance warning and allow him to slip away.

She gingerly pointed to a balding man in the corner with his back toward the front. The two lawmen approached.

"Mayor Keough!" Tipton said in a commanding tone.

Keough turned around expecting to see one of his supporters. He gulped when he saw Tipton. "What?!"

Tipton pulled out a document from his coat and handed it to

Keough. "You are under arrest for interstate voter repression, firearms and explosives violations, and conspiracy to . . ." The laundry list went on and on.

The mayor was stunned. "There must be some mistake!"

"Please hold out your hands," Tipton requested in a stern tone.

Keough shook his head. He didn't want to comply, but his hands came up automatically. Tipton skillfully slipped on some handcuffs. Keough's face went apoplectic. "Not in front of my supporters!" He pleaded. "The president will pardon me! I'm sure!"

Minutes later he was being escorted to the second SUV. It was still light enough to drive back to Medford. None of the feds wanted to spend a dreary night in Twin Oaks.

Across the street, Police Chief Marty Chiloquin had observed the takedown. FBI Ray Stone had called him earlier in the day and had given him a heads up.

***

At La Causa, everybody was eager to hear the election results, but the regularly scheduled programming was instead interrupted for breaking news. There was TV coverage of the arrest of Mayor Keough with a short back story.

Corkie went up to her husband. "What's this all about?"

"Marty said that the feds had an indictment against the mayor for all the dirty tricks he's been playing."

"Couldn't happen to a nicer guy."

At eight o'clock the first results were in. Statewide, the Yes on Proposition 105 initiative was losing 66% to 34%, with over forty percent of the ballots counted. That was great news for Corkie and the No on Proposition 105 campaign. In the mayor's race, Keough was ahead 72% to 38% with a huge under vote. Lots of people hadn't wanted to vote in the mayoral contest. Baumgartner and Warden were winning handily. Nationally, the Democrats kept picking up Congressional seats. Surprisingly enough, some of the red districts in Orange County, California, were going blue.

Corkie kept monitoring the results, giving updates every thirty minutes or so. Locally, the Yes on Proposition 105 was winning the county, but in Twin Oaks the margin was only 53% to 47%. This was a symbolic victory for La Causa and all the hard work that the volunteers had done.

By 11:30 Corkie closed down the party and told everyone to go home. There were still 15% of the ballots to be counted, but it looked like nothing was going to change. Proposition 105 would be defeated. She thanked everyone profusely and remembered to hand out the Subway gift cards.

Lorenzo and Corkie drove home in the rain. Corkie was sound asleep before they left the city limits.

## Chapter 58 – Thanksgiving

***Thursday, November 22, 2018***

There was more than inch of snow on the ground outside the Becerra home. Lorenzo had been in the kitchen all morning cooking an 18-pound turkey for their afternoon Thanksgiving dinner. He had experimented with a dry rub and had tented the bird under aluminum foil. He had prepared his signature corn bread and wild rice stuffing. The side dishes were Brussel sprouts, homemade cranberry sauce, mashed chayote squash, and of course, rice and beans. For dessert, one of the guests had brought a tres leches cake, and there was also a lemon meringue pie. For the wine drinkers, there was some of Holly's Red Sage merlot.

Corkie and their guests made themselves comfortable, noshing on the whole wheat crackers, salami, and Tillamook cheese. Chispa was playing dead, only to be revived when someone accidentally dropped a morsel of food on the floor. Marty Chiloquin had been invited, and to everyone's surprise, he had come. Holly and the Starmonts were also asked to attend, but they had prior commitments. Corkie was now back part-time at the community center. She had invited three young women who were social orphans in the community. The trio were Latinas.

"Congratulations, Señora Becerra, for being the first Latina on the city council," said Ofelia. "You make us very proud."

Corkie's face turned red and she nodded a polite thank you.

***

A few days after Election Day, the results became official. Proposition 105 had been sounded defeated. La Causa was disappointed that they didn't win the county, but happy that they had made a positive difference in the community and for the State. They had fought and they had fought hard. They had managed to educate the community. Keough was re-elected, and Baumgartner and Warden become first termers. Their Democratic candidates in the "non-partisan" city races were virtually no-shows.

After the election, Councilmember Kirby called the two incumbent city council members and the two newcomers and suggested that they have a special meeting. They all agreed and scheduled it for the following Tuesday. They gave public notice of the meeting per the law. On the agenda was a discussion about the mayor's arrest and impending removal from office.

Marsha Squires, the city attorney, was also present.

The first hurdle was deciding who would chair the meeting. Incumbents Alice Williams and Foster Grey were Democrats who often aligned themselves with Kirby, the Libertarian Republican. The only thing they had in common was their dislike of Keough. By prior arrangement, Williams moved that Kirby chair the meeting; it was seconded by Grey.

"Is that legal?" blurted out the newbie Baumgartner.

City Attorney Squires responded. "Yes, per your bylaws."

Baumgartner grumbled under his breath.

"I move that the position of mayor be declared vacant," Williams stated with conviction. This had all been scripted beforehand with Kirby. The motion was seconded by Grey.

“Why?” shouted out Warden.

“Councilman Warden, you are out of order,” Kirby gave the young pup a stern look.

“Ms. Squires, can you please explain to the council on what grounds a duly-elected mayor may be removed from office.”

“Per your own bylaws, for mental or physical incapacity, moral turpitude, criminal convictions . . .” Squires read the three paragraphs in their entirely.

“In light of Mayor Keough’s arrest and the allegations against him, he can no longer hold office,” Williams asserted.

“But he hasn’t been tried yet!” Baumgartner came to the mayor’s defense. “This violates Due Process.”

“Do you really want to wait until next year when he is tried?” Grey threw up his hands in exasperation. “We might as well abolish the council.”

After a heated debate, the question was called. The office of mayor was declared vacant by a vote of 3-2.

“I move that Councilmember Kirby be declared mayor for the remainder of the new term,” Williams said.

Baumgartner and Warden finally caught on. There was very little debate. They were the new kids on the block and the train had left the station without them.

This motion passed 3-2.

“Mr. Mayor, if I may,” Warden took a deep breath. “I’d like to change my vote from nay to aye and move that you be declared mayor by acclamation.”

"So moved. Any objection?" Kirby declared looking squarely at Baumgartner. Baumgartner did not have a clue what that meant. So he followed Warden's lead and kept his mouth shut.

"Motion passes." Everybody clapped. People got up and shook Kirby's hand.

"Anything else for the good of the Order?" the newly-appointed mayor asked.

"I move that your city council District Five seat be declared vacant," Williams quickly said. She didn't want Kirby to double-cross her. This had been part of the deal.

"Without objection," Kirby gave his colleague a wicked smile. He had tried to pull a fast one. "Anything else?

"I move that Corkie Becerra be appointed the city councilmember for District Five," Williams continued. That was the quid pro quo with Kirby. Williams wanted another woman council member and Kirby liked Corkie because she was always taking on the feds whom he despised.

***

At the Becerra home, the guests were seated around the table. They arranged their napkins. Lorenzo sat at one end of the table. Chiloquin at the other end.

"Before we begin our Thanksgiving feast, let us say Grace," they all reached out and held hands and bowed their heads.

"We are all blessed. Every day is a gift. We are thankful for our bounty. Many years ago the English settlers came to this continent. They were looking for a new life. A new beginning. New opportunities." Corkie and Lorenzo had decided to try to educate their guests on American customs and values. They knew that the Latina guests had to be at least bicultural in order to survive. They also wanted to show them that not everyone supported the U.S. president's racist and xenophobic views.

"The Native Americans are a very spiritual people. They saw these poor immigrants starving. They decide to share their food with these new arrivals . . ."

Two hours later, everybody was holding their stomachs as they left the Becerra home loaded down with leftovers.

"Good job, mi amor," Corkie laid her hand on Lorenzo's chest.

"Back at you, madam councilmember," he replied.

"Are you ready for some more pie?" she gave him a devilish smile.

***

There was a loud pounding on the front door. The clock radio read 11:00. Chispa barked. Corkie pulled the covers over her head.

"What in the heck is that?" she moaned, still half-asleep.

*Crap!* Lorenzo took a deep breath, threw on his robe, and put on his moccasin slippers. Chispa ran ahead of him.

"Just a minute!" he yelled out as he walked down the stairs.

There was a follow-up knocking. "Señor Becerra! Señor Becerra!" a female voice cried out. "Are you home?"

*Of course, I'm home. My house lights are on now!* He hurried. "Coming!" *¡Cómo friegas!*

Lorenzo unlocked the front door and opened it. There were gale force winds driving the rain toward him. In front of the door was Cristina Navarro, with a soaking wet shawl wrapped around her shoulders and face. Next to her was another woman in a heavy, hooded overcoat. Lorenzo could not see the woman.

"It's me!" the woman spoke loudly against the heavy winds. "Cristina. Gloria's friend."

"Oh, yes! Come in, come in," Lorenzo was getting pelted by the rain. He barely remembered her, but knew that Corkie and Holly were in constant contact with her.

He pointed to the living room. Water was dripping all over the floor. The second woman undid her coat. Lorenzo saw that there was another small person clinging to her.

"Sit down! Please sit down!" Lorenzo yelled in a frenzy. "Corkie! Corkie! Come downstairs quick!"

He could hear his wife muttering under her breath as she staggered down the stairs. She was still trying to wake up.

"Come in here, please!" Lorenzo pointed.

Corkie stepped forward. Her eyes opened wide. Her jaw dropped. She recognized the two diminutive figures who were with Cristina.

"They found Yessie," Cristina said sobbing. "Gloria has been saying a hundred Ave Marias every day. ¡Gracias a Dios!"

Corkie threw her arms around Gloria and Yesenia Ocaso. She never believed that they would find the young child abducted by ICE. Lorenzo joined in the group hug. He kissed the back of his wife's neck.

"This is a blessed Thanksgiving!"

The house seemed to lighten up. Positive energy and love abounded. The blustery winds then ceased to blow. But who knows when they would return again.

# PART III – THE APPENDICES

## THE OREGON SANCTUARY LAW

AB 2314, **commonly known as the Oregon Sanctuary Law,** was enacted in 1987. It was cited as ORS 181.850 for many years and then re-designated as ORS 181A.820.

While the success of HB 2314 was a victory for Oregon's diverse communities, it was passed amid Oregon's continued struggles with racial discrimination and white supremacist violence. There have been various attempts to repeal this law. Oregon became a focal point for the largest skinhead movement in 1988, mere months after ORS 181A.820 became law, when white supremacists beat an Ethiopian immigrant to death with a baseball bat in Portland.

More than ever, in light of the national xenophobia, hate speech, and racism, Oregon's Sanctuary Law remains as vital and necessary as it was thirty-plus years ago. This is due to the courageous behavior of Delmiro Treviño, the Rosa Parks of Oregon.

The Oregon Sanctuary Law is embedded in Chapter 181A — State Police; Crime Reporting and Records; Public Safety Standards and Training; Private Security Services website:www.oregonlegislature.gov/bills_laws/ors/ors181A.html

**Following is the current text of 181A.820, which is headed PUBLIC SAFETY PERSONNEL GENERALLY.**

**181A.820 Enforcement of federal immigration laws.** (1) No law enforcement agency of the State of Oregon or of any political subdivision of the state shall use agency moneys, equipment or personnel for the purpose of detecting or apprehending persons whose only violation of law is that they are persons of foreign citizenship present in the United States in violation of federal immigration laws.

(2) Notwithstanding subsection (1) of this section, a law enforcement agency may exchange information with the United States Bureau of Immigration and Customs Enforcement, the United States Bureau of Citizenship and Immigration Services and the United States Bureau of Customs and Border Protection in order to:

(a) Verify the immigration status of a person if the person is arrested for any criminal offense; or

(b) Request criminal investigation information with reference to persons named in records of the United States Bureau of Immigration and Customs Enforcement, the United States Bureau of Citizenship and Immigration Services or the United States Bureau of Customs and Border Protection.

(3) Notwithstanding subsection (1) of this section, a law enforcement agency may arrest any person who:

(a) Is charged by the United States with a criminal violation of federal immigration laws under Title II of the Immigration and Nationality Act or 18 U.S.C. 1015, 1422 to 1429 or 1505; and

(b) Is subject to arrest for the crime pursuant to a warrant of arrest issued by a federal magistrate.

(4) For purposes of subsection (1) of this section, the Bureau of Labor and Industries is not a law enforcement agency.

(5) As used in this section, "warrant of arrest" has the meaning given that term in ORS 131.005. [Formerly 181.850]

**Following is the wording of the original version of the law as passed and printed in Oregon Laws 1987:**

CHAPTER 487. An Act, HB 2314, Relating to law enforcement.

**Be It Enacted by the People of the State of Oregon:**

SECTION 1. (1) No law enforcement agency of the State of Oregon or of any political subdivision of the state shall use agency moneys, equipment or personnel for the purpose of detecting or apprehending persons whose only violation of law is that they are persons of foreign citizenship residing in the United States in violation of federal immigration laws.

(2) Notwithstanding subsection (1) of this section, a law enforcement agency may exchange information with the United States Immigration and Naturalization Service in order to:

(a) Verify the immigration status of a person if the person is arrested for any criminal offense; or

(b) Request criminal investigation information with reference to persons named in service records.

(c) For purposes of subsection (1) of this section, the Bureau of Labor and Industries is not a law enforcement agency.

Approved by the Governor July 7, 1987

Filed in the office of Secretary of State July 8, 1987

# HISTORY OF U.S IMMIGRATION LAW

The United States has long been considered a nation of immigrants. Attitudes toward new immigrants by those who came before have vacillated between welcoming and exclusionary over the years.

Thousands of years before Europeans began crossing the vast Atlantic by ship and settling en masse, the first immigrants arrived in North America and the land that would later become the United States. They were the ancestors of the Native Americans who crossed a narrow spit of land connecting Asia to North America some 20,000 years ago, during the last Ice Age.

By the early 1600s, communities of European immigrants dotted the Eastern seaboard, including the Spanish in Florida, the British in New England and Virginia, the Dutch in New York, and the Swedes in Delaware. Some, including the Pilgrims and Puritans, came for religious freedom. Many sought greater economic opportunities. Still others, including hundreds of thousands of enslaved Africans, arrived in America against their will.

Below are the events that have shaped the turbulent history of immigration in the United States since the birth of the country:

**January 1776:** Thomas Paine publishes a pamphlet, "Common Sense," that argues for American independence. Most colonists consider themselves Britons, but Paine makes the case for a new American identity. "Europe, and not England, is the parent country of America. This new world hath been the asylum for the persecuted lovers of civil and religious liberty from every part of Europe," he writes.

**March 1790:** Congress passes the first law about who should be granted U.S. citizenship. The Naturalization Act of 1790 allows any free white male person of "good character," who has been living in the United States for two years or longer to apply for citizenship. Without citizenship, nonwhite residents are denied basic constitutional protections, including the right to vote, own property, or testify in court.

**August 1790:** The first U.S. census takes place. The English are the largest ethnic group among the 3.9 million people counted, though nearly one in five Americans is of African heritage.

**1815:** Peace is re-established between the United States and Britain after the War of 1812. Immigration from Western Europe turns from a trickle into a gush, which causes a shift in the demographics of the United States. This first major wave of immigration lasts until the Civil War.

Between 1820 and 1860, the Irish—many of them Catholic—account for an estimated one-third of all immigrants to the United States. Some 5 million German immigrants also come to the U.S., many of them making their way to the Midwest to buy farms or settle in cities including Milwaukee, St. Louis and Cincinnati.

**1819:** Many of the newcomers arrive sick or dying from their long journey across the Atlantic in cramped conditions. The immigrants overwhelm major port cities, including New York, Boston, Philadelphia and Charleston. In response, the United States passes the Steerage Act of 1819 requiring better conditions on ships arriving to the country. The Act also calls for ship captains to submit demographic information about passengers, creating the first federal records on the ethnic composition of immigrants to the United States.

**1820:** Between 1820 and 1860 the Irish constituted over one-third of all immigrants, especially due to Ireland's Potato Blight.

**1849:** America's first anti-immigrant political party, the Know-Nothing Party forms, as a backlash to the increasing number of German and Irish immigrants settling in the United States.

**1875:** Following the Civil War, some states passed their own immigration laws. In 1875 the Supreme Court declares that it is the responsibility of the federal government to make and enforce immigration laws.

**1880:** As America begins a rapid period of industrialization and urbanization, a second immigration boom begins. Between 1880 and 1920, more than 20 million immigrants arrive. The majority are from Southern, Eastern and Central Europe, including 4 million Italians and 2 million Jews. Many of them settle in major U.S. cities and work in factories.

**1882:** The Chinese Exclusion Act passes, which bars Chinese immigrants from entering the U.S. Beginning in the 1850s, a steady flow of Chinese workers had immigrated to America.

They worked in the gold mines and garment factories, built railroads, and took agricultural jobs. Anti-Chinese sentiment grew as Chinese laborers became successful in America. Although Chinese immigrants made up only 0.002 percent of the United States population, white workers blamed them for low wages.

The 1882 Act is the first law in American history to place broad restrictions on certain immigrant groups.

**1891:** The Immigration Act of 1891 further bars certain groups from entering the United States: barring the immigration of polygamists, people convicted of certain crimes, and the sick or diseased. The Act also created a federal office of immigration to coordinate immigration enforcement and a corps of immigration inspectors stationed at principal ports of entry.

**January 1892**: Ellis Island, the United States' first immigration station, opens in New York Harbor. The first immigrant processed is Annie Moore, a teenager from County Cork, Ireland. More than 12 million immigrants would enter the United States through Ellis Island between 1892 and 1954.

**1907**: U.S. immigration peaks, with 1.3 million people entering the country through Ellis Island alone.

**February 1907:** Amid prejudices in California that an influx of Japanese workers would cost white workers farming jobs and depress wages, the United States and Japan sign the Gentlemen's Agreement. Japan agrees to limit Japanese emigration to the United States to certain categories of business and professional men. In return, President Theodore Roosevelt urges San Francisco to end the segregation of Japanese students from white students in San Francisco public schools.

**1910:** An estimated three-quarters of New York City's population consists of new immigrants and first-generation Americans.

**1917:** Xenophobia reaches new heights on the eve of American involvement in World War I. The Immigration Act of 1917 establishes a literacy requirement for immigrants entering the country and halts immigration from most Asian countries.

**May 1924:** The Immigration Act of 1924 limits the number of immigrants allowed into the United States yearly through nationality quotas. Under the new quota system, the United States limits immigration visas to 2 percent of the total number of people of each nationality in the United States at the 1890 census. The law favors immigration from Northern and Western

European countries. Just three countries, Great Britain, Ireland and Germany account for 70 percent of all available visas. Immigration from Southern, Central and Eastern Europe was limited. The Act completely excludes immigrants from Asia, aside from the Philippines, then an American colony.

**1924**: In the wake of the numerical limits established by the 1924 law, illegal immigration to the United States increases. The U.S. Border Patrol is established to crack down on illegal immigrants crossing the Mexican and Canadian borders into the United States. Many of these early border crossers were Chinese and other Asian immigrants, who had been barred from entering legally.

**1942:** Labor shortages during World War II prompt the United States and Mexico to form the Bracero Program, which allows Mexican agricultural workers to enter the United States temporarily. The program lasts until 1964.

**1948:** The United States passes the nation's first refugee and resettlement law to deal with the influx of Europeans seeking permanent residence in the United States after World War II.

**1952:** The McCarran-Walter Act formally ends the exclusion of Asian immigrants to the United States.

**1956-1957**: The United States admits roughly 38,000 immigrants from Hungary after its failed uprising against the Soviets. They were among the first Cold War refugees. The United States would admit over 3 million refugees during the Cold War.

**1960-1962**: Roughly 14,000 unaccompanied children flee Fidel Castro's Cuba and come to the United States as part of a secret, anti-Communism program called Operation Peter Pan.

**1965:** The Immigration and Nationality Act overhauls the

American immigration system. The Act ends the national origin quotas enacted in the 1920s which favored some racial and ethnic groups over others.

The quota system is replaced with a seven-category preference system emphasizing family reunification and skilled immigrants. Upon signing the new bill, President Lyndon B. Johnson, called the old immigration system "un-American," and said the new bill would correct a "cruel and enduring wrong in the conduct of the American Nation."

Over the next five years, immigration from war-torn regions of Asia, including Vietnam and Cambodia, would more than quadruple. Family reunification became a driving force in U.S. immigration.

**April-October 1980**: During the Mariel boatlift, roughly 125,000 Cuban refugees make a dangerous sea crossing in overcrowded boats to arrive on the Florida shore seeking political asylum.

**1986:** President Ronald Reagan signs into law the Simpson-Mazzoli Act, which grants amnesty to more than 3 million immigrants living illegally in the United States.

**2001**: U.S. Senators Dick Durbin (D-Ill.) and Orrin Hatch (R-Utah) propose the first Development, Relief and Education of Alien Minors (DREAM) Act, which would provide a pathway to legal status for Dreamers, undocumented immigrants brought to the United States illegally by their parents as children. The bill—and subsequent iterations of it—do not pass

**2012**: President Barack Obama signs the Deferred Action for Childhood Arrivals (DACA) which temporarily shields some Dreamers from deportation, but doesn't provide a path to citizenship.

**2017:** President Donald Trump issues two executive orders—both titled "Protecting the Nation from Foreign Terrorist Entry into the United States"—aimed at curtailing travel and immigration from six majority Muslim countries (Chad, Iran, Libya, Syria, Yemen, Somalia) as well as North Korea and Venezuela. Both of these travel bans are challenged in state and federal courts.

**2018:** In April 2018, the travel restrictions on Chad are lifted. In June 2018, the U.S. Supreme Court upholds a third version of the ban on the remaining seven countries.

Sources:

Immigration Timeline, The Statue of Liberty-Ellis Island Foundation.

LBJ on Immigration, LBJ Presidential Library.

The Nation's Immigration Laws, 1920 to Today, Pew Research Center.

## ICE AND FAMILY SEPARATION

Long before the Trump White House implemented its "zero tolerance" immigration enforcement policy in 2018, his administration was already separating children from their parents as part of a pilot program conducted in the El Paso, Texas area and along other parts of the border. Under the El Paso program, begun in mid-2017, adults who crossed the border without permission – a misdemeanor for a first-time offender – were detained and criminally charged. No exceptions were made for parents arriving with young children. The children were taken from them, and parents were unable to track or reunite with their children because the government failed to create a system to facilitate reunification. By late 2017, the government was separating families along the length of the U.S.-Mexico border, including families arriving through official ports of entry.

On May 7, 2018, the U.S. Department of Justice (DOJ) announced it had implemented a "zero tolerance" policy, dictating that all migrants who cross the border without permission, including those seeking asylum, be referred to the DOJ for prosecution. Undocumented asylum seekers were imprisoned, and any accompanying children under the age of 18 were handed over to the U.S. Department of Health and Human Services (HHS), which shipped them miles away from their parents and scattered them among 100 Office of Refugee Resettlement (ORR) shelters and other care arrangements across the country. Hundreds of these children, including infants and toddlers, were under the age of 5.

Prior to the Trump administration, families were generally paroled into the country to await their immigration cases or detained together.

The following is a timeline of family separation under President Trump, beginning less than two months after he took office, following a campaign in which he called Mexican immigrants rapists and criminals.

**2017**

**March 3, 2017** – The Trump administration is considering a proposal to begin separating children from their mothers at the border as a way to deter future migrants, Reuter reports. The policy would allow the government to keep parents in custody while they await asylum hearings or contest deportation.

**Nov. 25, 2017** – The Houston Chronicle reports that the Trump administration has, since at least June, been separating children from parents who cross the border. The paper identifies 22 cases of parents whose children were taken without due process.

**2018**

**June 9, 2018** – A man from Honduras who suffered a nervous breakdown after being separated from his wife and child at the border died by suicide in a Texas jail in May, *The Washington Post* reports. The government has no comment on the man's death.

**June 14, 2018** – CNN reports that a Honduran woman was breastfeeding her daughter in detention in McAllen, Texas, when federal authorities snatched the child away from her. "The government is essentially torturing people by doing this," says Natalia Cornelio, an attorney with the Texas Civil Rights Project.

**June 15, 2018** – For the first time, DHS publicly acknowledges that it separated nearly 2,000 children from their parents or legal guardians between April 19 and May 31. The government's protocol for reunifying families has yet to be made clear.

**June 17, 2018** – Journalists and human rights advocates tour an old warehouse in McAllen, Texas, where hundreds of children are being kept in a series of cages made of metal fencing. The Associated Press report that overhead lighting stays on around the clock, children are sleeping under "large foil sheets," older children are forced to change the diapers of toddlers and that children have no books or toys. One toddler is seen crying uncontrollably and pounding her fists on a mat. "If a parent left a child in a cage with no supervision with other 5-year-olds, they'd be held accountable," says Michelle Brané, director of migrant rights at the Women's Refugee Commission.

**June 17, 2018** – Former First Lady Laura Bush calls the administration's practices "cruel" and "immoral" in a commentary published by *The Washington Post.*

**June 17, 2018** – Homeland Security Secretary Kirstjen Nielsen tweets falsely: "We do not have a policy of separating families at the border. Period."

**June 18, 2018** – *ProPublica* publishes a now-viral audio clip, where Central American children separated from their parents are heard sobbing in jail-like cages, crying "Mami" and "Papa" over and over. Guards can be heard making jokes about the desperate children. "I don't want them to deport him," one child cries. "Daddy!" another screams.

**June 20, 2018** – Reacting to mounting public pressure, President Trump signs an executive order directing DHS to stop separating families except in cases where there is concern that the parent represents a risk to the child. Trump falsely blames Congress, the courts and previous administrations for his family separation policy, claiming that now "[y]ou're going to have a lot of happy people." CBS News reports that 2,342 children were separated at the border from more than 2,200 adults between May 5 to June 9.

**June 26, 2018** – Following a class action suit filed by the ACLU, U.S. District Judge Dana Sabraw issues a preliminary injunction requiring U.S. immigration authorities to reunite most separated families within 30 days and to reunite children younger than 5 within two weeks. Judge Sabraw also prohibits further separations unless the parent poses a danger to the child or has a criminal history or communicable disease. "The court made clear that potentially thousands of children's lives are at stake, and that the Trump administration cannot simply ignore the devastation it has caused," says ACLU attorney Lee Gelernt.

**July 3, 2018** – NBC News reports that in the wake of Judge Sabraw's injunction, the Trump administration is forcing migrants to choose between leaving the country with or without their kids, effectively preventing them from asking for asylum.

**July 13, 2018** – The Trump administration says in a court filing that 2,551 children between the ages of five and 17 remain separated from their parents, almost a month after the "zero tolerance" policy was revoked.

**July 26, 2018** – More than 900 parents have yet to be reunified with their children by the court's deadline. "It's the reality of a policy that was in place that resulted in large numbers of families being separated without forethought as to reunification and keeping track of people," says Judge Sabraw. More than half of those parents – 463 – have been deported to their home countries without their children.

**Oct. 11, 2018** – Helen, a 5-year-old girl from Honduras, was persuaded to sign away her rights after being separated from her grandmother, *The New Yorker* reports. "One of the things Helen's story really showed us is that the Trump administration never stopped separating children from their families," says Jess Morales Rocketto, of Families Belong Together. "In fact, they've doubled down, but it's even more insidious now, because they are doing it in the cover of night."

**Oct. 11, 2018** – As the grueling process of reunifying families continues, Amnesty International publishes a report that cites U.S. Customs and Border Patrol data indicating that 6,022 "family units" had been separated between April 19, 2018, and August 15, 2018 – a much greater number than previously stated. "Right now, hundreds of children are languishing in tent cities on the border," says Margaret Huang, executive director of Amnesty International USA. "Even more children are locked behind bars in family detention centers. This is nothing short of unconscionable."

**Oct. 15, 2018** – The government report to a court that a total of 2,654 children have been separated from their parents, and of that number, 2,363 have been discharged from ORR custody. But 125 children made the tough decision to pursue asylum in the U.S. without their parent, while another 120 children who hadn't waived reunification were still in ORR's care, waiting to be reunited.

**Nov. 17, 2018** – Families are still being separated at the border, *ProPublica* reports. As justification, Border Patrol agents are using vague or unproven allegations of suspected gang activity to separate parents from children.

**Dec. 20, 2018** – Appearing before the House Judiciary Committee, Homeland Security Secretary Nielsen once again falsely claims the administration has no family separation policy. "I'm not a liar, we've never had a policy for family separation," she says. If there were one, she adds, it "would mean that any family that I found at a port of entry I would separate, it would mean that every single family that I found illegally crossing, we would separate. We did none of those."

**2019**

**Jan. 17, 2019** – The Department of Health and Human Services' inspector general finds that thousands more children than previously known may have been separated from their parents since 2017. The numbers began to increase in the summer of 2017, when DHS referred more and more separated children to ORR. The number of children separated is unknown because of the lack of a formal tracking system coordinated among the agencies involved.

**Jan. 17, 2019** – The list of families to be reunified is "still being revised" nearly six months after reunification is ordered by a federal court, *The New York Times* reports.

**Feb. 14, 2019** – A report by the Texas Civil Rights Project finds that as family separations continue, a significant number of children have been separated from relatives other than parents or legal guardians. Such separations are not counted by DHS in its statistics.

**Feb. 27, 2019** – The federal government received more than 4,500 complaints about the sexual abuse of immigrant children held in detention from October 2014 to July 2018, *The New York Times* reports. Of the 1,303 cases considered the gravest, 178 included accusations of sexual assault by adult staff members. Those allegations included rape, fondling, kissing and watching children shower.

**March 8, 2019** – A federal judge agrees to expand the ACLU's class action lawsuit – which earlier resulted in a reunification order – to include families that had been separated months earlier than those previously disclosed.

**March 9, 2019** – The Trump administration reports to a federal court that it has separated 245 children from their parents and other relatives since President Trump rescinded the family separation policy nearly nine months earlier. Government officials say they are following guidelines allowing separations when an adult poses a safety risk to the child. But *The New York Times* reports that in some cases children were removed from parents who had minor previous offenses, including one for possessing a small amount of marijuana.

**April 6, 2019** – The government says in court documents that it may take two years to identify potentially thousands of children who've been separated from their families at the southern border.

**May 8, 2019** – The administration acknowledges it has separated 389 families since June 2018, when a court ordered it to end the policy. Advocates contend the number is significantly higher, noting that at least 40 separations occur daily along the California border, with others continuing in Texas, New Mexico and Arizona.

**May 18, 2019** – The Trump administration acknowledges that it may have separated at least 1712 additional children before the "zero tolerance policy" went into effect in May 2018.

**June 2, 2019** - NBC News reports that in July 2018, some 37 children boarded a van for a 30-minute drive to the Port Isabel Detention Center in Los Fresnos, Texas, to be reunited with their parents. Some were as young as 5. But once there, they were forced to wait in the van, in the hot sun – some for as long as 39 hours.

**June 20, 2019** – The Associated Press ignites public outcry when it reports that at a facility near El Paso, roughly 250 infants, children and teens have been locked up for 27 days without adequate food, water or sanitation. Some were separated from adult caregivers after arriving at the border. At least 15 were suffering from the flu. "In my 22 years of doing visits with children in detention, I have never heard of this level of inhumanity," says Holly Cooper, an attorney who represents the detained youth.

**July 8, 2019** – *ProPublica* reports that the U.S. is now using databases from foreign police and militaries to find out if asylum seekers have gang affiliations. Attorneys representing asylum seekers along the border question how frequently the databases are used and whether they may be wrongly labeling migrants as criminals. The report points to a Salvadoran man named Carlos, who was separated from his family after immigration agents accused him of being in a gang. "I told them I've never been in a gang," he said. "And the agent said your government is saying you are."

**July 12, 2019** – The House Committee on Oversight and Reform held a hearing where witnesses described the trauma caused by the Trump administration's family separation policy, and stated that the administration was not transparent regarding the purpose of the separations, and that the "nightmare" of separating families continues. What's more, witnesses pointed out that the administration's policies are continuing to cause problems at the border – not helping to resolve them.

**July 15, 2019** – NPR_reports that after a doctor told Border Patrol agents that a 3-year-old girl from Honduras who suffers a heart condition should remain in the U.S., an agent gave the family a choice: One parent could stay with the child, but the other would have to return to Mexico. The agent told the girl to choose. After the doctor appealed to another agent, the family was released together.

**July 30, 2019** – The ACLU files a motion in the U.S. District Court of San Diego, asking a federal judge to block the Trump administration from continuing to separate families at the border. Since the nationwide injunction was issued on June 26, 2018, more than 900 parents and children – not excluding babies – have been separated at the border. The ACLU alleges that families have been separated for minor transgressions such as traffic offenses. “It is shocking that the Trump administration continues to take babies from their parents,” ACLU attorney Lee Gelernt says. “The administration must not be allowed to circumvent the court order over infractions like minor traffic violations.”

**Aug. 21, 2019** – DHS and the U.S. Department of Health and Human Services (HHS) announce a new rule that would end the *Flores settlement*. The settlement is a consent decree in place for more than two decades that limits the length of time migrant children can be detained by U.S. Customs and Border Protection (CBP) to 20 days, requires the government to comply with certain standards of care, and states that children must be placed in the “least restrictive” setting appropriate for their age and needs. The Trump administration’s rule would allow it to indefinitely detain migrant families who crossed the border without authorization.

**Aug. 22, 2019** – *The New York Times* reports that “there is a stench” where detained migrant children are held in a Texas CBP facility. The children have not been able to bathe since crossing the border, and their clothes are soiled with snot and tears. Moreover, the children do not have access to soap, toothbrushes or toothpaste. A reporter described the facility’s conditions as “a chaotic scene of sickness and filth.” One attorney who has for years inspected government facilities that hold migrant children says, "So many children are sick, they have the flu, and they're not being properly treated."

**September 2019** – A reports issued by the HHS Office of Inspector General states that "intense trauma" was common among children who had entered Office of Refugee Resettlement (ORR) facilities in 2018, with children who had been "unexpectedly separated from a parent" facing additional trauma. The report highlights that children exhibited "fear, feelings of abandonment and post-traumatic stress" along with anxiety and loss resulting from the separations. Suffering from acute grief, the children would also cry inconsolably.

**Sept. 5, 2019** – Judge Sabraw order the Trump administration to reunite 11 children with parents who were deported under its family separation policy. He says some migrants were pressured to consent to their deportation while they were separated from their children, and that immigration officials gave them false or confusing information. He orders the government to allow the migrants to return to the U.S. for an opportunity to pursue asylum claims.

**Sept. 27, 2019** – U.S. District Judge Dolly Gee of the Central District of California rejects the administration's plan to end the *Flores* settlement. Advocates previously lamented that terminating the settlement would be "cruel beyond imagination," citing the cases of at least seven children who died in detention.

**Nov. 6, 2019** – U.S. District Judge John Kronstadt orders the government to provide mental health screenings and treatment to separated parents, citing "extensive evidence" of the "substantial trauma" that these families suffered due to the Trump administration's policy.

**Nov. 25, 2019** – The DHS Office of Inspector

General reports that the agency failed to properly track and reunify families during the family separation crisis, citing "poor data entry, data tracking, information sharing and IT systems capabilities."

**Dec. 9, 2019** – The U.S. government has separated more than 1,100 migrant families at the border since June 2018, when Trump issued an executive order to halt separations, *The Intercept* reports. The government's own data suggests the number could be even higher, due to wildly inconsistent record keeping.

**Dec. 16, 2019** – The Trump administration knew migrant children would suffer from family separations but ramped up the practice anyway, *The Texas Tribune* reports.

**2020**

**Jan. 10, 2020** – The SPLC sues the Trump administration on behalf of two immigrant parents and their children separated at the border. The lawsuit describes the deliberately cruel government actions that harmed these families. Covington & Burling and Coppersmith Brockelman law firms serve as co-counsel.

**Jan. 13, 2020** – After the ACLU in July 2019 filed its motion to stop family separations, Judge Sabraw refuses to issue new guidelines to further limit the government's ability to separate migrant families, instead allowing immigration officials to use their discretion to decide whether to separate children from their parents in certain – mostly spurious – circumstances.

**Jan. 18, 2020** – The Los Angeles Times reports that the official government count of children separated from their parents or guardians under the family separation policy is 4,368. Meanwhile, attorneys say it still proves incredibly difficult to reach hundreds of parents of children separated from them. They also say that known flaws in government tracking systems mean that the total number of separated families is likely higher.

**March 18, 2020** – GAO issues a report stating that arrests of families (parents or guardians traveling with children under 18) grew from about 22 percent of total southwest border apprehensions in fiscal year 2016 to about 51 percent of such apprehensions during the first two quarters of fiscal year 2019.

**May 29, 2020** – Yet another HHS Office of Inspector General report is published revealing that CBP separated more asylum-seeking families at ports of entry than previously reported, and

for reasons other than what had been outlined in public statements. CBP claimed it had only separated seven asylum-seeking parents from children between May 6, 2018, and July 9, 2018. But in reality, at least 60 asylum-seeking families were separated in May and June 2018, at 11 ports of entry.

Source: Southern Poverty Law Center, June 17, 2020

Migrant Children Can No Longer Be Secretly Held in Hotels, But Advocates Continue to Worry Children May Still Be Expeditiously Expelled Without Any Due Process

By Immigration Prof

Guest blogger: Violeta Velazquez, law student, University of San Francisco:

On September 4, 2020 District Court Judge Dolly Gee ordered the Trump Administration to halt using hotels to hold migrant children caught at the border before expelling them. In her decision, Judge Gee stated that keeping children in hotels violated fundamental humanitarian protections under the Flores Settlement Agreement.[1]

The Flores Agreement stems from a 1977 case, *Flores v. Reno*[2], which requires the government to release children from immigration detention without unnecessary delay to their parents, other adult relatives, or non-secure licensed facilities, generally through the Office for Refugee Resettlement (ORR) within three to five days. [3]The agreement also stipulates that unaccompanied migrant children must have access to lawyers, safe and sanitary facilities, and other safeguards while the government seeks their prompt release. [4]

The 9th Circuit Court of Appeals upheld the lower court's decision to ban the use of hotels on October 4, 2020[5]agreeing with District Judge Gee that the practice of holding immigrant children in hotels and quickly expelling them without access to lawyers violated the Flores Settlement Agreement.

Since the Pandemic began back in March, The Trump administration began instituting a shadow immigration system near the U.S. - Mexico Border, in which private contractors would detain migrant children in hotels without access to lawyers for about three to five days, though sometimes for weeks, before deporting them back to their home countries. In many instances, parents or relatives were unable to find out the whereabouts of the child. In one case, a desperate father living in Texas called the Honduran Consulate, only to be told his son was on an express deportation list, but given no further details as to his whereabouts.[6] His son was able to call him on one occasion, but was forbidden to tell him where he was located.[7] In that case, thankfully the father was able to obtain legal assistance from KIND, who was able to get his son transferred to  a shelter for minors. But this was the exception.[8] For most of the minors who were kept in hotels, they would be quickly expelled after entering the U.S.

Since March, the U.S. has placed at least 577 unaccompanied children in hotel rooms without before deporting them without a chance to request asylum or other protections per the Flores Settlement Agreement.[9]

The Trump administration claims it's allowed to quickly expel immigrants including children under a COVID Rule, issued by the CDC in March, Title 42 of the Public Health Safety Act. This act allows the temporary suspension of entry of any persons that might introduce a disease into the United States.[10] In total, the U.S. under this rule has expelled about 147,000 immigrants since March which includes about 8,8000 unaccompanied children.[11]

Though the Trump administration claimed it had to expel all people crossing the border including unaccompanied children, due to public health and preventing the spread of Covid-19, it's quite clear that this is a pretext for restricting asylum. In the case of the unaccompanied children, The Trump administration had actually been testing all the children before sending them back to their home countries.[12] Essentially, the children had already been tested and proven not to be infected with COVID-19 virus, but were still being boarded onto planes and deported anyways.

While the decision by the Appeals Court to uphold District Judge Gee's decision gives protection to accompanied and unaccompanied minors who now must be placed in licensed facilities, many advocates continue to express concern about expeditious expulsions without due process continuing. One immigration attorney, Taylor Levy speaking to CBS news said, "The true problem here is not the hotels, it's the expulsions. Just because [the Department of Homeland Security] has stopped using hotels does not mean that children are not being expeditiously expelled without any due process, without any chance to seek asylum."[13]

This administration has proven to be relentless and cruel when it comes to attacking immigrants including their right to seek asylum. They have no regard for families, women, or children. While this is an important decision and victory, immigrants' rights advocates will likely continue to remain vigilant and ready to call out this administration's attacks on immigrants.

[1] "Judge Orders DHS to Stop Holding Illegal Immigrant Families in Hotels." Washington Times. September 4, 2020.
https://www.washingtontimes.com/news/2020/sep/4/judge-orders-dhs-stop-holding-illegal-immigrant-fa/
[2] *Reno v. Flores*, 507 U.S. 292 (1993).
[3] The Flores Settlement and Family Incarceration: A brief History and Next Steps Fact Sheet." Human Rights First. October 2018.
https://www.humanrightsfirst.org/sites/default/files/FLORES_SETTLEMENT_AGREEMENT.pdf

[4] "U.S. stops holding migrant children in hotels, but says they can still be expelled." CBSNews. October 2, 2020. https://www.cbsnews.com/news/u-s-stops-holding-migrant-children-in-hotels-but-says-they-can-still-be-expelled/
[5] "Appeals Court Upholds Ban on Holding Migrant Kids in Hotels." ABCNews. October 4, 2020. https://abcnews.go.com/Politics/wireStory/appeals-court-upholds-ban-holding-migrant-kids-hotels-73423799
[6] "Shadow Immigration System: Migrant Children Detained In Hotels By Private Contractors." NPR. August 20, 2020. https://www.npr.org/2020/08/20/904027735/shadow-immigration-system-migrant-children-detained-in-hotels-by-private-contrac
[7] *Id.* at 6
[8] *Id.* at 6.
[9] *Id. at 5*
[10] "ICE is making sure migrant kids don't have COVID-19, then expelling them to "prevent the spread" of COVID-19." The Texas Tribune. August 10, 2020. https://www.texastribune.org/2020/08/10/coronavirus-texas-ice-migrant-children-deport/.
[11] *Id.* at 5. [12] *Id.* at 5.
[13] "Appeals court rules Trump administration can't detain young immigrants in hotels." The Hill. October 5, 2020.

## ABOUT THE AUTHOR

Rocky Barilla lives in the San Francisco Bay Area with his wife, Dolores, and dozens of feathered friends who visit their back yard daily, ranging from Anna's hummingbirds to red-tailed hawks. The couple live part of the year in the paradise of Zihuatanejo, Mexico.

Rocky was formally educated at the University of Southern California and Stanford University. He also spent two academic quarters in Vienna, Austria. His passions are 19th century French literary fiction, Mexican history, global traveling, studying foreign languages (currently, Greek and Italian), ceramic painting, and cooking. For fun and exercise, he and his wife Dolores do Zumba.

Rocky has been actively involved in human rights, immigration, and multicultural issues, especially involving Latinos and other people of color. He was heavily involved in the Oregon Sanctuary State movement in the 1970's and '80's.

His first book "A Taste of Honey" won second place at the International Latino Book Awards (2015) for Fantasy Fiction and won First Place at the Latino Books into Movies Awards (2015) for Fantasy Fiction.

"The Devil's Disciple," Rocky's second book, also won second place at the International Latino Book Awards (2016) for Mystery and was an award winner at the Latino Books into Movies Awards (2018) for Mystery/Suspense.

Rocky's third book is "Ay to Zi." It is a romance that is set in Zihuatanejo, Mexico. It was the Second Place Winner of the International Latino Book Awards (2017) for Romance and an award winner at the Latino Books into Movies Awards (2018) for Romance.

"Harmony of Colors," his fourth book was published in 2017. It is a bittersweet romance filled with cultural clashes and a struggle for the American Dream. It was the Second Place Winner of the International Latino Book Awards (2018) for Latino-Themed Fiction.

“Esmeralda,” a magical realism/fantasy novel, was published in 2018 and was the 2019 International Latino Book Awards First Place Winner for Fantasy Fiction.

He wrote “STARS” in 2019 which is an International Latino Books Award winner for Fiction – Romance.

His mantras are “Life is Good,” “Do Good Deeds,” and “Be Grateful.”

Made in the USA
Monee, IL
19 November 2020

48407667R10203